LARA'S SHADOW

NOVELS BY ALAN FLEISHMAN

Goliath's Head

A Fine September Morning

Lara's Shadow

LARA'S SHADOW

A NOVEL

ALAN FLEISHMAN

BB
B. Bennett Press
San Carlos California

Published by B. Bennett Press
San Carlos, California

Book design by Burche-Bensson
Cover photos used under license from Shutterstock:
Front Cover - © spfotocz
Spine - © Boris Znaev
Back Cover - © Aekkaphob (soldier), NiklsN (girl)

ISBN-10: 1505906504
ISBN-13: 978-1505906509

PRINTED IN THE UNITED STATES OF AMERICA

First Edition

www.alanfleishman.com

To Konrad von Emster and Mary Ann Kearns
who showed me what courage looks like.

To my darling wife Ann.
Though this story is not autobiographical, it was during this time
and in this place that we met, married, and began a
lifetime love affair.

And to Lieutenants Denny Lemaster, Jim Pearson, Tom Buck,
Dan Macquarie, Kelly Weems, Gene Shapiro, Todd Parker,
Sergeant Billy D. Graves, Major John Gleason,
Chaplain Dallas Roscoe and all of the troopers of the
First Battalion, Sixty-Fourth Armor with whom I soldiered.
All of them served our country. Some of them died for it.

PART ONE

1963

Some people forgive too easily, and some can't forgive at all. But the truly tormented are those who can never forgive themselves.

ONE

Eli Schneider hated Germans as hard as anyone could hate. Even by 1961, he could not forgive a single one of them for their atrocities. He was, after all, a Jew, one with good reason to cling to his hate. The rest of America moved on, more worried about a Cold War clash with the Soviet Union than an old war long over.

Now here he was in Bavaria on a gloomy gray October morning, a new lieutenant in the U.S. Army with orders to defend those bastards. How could anyone expect him to do that? But he had no choice. He owed a debt to his adopted country, one he intended to repay by being the best soldier he could be.

Brakes screeched and the troop train slowed to a stop at the town of Kronberg. Eli hitched up his pants and smoothed the jacket of his army green uniform, rumpled from the overnight train ride from the port of Bremerhaven. He stepped onto the station platform, his heart racing.

The driver who was there to meet him wore the single chevron of a Private First Class on the arms of his starched and tailored fatigue jacket. He couldn't have been more than nineteen, but he carried himself with the confidence of a veteran. He saluted smartly, and then hoisted Eli's crammed duffel bag into the back of a topless jeep. Eli hopped in and they sped away, a chilling breeze blowing through.

"Hold on to your teeth," the driver warned just as the jeep hit the rough cobblestoned street. He offered an apologetic grin. He was personable, but appropriately deferential in addressing an officer. He offered that he was from Hays, Kansas and asked where Eli was from. "Manhattan Beach in Brooklyn," he answered. He tried to sound friendly, still uncomfortable with the military's class distinction between officers and enlisted men.

His stomach rumbled. He hadn't eaten since a boxed breakfast on the troop train at four o'clock in the morning. He could still taste the cold bacon and overcooked eggs. He would have given his right ring finger for a cup of coffee about now. As if by magic, the driver said, "There's a thermos of hot coffee under the seat if the Lieutenant would like some." Eli declined, afraid he'd spill it on his uniform.

They lurched around a corner near a church with an onion-shaped steeple, and then sped through a medieval stone arch, the remnant of an old city wall. Even at this early hour, a few squat old ladies in plain colorless coats carried their bags of groceries along the sidewalk. Two younger women in equally colorless outfits peddled their bicycles. An occasional gray fieldstone house wedged itself between the rows of dull gray stucco ones, each adorned with dark shutters and topped with steep gray slate roofs. Eli felt like he was in the middle of a Grimm's Fairy Tale illustration.

The hum of a pair of aged Volkswagens rippled the silence of the morning. Then a convoy of five American army trucks thundered past traveling in the opposite direction, spewing their toxic exhaust. When the jeep braked a few minutes later for a traffic light, two other jeeps and three armored personnel carriers crossed in front, gliding through town as naturally as swans on a pond. The flow of U.S. Army vehicles on quiet German streets didn't seem unusual to Eli's driver, who waited patiently for them to pass. "Fifteenth Infantry heading out," he said.

The respectful young man chatted all of the way, giving Eli a guided tour of Kronberg. "The base is right outside town, a couple of kilometers," he said when they crossed an ancient stone bridge over the Main River. "Holden Barracks used to be a German army base, ever since before the First World War. Sturdy. Much better quarters for enlisted men than back in the States."

Eli wanted to make a good first impression, even if his driver was only a private. He tried to look self-assured, one foot dangling casually on the jeep's entry step. He kept his comments clipped, but it was hard to conceal the anticipation of his first duty assignment. A little more than two months earlier, the Communist East German government ignited a crisis with the United States and its allies when it constructed a barrier of barbed wire and concrete to keep its citizens from fleeing into West Berlin and freedom. Since the end of World War II, more than three million East Germans escaped through the Allied sector of the divided city, an embarrassment to the Soviets and a brain drain for East Germany. Now here he was in the middle of the action, with a tank battalion near the border, no less.

"Were you here when the wall went up?" Eli asked.

"Yes, sir," the Private answered, pride in his tone. He sat up a little straighter behind the wheel. "The whole battalion, all seventy-two tanks, right up there on the border, just waiting. We was there for five days. It's been crazy ever since. More and more troops pouring in from the States. It's getting crowded in the barracks. We've had to double up. You're the third lieutenant I've fetched at the *bahnhof* this week."

Four days after the wall went up in Berlin, President Kennedy ordered forty thousand additional U.S. military personnel rushed to Germany to bolster the 235,000 already there. Eli was one of them. Some Americans cheered Kennedy's actions; others searched for the nearest bomb shelter. The world waited to see if Soviet Premier Khrushchev would carry out his threat to close the lone hundred mile corridor connecting the isolated sector of West Berlin with the rest of West Germany.

Just four months ago Eli was graduating from small Carlyle College in upstate New York. Of relevant consequence, on graduation day he also earned a U.S. Army commission and a pair of gold lieutenant's bars. He was eager to serve, and ready to go anywhere the Army sent him, even Korea - anywhere but Germany. He wondered how he would survive these next two years. What would the Germans do to him when they found out he was a Jew? And what would he do to them?

"What are the German people like?" he asked.

"They're okay. Glad we're here to protect 'em and spend our money. But not too crazy about us taking their women." The driver smirked, intentionally conveying his own experience. "Hell, there are ten thousand Germans in this town, and almost as many Americans, what with the soldiers and their families."

"And how do they treat Jews these days?" It just spurted out. Eli wanted to take his question back as soon as he asked it, not eager to expose his sensitivity. He hoped his driver would take the reference to Jews as a generic question.

The driver's smile melted. He glanced over at Eli, and then quickly fixed his eyes back on the road. The jeep slowed for a big hay wagon pulled by a pair of oxen, a toothless old farmer and his skinny gray-haired wife perched on top. "No problems as far I know," the driver answered. "There are a couple Jews in our company. They get laid as often as any of us." That seemed to answer the question definitively, in the only way that mattered.

Eli pictured for a moment the farewell dinner at Grandma Sara's the weekend before he left for the Army. The whole family came to see him off. After the last of the brisket was consumed, the men sat around the big mahogany dining room table smoking, while the women cleared the dishes. Each of Eli's uncles issued grave warnings about the born malice of Germans. His adoptive father, Jake Gross, was beside himself. "They're still a bunch of

Nazis," he fumed. "You know what they do to Jews, don't you?" His Uncle Josef was more fundamental, as always. "You can *shtup* the women all you want," he growled. "But don't you dare bring one of them whores home with you." The dark discussion ended when Auntie Ester brought forth the sponge cake.

The driver came to a stop beside the guard house at the entrance to Holden Barracks. A polished and starched Military Police guard stepped out, a pistol on his hip and helmet on his head. He gave them the once over, crisply saluted Eli, and motioned for them to pass.

The jeep pulled up in front of one of several two story cream stucco buildings with steep slate roofs. "Here we are, sir. Welcome to the headquarters of the First Tank Battalion, Sixteenth Armor. You'll find the Adjutant's office just inside the front door to the left." The Private lifted Eli's duffle bag from the back and placed it on the ground. "Good luck, Lieutenant," he said. "You're going to do fine." He gave a proper salute. Then he jumped back in his vehicle and sped off toward the motor pool.

Eli fixed his tie, checked the spit shine on his shoes, and squared his uniform hat. A platoon of infantry marched past in the street, their sergeant calling out cadence. A couple of enlisted men going in the opposite direction strode by on the sidewalk. They straightened up and saluted when they saw Eli. In the distance, he heard the roar of a revving tank engine. The smell of army grease and gunpowder clung to the falling tree leaves.

He looked up at the building that had housed elements of the *Wehrmacht*, once the fiercest fighting force on the planet. He took a deep breath. Then he marched up the two stone steps, opened the heavy oak door, and entered another life.

The battalion commander, Colonel Stratton, could have played the leading man in a war movie - good looking with a subtle swagger and a vibrant voice. He knew Eli's background without even glancing at his personnel jacket. "Honors in Econ. Fifth in your ROTC class. Third at the Armor School. Good record, Schneider."

After a few welcoming comments and benign questions, the colonel turned to military matters. He stood up and came around from behind his desk, circling the chair in which Eli was seated. He stopped in front of a large topographic map of Bavaria affixed to an easel, and pointed his finger at one particular spot. "When the balloon goes up, we block the Ruskies right here." It only took Eli a flash of a second to understand Stratton meant war with the Soviet Union. He said it with a startling combination of certainty and indifference, as though he was talking about a trip to the grocery store, not the possibility of infinite deaths, including his own. Eli did his best to maintain a stony demeanor, but his knees were knocking.

An hour later, his new cigar-chomping company commander also talked about the balloon going up, with similar indifferent certainty. Late in the morning his new platoon sergeant, a grisly Korean War vet, did the same. Eli didn't flinch, but the casual way they all accepted the inevitability of war unnerved him.

Nonetheless, for the first time he felt like a real officer. The eight weeks he spent at the Armor School at Fort Knox had been mostly fun and games, playing war, drinking beer, and chasing women. Now Soviet armor stood just fifty kilometers away, right across the border with East Germany.

That afternoon Eli met his first German up close when he checked into the Bachelor Officers Quarters at the edge of the base, across the street from the imperial fieldstone Officers Club. The BOQ manager was a caricature of a Gestapo agent: balding head, thin mustache, silver wire-rimmed glasses, and a devious English accent. He bowed slightly in formal deference when Eli introduced himself. Eli filled out some official looking Army forms while the manager waited patiently, staring, a stilted smile embossed on his cold face. Then the manager led him out of the office and down the hall, their heels echoing in unison on the glistening stone tile floor.

The German tried to make small talk while they walked. As they climbed the stairs to the second floor, he turned his pellet-like eyes on Eli. "So Lieutenant, your name is Schneider."

"Yes, Eli Schneider."

"That is a German name, no?"

A chill prickled Eli's spine. He was being interrogated. A friend once told him he had the map of Israel painted all over his face. His curly black hair, dark eyes, and Semitic nose surely exposed his pedigree. He glared back at the Gestapo agent. "It's Jewish," he answered as evenly as he could.

The manager nodded, lips pursed, silent. He unlocked the door to Eli's new quarters and ushered him in with an extravagant gesture, and then handed him the key. "Welcome to Kronberg," he said. Eli shivered.

That night, he lay awake wondering what in hell he was doing in this den of wolves. He brooded over the German BOQ manager's malevolent manner, and how indifferent everyone was about the balloon going up. If there was a shooting war with the Russians, he wanted to be in it. He would do his duty to the fullest, but then get the hell out of this goddamn country as fast as he could. In the meantime, he intended having little to do with Germans, even the *frauleins*.

Three days later, the battalion went on alert. American and Soviet tanks and infantry had stumbled into a face-off at Checkpoint Charlie, the one remaining crossing connecting East and West Berlin. After a tense twenty-four hours, both sides stood down, and a nervous calm settled in. But the cement wall hardened in place, doing its job, stopping the flight of East Germans. Allied and Soviet forces, both armed to the teeth, continued to growl at each other all along the mined and fenced no-man's land separating East and West Germany.

By the end of his first thirty days, Eli had adopted the fatalism of every other man in the battalion; given time, war with the Soviets was certain. So he worked hard, played occasionally, and sealed the thought of his own demise in the same vault where he buried other horrors.

Sixteen months later a lot had changed, but not his feeling about Germans.

TWO

Eli should not have been tempted by the promise of a date with another German girl. But on that February day in 1963, he was so bone-weary, and his roommate Harry Ashby was ever so persistent.

The battalion just returned from three weeks at Grafenwehr, the tank gunnery range to the east of Nuremberg. Usually the men and equipment traveled to their home base by train. But this time Colonel Stratton, the battalion commander, ordered a one hundred seventy kilometer road march instead, right in the dead of winter. "Wars aren't always fought in sunshine," he snapped when one of the company commanders gave him a troubled look.

The battalion's seventy-two tanks and support vehicles rolled out at first dim morning light, the fog and wet mist so thick you could barely see the tank in front of you not twenty meters ahead. When the fog lifted, snow began to fall, caking on the roadway and freezing. Diesel exhaust from the tanks in front of Eli enveloped him, streaking his eyeballs red. The frozen metal of the tank turret numbed his hands through his gloves. The column moved at a snail's pace, cold chewing on his exposed nose. He wrapped his wool scarf tight over his face so only his eyes showed, but that didn't help much.

Late in the morning one Delta Company tank slid out of control, skidding sideways down a bank into an apple orchard. It took three hours and two tank retrieval vehicles to hoist it back on the road. In the afternoon, a two-and-a-half ton truck from Alpha Company overturned, injuring three enlisted men. Then a jeep from Headquarters Company crashed into a honey wagon, scattering frozen feces across the pristine snow blanket.

Eighteen hours after they left Grafenwehr, lead elements of the Sixteenth Armor ground through the back gate of Holden Barracks onto Panzerstrasse.

Eli and Harry dragged themselves up the worn wooden stairs to their third floor apartment, combat boots thumping in tired unison. *Frau* Giesler's fried pork chops saturated the stairway corridor. Normally the landlady's cooking made Eli's stomach growl, but right now he was too exhausted to lift a fork to his mouth.

He fished the keys out of his pocket, opened the heavy wooden door, and dumped his duffel bag inside. Harry did the same. "The first thing I need is a hot bath," Eli said. "The second thing I need is a hot woman."

"That should be the first thing you need, dear fellow." Harry wandered to the refrigerator for a beer. He grabbed another for Eli and handed it to him.

"And no prospects."

"Well you shouldn't be sitting home alone on a Saturday night. Let Margot fix you up with her friend. What do have to lose?"

"Another Nazi daughter? No thanks." They had already had this conversation before. Eli could only guess what a friend of Margot's would be like - one more whore eager to hook an American G.I.

Eli flipped the stopper wire off the bottle of Kulmbacher beer and took a long gulp. Then he took off his parka, fatigue jacket, wool scarf, and winter wool hat, and dropped them in a pile on the kitchen linoleum. Harry followed him into the living room, too weary to doff his outerwear, except for his hat. Eli collapsed in the prehistoric blue easy chair. Harry flopped on the battered brown army-issue sofa and closed his eyes.

Eli thought he was asleep. Then Harry spoke again, an articulated mumble. "The problem with you, Eli, is you're too damned picky. You'd get laid every night if you lowered the bar a little."

"I don't like Krauts. So shoot me," Eli mumbled back.

"And you sure let them know it."

And why not? As far as Eli was concerned, they were all still Nazis. Murderers. His first conquest of a *fraulein* felt like rewarding retribution. "I'm a Jew," he said after they finished their business, trying to humiliate the girl. But she just gave him a perplexed look as though his revelation was of no fathomable significance. He only dated two more after that first one, neither more than three times lest she attach herself to him.

"Maybe I'm just tired of them," Eli sighed. "Would it hurt so much if they shaved their armpits once in a while? Or took a bath?" He didn't notice his own rank field aroma.

"I'll have Margot tell her to take a bath and shave," Harry quipped. Then he was more serious. "I hear Lara's got some class."

Eli forced his eyes open. "Then what's she doing going out with American soldiers?"

"She usually doesn't, but Margot likes you."

"But does she put out?"

"Have you met one who doesn't?" Harry rubbed the back of his hand slowly as if trying to rub away his abundant freckles.

"Are you seeing Margot tonight?" Eli asked.

"I need some sleep first. She'll wait until tomorrow."

Eli stared at the snow piling up on the window ledge outside, mesmerized. His eyes closed, and then struggled to open. The radiator thumped as scalding water steamed through. *Frau* Giesler must have heard them come in, and knew they would crave warmth.

"Tell her okay, I'll give her friend a fling."

Harry smiled. They both closed their eyes and descended into a deep sleep.

Eli would have denied it, but what he really wanted was a good American girl who would love him without reservation, and who he could love back in the same way. He understood he wasn't going to find her among the few American schoolteachers he met at the Officers' Club. The ones who interested him were either too old, unwilling, or already taken. And by now the German girls disgusted him, so he mostly stayed away, resigned to living like a monk for the nine months until he rotated home.

THREE

"Lighten up," Harry scolded his friend. "Lara's looking forward to meeting you. Don't screw it up."

"I hope that means I'm going to get laid tonight," Eli answered. He looked in the mirror and straightened his tie, his good navy blue one with the red diagonal stripes. Then he slipped on his herringbone sports jacket.

"I'll pick the girls up at Margot's, and meet you at the Cave in half an hour," Harry said. This was necessary, Margot had explained to Harry, because Lara's father forbade his twenty-four year old daughter to date American G.I.s. What would her father say, Eli wondered, if he found out she was not only on a date with an American, but a Jewish one at that? More importantly, what would Lara say? Eli had no intention of telling her.

"Don't forget a condom," Harry teased.

Eli checked his pants pocket. "Loaded and ready to go."

Harry touched him on the forearm, and turned serious for a moment. "Eli, be a gentleman, please," he warned. "Lara's a nice girl."

Anyone who knew Eli before Germany would have been surprised he needed such a warning. He had been raised right. In high school and college, he was the kind of respectful young man mothers prayed for and fathers trusted their precious daughters with. Eli was a gentleman to a fault. He was the only one at Carlyle College who didn't know Sonia Pike had been passed around. He dated her for two months before she thrust herself on him in frustration. The same thing happened with Nicky Morris, a childhood friend from Berkinbury who he dated in the summer before he went in the Army. He wasn't a complete saint when he finally recognized these rare opportunities.

Recently there was Angela Barton, an American schoolteacher in Kronberg he saw a few times late last summer. He could have fallen for Angela, but she rotated home in September. They wrote a couple of times, and then stopped, both losing interest at such a distance.

It was peculiar how, when he was with one of the schoolteachers, his naturally chivalrous manners asserted themselves. German girls were a different matter entirely. He didn't care for their Nazi parents, and didn't respect the daughters who were little better than prostitutes, trading their favors for a good time. He could have lived without these big boned farm girls but for the occasional need for physical gratification. Yet each of these uncommon encounters left him more empty, more lonely, and angry with himself.

He had to admit his mother and grandmother would be disappointed in him if they knew he disrespected any girl, even a German girl. And his cousin Rose would have his head. But tonight he muffled his conscience when he parked his beat up blue Volkswagen along the river in Sulzfeld, right next to Harry's prize.

Harry's brand new Chevy Impala convertible was his graduation present from his mother, heiress to the Billingham railroad fortune. By graduation time, Harry's father barely spoke to his disappointing son.

The elder Ashby headed one of the most prominent law firms in Manhattan. Harry's two older brothers graduated from Yale law school, just like their father, and immediately joined the firm. On the other hand, Andover Academy expelled Harry in his senior year for sleeping with the principal's daughter. His poor grades forced his father to make a generous donation to Westbridge College, a small second tier school in Connecticut, just to get him admitted. Harry liked his parties, and might have flunked out were it not for his father's continuing donations. He took ROTC in a fit of patriotism and defiance, the first in the Ashby family to so serve since the Civil War. His father was furious with him.

Eli felt lucky to have found a friend like Harry. Though Harry was a true Scarsdale blue blood, the two young officers were similar in one important way. They were both misfits. Maybe that's what made Eli so eager to protect his friend. The two of them started as platoon leaders together in Bravo Company, arriving in Germany within days of each other in October 1961. Each was driven by his determination to prove himself worthy.

While Eli took quickly to the army, and knew instinctively how to earn the loyalty of the men he led, Harry didn't. So Eli spent hours tutoring him on map reading, tank gunnery, communications, and tactics. They often talked late into the night over beer and pretzels in their BOQ rooms. Harry learned quickly and well. After a few months he was technically as good as any platoon leader in the battalion. But he still couldn't feel what it was like to be a poor white boy from the Ozarks, a black kid from Chicago, or a Chicano from a San Antonio barrio. Eli had no such difficulty.

Last summer they moved into their off-base apartment at 7 Lindenstrasse in Kronberg, across a small park from the stone tower marking the old city gate. Harry wanted to get to know the Germans better. Eli went along with the move to be with Harry, and to enjoy more comfortable quarters.

Through Harry, Eli met a few German girls eager to please an American army officer. He also introduced Eli to three German guys their age, the only ones Eli knew. They hung out together for a short while, but Eli couldn't hide his contempt for all things German. After Harry met Margot, it came down to just Eli and the one named Willy Speer.

Eli locked his car, though no right-minded thief would think of stealing it, not with Harry's beauty parked right beside it. He avoided the icy patches on the cobblestone street and the half-melted, gritty snow mounds gathered in corners by the houses. When he reached the entrance to the Cave a block away, he bounded up the three stone steps and pushed open the red door.

He was nervous about meeting Lara, mostly because he didn't want to embarrass Harry by making a fool of himself. And he didn't want to offend Margot. He liked Margot enough to now and then forget she was German.

Sometimes Eli envied Harry for having Margot. She adored him, and he made no secret that Margot's performance between the sheets exceeded all of his previous experiences. Eli didn't want to think of the hurt Margot faced when Harry rotated home in November at the end of his tour of duty. Margot was not some-one you brought home to Mother's Scarsdale society. She was coarse, big boned, and cursed using every bit of the colorful G.I. slang she learned working as a sales girl at the Holden Barracks Post Exchange. Her sarcastic, foul-mouthed humor always made Eli laugh.

To be honest about it, Eli couldn't understand why Margot had such a hold on Harry. He could have had his pick of many Ger-man girls, or just about any American schoolteacher he wanted, for that matter. He was not a handsome man. In fact he was kind of goofy looking, toothy and gangly with tussled red-brown hair and strawberry freckles. But Eli envied how comfortable Harry was with girls, and how comfortable they were with him. He was kind, considerate, and made them laugh. It also didn't hurt that he drove that big white Impala convertible.

The Cave was a bar not more than ten kilometers from Kronberg, frequented by young Germans and single American Army officers. On Saturday nights Eddie, the stout owner, brought in a small German dance band with a singer who imagined himself a cross between Elvis Presley and Perry Como. But the noises the group produced sounded more like a faded German brass band playing a polka.

When Eli walked in the door, the music hadn't started playing yet, but the room already buzzed like a beehive with the queen bee in heat. Eddie rushed over to greet him with a familiar "*guten tag,*" and a hearty handshake. Eddie tried to make his place a hip club like clubs he envisioned existed in America. He failed, but the Cave did have its own unique *Deutche* farm-country character. Chrome-legged lime green and orange plastic chairs surrounded chrome-legged, lime green Formica-topped tables. A thick cigarette haze fused with muted blue lights.

Young German women on the make already occupied more than half of the tables, some sitting with German men, some with American Army officers, and a few unattached and available. Eli caught a glimpse of a few of his fellow officers at the bar - Richard Kaine, Hank Swisher, and Mario Franco.

He spotted Margot and Harry at a table in the back corner. Margot waved him over. When he drew close enough to see Lara, he was only faintly aroused. Margot was one of a kind, and Eli didn't expect Lara to be a duplicate, but he was not prepared for an opposite.

Big-bosomed Margot wore a flowered blouse so tight it pulled on the buttons, and gaped open so you could see her black bra underneath. Cold as it was outside, the blouse was nearly sleeveless, revealing a little of her hairy underarms and muscular limbs.

Her tight leather skirt climbed up to her thighs, and her mouse-brown hair looked like she had just climbed out of bed with no time to comb it.

Lara, on the other hand, had the lithe frame of a ballet dancer. She reminded him of Leslie Caron. Her white blouse, peach cardigan sweater, and pleated gray skirt covered her properly. Her fine, muddy blonde hair hung loosely behind her ears, and her small dark brown eyes glistened. A kind, gentle smile lay on her lips even when no one was watching.

A cigarette dangled from Margot's lips while she introduced Eli and Lara. "I am pleased to meet you, *Leutnant*," Lara said. She stood and held out her hand giving Eli the customary firm, single-pump German handshake, a genuine smile on her face. When she spoke, it sounded more like lyrical French than guttural German. But make no mistake, Eli cautioned himself, she is no fragile *fraulein*.

Lara fidgeted with her glass of white Franken wine and tried to look amused when Harry, Margot, and Eli joked about Margot's bald boss and the battalion officers' frigid wives. Lara laughed when the others laughed. Eli smoked one cigarette after another. Each time he offered Lara one of his American Pall Mall's she reached for it like a starving chick grabbing a worm. Margot and Harry filled in the conversation until they got bored and went off to dance.

When the band began playing a passable rendition of *Blue Moon*, Eli asked Lara to dance. On the way to the dance floor, he caught enough of a view from behind to appreciate her adorable round rump, her most generous feature.

Lara may have looked like a ballerina, but she danced like a cow. She kept stepping on Eli's toes, and then apologized profusely. "No, no. It is my fault," he insisted. "I am not a very good dancer." Actually Eli considered his dance moves one of his more admirable traits.

Most of the other couples on the dance floor cuddled close, whether Germans or Americans. Margot and Harry were so entwined they looked like they were going to have sex right there. Lara didn't notice, concentrating hard on the movement of her own feet and Eli's. She compounded her clumsy dancing by keeping him at rigid arm's length as though they were in the nineteenth century doing a Viennese waltz.

By the end of their second dance, Eli learned Lara liked American authors, some of the same ones he liked: Steinbeck, James Michener, and Leon Uris. He tried not to react to the last one when she said she loved *Exodus,* a story about Jews. She also liked American movies and went to nearly every one that came to Kronberg's movie theater. She worshipped Humphrey Bogart and Ingrid Bergman. Eli, hoping to score through flattery, insisted they were his favorites too.

After the third dance he learned she was born and raised in Kronberg; she lived with her mother, father, and younger sister Katrin, and was now apprenticing to a photographer in town who owned a shop near the fountain just around the corner from the *Rathaus* - the city hall. Eli told her he was Executive Officer of Charlie Company, and came from Brooklyn. He didn't tell her he was born in the town of Uman in the Ukraine, or that he was a Jew.

"I like American jazz," she said, a twinkle in her eye.

"Me too." Eli meant it this time.

"Yah. Chubby Checker, Beach Boys, Elvis Presley."

Eli didn't want to tell her that those were not jazz musicians, but his speechless serious face must have given him away. Then she started laughing. "I tell a joke, yah? For truth, my favorites are Dave Brubeck, Dizzy Gillespie, and Mel Torme. I have their records."

Eli laughed too, and on the next song Lara snuggled close to him when the male vocalist gave a passable rendition of Elvis Presley's *Love Me Tender*. This time they didn't step on each other's toes. He liked the feel of holding her slender body in his arms. Her hair smelled like eucalyptus, not harsh soap like other German girls he knew. He pulled her closer. They swayed to the music, pressed together. She aroused more than just his interest. But when the next song started, Lara resumed her rigid distance, notifying Eli he hadn't really made much progress.

Margot and Harry cut out early, eager to get down to business. They would probably be in bed in the apartment by the time Eli got back, even if he got lucky. On the way out, Harry whispered "good luck" in his ear, and gave him a wink. Lara pretended not to notice.

Eli tried to push one more glass of wine on her, hoping inebriation would achieve where charm had failed. She declined, but kept up a stream of chatter in near-perfect English. "My mother and Margot's mother met just before the end of the war. They were both clearing away bricks and rubble after British planes dropped bombs on Kronberg." She said it as matter-of-factly as if she were describing a change in the weather.

"It must have been horrible." Eli did his best to fake a sympathy he didn't feel. Then he offered her another cigarette. She grabbed it. He lit it for her and she continued.

"Margot and I, we were only six years old, playing close by while our mothers worked. Sometimes we helped. Then we go to school together all the way until high school. And then I go on to *gymnasium* and Margot to vocational school. It broke my heart to separate us. But now we are still best friends." She smiled.

They left The Cave soon after. Lara bundled up in her brown scarf and heavy honey-brown loden coat. She pulled on a brown beret-type hat half way covering her ears. The weather had warmed a little in the week since the battalion returned from Grafenwehr, but not enough to use his car as a lair. The ancient Volkswagen barely put out enough heat to prevent frostbite. He hated having to buy any German product, but this old rattletrap was all he could afford. He apologized to Lara for it as he opened the door for her. "It is a very nice car," she replied.

Eli always held his breath when he turned the key, wondering how many cranks it would take before it started. This time it only took two tries, but it would be ten minutes before the worthless heater began producing any warmth.

Lara had not encouraged Eli all evening, and she only mildly aroused him. But she was all that was available at the moment, so as they approached Kronberg, he gave it a last try. "I have a great collection of jazz records," he said, trying to sound sincere. "Brubeck, Dizzy, Duke Ellington. Our apartment is close by, right around the corner from the tower."

"I must be home." She looked straight ahead as she spoke, her gaze fixed on some figment far beyond the windshield.

"Margot and Harry are probably there."

"Nein, danke." She braced as if expecting a physical assault.

Eli let out a sigh loud enough to deliver a message. "Alright, so where do you live?"

Lara exhaled. "Take me to the corner on this side of the *Alte Brucke*, please."

He kept driving, letting his silence speak. "I am sorry," she finally said, looking over at him. "This is my first time on a date with an American in a very long time."

Eli turned the corner by the tower and drove toward the old bridge - the *Alte Brucke*. A half block away he slowed down. "Where should I stop?" he asked.

"There by the candy store," she said, pointing.

He did as he was told, pulling over and shifting into neutral, but letting the car idle to keep the heater going.

"Which is your house?" he asked.

"Oh, I live just on the other side of the bridge."

"Well, let me drive you there," he said, moving to put the car in gear.

"No, no," she cried out, and moved her hand to stop him from shifting.

He gave her a frown, intentionally showing his confusion. He let his hand linger on the gear shift, her hand resting on his.

"My father does not like me to date with American soldiers," she said. She bit her lower lip, embarrassed, her eyes asking for him to understand.

"Doesn't like Americans, huh. And why is that?"

"He thinks he is protecting me. People say bad things about German girls who date American soldiers." She squeezed his hand before lifting hers. "I am sorry to say this."

Eli looked over at her. Her dark eyes shined in the glow from the streetlights on the bridge. She looked so cute in that silly brown beret. He reached his arm around her and pulled her toward him. She held her face up, and he kissed her. Her warm, soft lips tasted like brown sugar. She pressed back against his lips. He pushed the hat off her head and ran his fingers through her silken hair. She pulled away and looked into his eyes. She let out a long sigh and touched her hand to the back of his head. Then she pressed her lips against his again.

The front seat of a tiny 1956 Volkswagen with a gear shift between the two front bucket seats was hardly the place to make a move, but Eli had to try. He ran his tongue along her lips. Then he unbuttoned the top button of her loden coat and slipped his hand inside, searching for a breast. Whether it was something about her, or simply the hangover from three weeks in the field, he was ready to devour her right there.

Lara pulled away, grabbing at the handle of the car door. "I must go now," she said, a tremble in her voice. "Thank you for a nice evening." With that, she bolted from the car and scurried over the *Alte Brucke*, her heels clicking on the medieval cobble-stones.

Eli watched her until she disappeared over the hump of the arch in the middle of the bridge. He was upset. He couldn't tell if she was just a tease, or if he scared her. Either way, this night had been a waste of time, and he wasn't going to waste any more of it. She wasn't worth it. Too bad. She might have been interesting. It was time to find a more willing *fraulein*, one whose father didn't hate Americans so much.

The taste of brown sugar lingered on his lips.

FOUR

Slushy rain pounded against the windows. Eli prayed they wouldn't call an alert. This was a Sunday morning to stay inside, savor the stillness, and catch his breath after the three weeks in the field at Grafenwehr.

Harry hadn't come home last night, which was okay with Eli. He and Harry worked out a bachelor's agreement right from the beginning; if one of them had a lady friend spend the night, the other one slept on the couch. But now with Harry bedding Margot on such a regular basis, that no longer worked. So at times Harry and Margot, with no urging from Eli, rented a hotel room in the small town of Marktbriet, a safe distance from Kronberg. Harry still tried to protect Margot's reputation, though who knows why? Margot didn't seem to care about her reputation one way or the other as long as she could be with Harry.

A touch of the blues poked at Eli from the moment he woke up. Maybe the dismal weather brought on a little touch of homesickness. Or maybe it was the loneliness of the empty apartment. It had nothing to do with his failure to seduce Lara, he told himself. He had experienced such failures before. He did regret missing a chance to squeeze her adorable buns, but not enough to waste any more time on her. Why was he even thinking about her at all?

A package from Grandma Sara arrived while he was in the field. She sent him another warm woolen sweater she knitted for him, this one a deep forest green. Like all of her knitting projects, one sleeve was longer than the other, the front shorter than the back, and many a stitch missed. He didn't mind. When he pressed the sweater to his cheek, he could feel her gentle touch.

A door slammed in the stairway below, probably the family returning home from church. *Herr* Giesler's law office occupied the first floor of the gray stone building. The Giesler living quarters occupied the second floor, Harry's and Eli's small apartment the third. Eli avoided his neighbors. Occasionally he exchanged grunts with *Frau* Giesler when they passed on the stairway, but Harry handled all of the necessary tenant-landlord interaction. Last Christmas evening *Frau* Giesler invited them for coffee and kuchen. Harry went. Eli didn't.

On a dark day, light from outside struggled for a foothold. Harry's German souvenirs littered the apartment, catching dust: Hummels, carved wooden figures, pewter-topped ceramic beer steins, and a cuckoo clock that drove Eli nuts. Eli marked his own presence mostly with his collection of jazz records and Book-of-the-Month-Club selections stacked in the bookcase. He wanted no souvenirs to remind him of Germany when he went home.

He picked out a Modern Jazz Quartet album and loaded it on the record player he bought in the Post Exchange when they moved into the apartment. The quartet's *Autumn in New York* reflected the quiet blues he felt at the moment. He listened while he ate his toast and drank his dark coffee - no milk and one cube of sugar. Then he sat down at the big black desk to write Grandma Sara and Grandpa Avi a letter. In the note she enclosed with the sweater, Grandma again asked if he was eating well, and if he was safe. She also wanted to know if he had a gun. She, like his mother, worried more about local Nazis than a Soviet invasion.

Sleet hammered against the windows without letup. He looked at the framed picture of Grandma and Grandpa on the end of the desk, taken of them dancing at his bar mitzvah eleven years ago. They were so much younger then. The last time he saw them, just before he shipped out, they looked old and frail. Grandma was now eighty and Grandpa eighty-one. Eli feared one or both of them could be gone before he returned home.

He thought about how hard he tried on the day of his bar mitzvah to look as happy as his mother, father, Grandma, Grandpa, and all of his aunts and uncles. He didn't want to disappoint them, but he could never forget he was an orphan, and that his real mother and father were murdered. Even now at twenty-four years old, he still harbored a dread that those who loved him most could be taken from him at any moment.

His new life began the day Grandma and Grandpa found him. He was a little boy of eight, scared and all alone except for his desperate attachment to the other twenty European war orphans who flew with him from Vienna. In the days after they landed, they were hustled from one location to another, terrified, confused, and hungry.

Then one morning, a nice woman he didn't know led him down the hall of an orphanage in the Bronx. At the end of the hall, he spied a gray haired, wrinkled old man and old woman clutching each other's hands, their gazes fastened on him. He stopped and examined them. He recognized the old man though he never met him before. Yet he knew as soon as he looked into the old man's glistening eyes that he belonged to him. He moved cautiously into the outstretched arms. The old man clutched him close and whispered in his ear, "I will be your Grandpa Avi."

That afternoon they took him home with them. And the next day he met their daughter Yakira and her husband Jake. "They are your new mother and father," his new grandfather told him, his strong voice providing the comfort of certainty. It took Eli many months before he could call them Mother Kira and Father

Jake. It was even longer before he could feel it inside of him. Now they were just Mom and Dad.

One cloudy September day soon after his thirteenth birthday, Grandpa Avi took young Eli for a walk along the water in Manhattan Beach, the part of Brooklyn where they lived. They sat down on a bench by the wood-planked walkway skirting the sand. The beach was nearly deserted on such a cool, overcast morning.

The old man took his grandson's hand in his own and didn't let go. "It is time you know where you came from." His serious tone of voice made Eli uncomfortable.

"I came from Brooklyn," he insisted.

"Before Brooklyn."

His grandfather looked right at him. Eli stared at the sea gulls sprinting through the spray at the water's edge. Small, quiet waves lapped the shore. He pulled his light jacket shut.

"You were born in a place far away," Grandpa began, as if telling a bible story. "A town called Uman in Russia." He took a deep breath. "Your father's name was Joshua, and your mother was Leya. You had two big sisters named Rebekah and Anya. Your grandfather was my brother, Lieb, and your dear grandmother was named Golde."

Grandpa Avi let go of his hand and reached into the outer pocket of his tan windbreaker. He pulled out an envelope containing a small, worn black and white photo. He handed it to Eli. An aged man with a beard and an aged woman in a simple dress posed in back next to a younger clean-shaven man. An attractive dark haired woman sat in a chair holding an infant. Equally attractive dark-haired young girls stood on each side of her.

Eli glanced at the photo for only an instant. "I don't know these people."

"Let me tell you about them." The old man took back the

photo and returned it to its envelope. "I will save this picture for you."

"I don't want it."

"Your mother and father loved you so much they gave you to a Christian woman to save your life. You were only two years old."

Eli winced. He glimpsed in a foggy memory someone old, maybe his Grandpa Lieb, handing him to a stranger, an older woman.

"Her name was Valerya Shumenko, the wife of a dear family friend," Grandpa Avi continued. "You called her Auntie Via. She hid you and took care of you until the war in the Ukraine passed."

Auntie Via - a name and a person he had willed himself to forget from the moment he arrived in America, as he refused to remember everything before America. "Why did they give me away?" Eli demanded, agitated. But he already knew the answer to that.

Grandpa patted his hand and resumed the story. Without giving him the details, Avi told the boy how the Germans overran Uman in the early days of their invasion of Russia. Then they killed Eli's mother, father, sisters, Grandpa Lieb, Grandma Golde, and all of the Jews in their town, the same town where Grandpa Avi and Grandma Sara grew up. "They shot every one of them and buried them in a beautiful ravine called Sukhi Yar." Grandpa gulped and looked out to sea, quiet until he gathered himself.

Eli was one of the fortunate few who survived, hidden and raised by Auntie Via. The Nazis murdered her husband, and her two sons died fighting in the war. To protect Eli, she changed his name to Ilya, a Russian name, and claimed he was her dead son's child. She became his *babushka* - his grandmother.

Eli wished Grandpa Avi would stop the story, but he didn't. "Auntie Via was a remarkable woman," he went on. "Soon after the war ended, when the Communists hadn't yet sealed the borders, she walked with you half way across Europe. To a Displaced Persons Camp for orphans, in Austria. She died right after that. Then they flew you to America with some other orphans. President Truman himself ordered it." He patted Eli on the leg.

Eli said nothing, looking down at his hands mostly. Finally he spoke. "Who is Auntie Zoya?"

Avi shook his head, puzzled. "I don't know. Who is she?"

"I don't know either," Eli snapped back. But clearly he did know.

By the time Grandpa finished, Eli felt angry and ashamed, guilty that he alone survived. Why him?

That day was the first day he felt a mad rage at the Nazis and all things German. It mounted from there. He developed a hunger to learn all he could about Hitler, and the war - particularly the war on the Eastern Front. One might say that for a while revenge obsessed him, even into adulthood. When in May 1962 the Israelis executed Adolf Eichmann, a major Nazi organizer of the Holocaust, Eli bought all of his buddies a round of drinks at the Officers Club. His Gentile guests appreciated the gesture, but had no idea they were celebrating a hanging.

In spite of the abundance of family love he received, Eli grew up feeling he belonged nowhere and to no one. He feared abandonment would happen again. So he smiled a lot, and strived to make his American family so proud of him they would never desert him.

When he first landed in America he spoke no English. Two years later, he was fluent. And when he graduated from junior high school, he won the coveted English Merit Award given to the most outstanding English student. He excelled in everything he tried, and grew up more American than any American born kid. He worshipped the Brooklyn Dodgers, Audie Murphy, General George S. Patton, and especially his Uncle Henry, a decorated Marine fighter pilot wounded in the Pacific during World War II.

In grade school and junior high school, he tried to hide the fact he was a Russian orphan, but the other kids knew, and sometimes made brutal fun of him. Salvation came when, just before he entered high school, Mother Kira decided they should move from the other end of Brooklyn to Manhattan Beach to be closer to Grandma Sara and Grandpa Avi who were getting old and needed more help.

In high school, Eli reinvented himself, changing his name from Elias to Eli because it sounded more American and more grownup. He created the first eight years of his life as he wanted them to be, sometimes convincing even himself he was born in a small town in Pennsylvania coal country. He told none of his new friends the truth, not even Harry. He dropped all of the old friends who knew his real story.

Eli enjoyed many good moments in his growing-up years, but at times he felt empty and detached despite everything Mother Kira and Father Jake did to love him. They tried so hard to give him attention he didn't deserve, and gave him anything to make him happy. No one wanted to discipline him. As a consequence, now and then he got out of hand. That's when Grandpa Avi stepped in and with a single look reminded him why he was still alive. Then Eli berated himself for his ingratitude, and redoubled his efforts to make them all proud of him.

He won a scholarship to Carlyle College, a well-regarded little Ivy in upstate New York not far from Syracuse. Grandpa Avi and Grandma Sara cried sweet tears on the day he graduated four years later. In his senior year, he was elected president of his fraternity, captain of the wrestling team, and starred in cross-country. Eli and his date, the perfectly pretty Bobbi Larsen, were voted King and Queen of the Homecoming Court. Girls found him attractive, and guys followed his leadership. But he never let anyone other than his cousins Max and Rose get too close to him.

When college graduation came around, most of Eli's friends set about picking graduate schools or winning their first corporate jobs. Eli knew where he was going - into the Army. By then he was a fervent Nazis hater, a resolute anti-Communist, and an idealistic disciple of the dashing young President John Kennedy.

Even with all he accomplished and all of the friends he made, most of the time he still didn't feel at home anywhere. Then they pinned gold bars on his shoulders, and things changed. In the Army, no one cared if he was a Jew as long as he could fight. The dog tags hung around his neck carried the embossed "J" for Jewish, and that was okay with him.

The sleet turned to rain, and let up a little. Eli could no longer hear it pounding on the slate roof above. He began the letter. *Dear Grandma. Thank you so much for the sweater. I love it, and am wearing it now as I write to you. Grandpa, thank you for the five dollars you sent with it. I will do as you suggested and spend it on something fun.*

When he finished the letter, he sealed it in an envelope and began another, this time to his cousin Max. All Max wanted to know was how Eli was doing with the women. Max was a lieutenant in the Navy, serving on the guided missile cruiser Burlington sailing out of Pearl Harbor. He was thoroughly enjoying himself. Max didn't really like ships; he went to Naval Officer

Candidate School after college mostly to avoid the draft, but partly because he liked the Navy's uniforms.

By mid-afternoon the rain stopped, but the skies stayed gloomy German-winter gray. Where was Harry? He was usually home by now. Eli put a Duke Ellington album on the record player, hoping the Newport concert would brighten his mood. He shined his brass and his tanker's combat boots, even down to the wrap-around straps. He read six chapters of *The Agony and the Ecstasy,* and smoked through a complete pack of Pall Malls. By the time he lit the last one, Stan Kenton's orchestra was playing the song *Laura.* Lara Kohler's cute smile shot through his mind for a split second, that and the sweet taste of brown sugar when he kissed her. He pushed her out of his thoughts.

By late afternoon, boredom was about to embalm him when he heard the door lock turn. "You look like hell," Eli wisecracked when Harry wobbled into the living room.

"Margot wore me out." Harry plopped down on the sofa. "So, did you score, old sport?"

"Score? Hell, I didn't even get to bat." Eli got up and turned the stereo down low. "That girl's a teaser."

Harry lit a cigarette and blew a cloud toward the ceiling. "Well, my friend, apparently Lara likes you, though heaven knows why. She told Margot you look like Paul Newman."

"You've got to be kidding me." The reference to Paul Newman embarrassed Eli. He searched for an appropriate retort, but came up empty. So he said, "Paul Newman was half Jewish, you know."

"Dear god, don't start again." Harry let out a long theatrical sigh. "In my current state, another Nazi lecture will surely drive me absolutely mad."

"Her father hates Americans. Wonder what that's about."

Harry's devilish grin returned. "Need you ask? Are your intentions anything other than dishonorable, my friend?"

"But you always say I'm such a fine gentleman," Eli dead-panned.

"You and the whole Third Infantry Division," Harry shot back. "Hell, the only guy I know who's hornier than me is you."

"And you're well taken care of." Eli's voice carried a touch of envy, and it was about more than Harry being taken care of. Harry had Margot.

That night, as they did every night, Eli and Harry laid out their fatigues on the top of their footlockers, and tucked a pair of warm, wool socks into their tanker's boots. They donned their long underwear and crawled in bed. Eli turned out the light.

"Lara does have a nice ass," Harry said into the dark.

"I think she wears a chastity belt," Eli answered. "Ask Margot if she knows where she hides the key."

"I think she hides it behind the bush."

Eli could hear Harry smiling.

FIVE

At four o'clock Monday morning, the cruel shrill of the phone ruptured a sound sleep. Eli grabbed it before the end of the first ring. "Alert," the voice on the other end of the line hollered. By the time Eli hung up the phone, Harry was already into his fatigues, grabbing for his tanker's boots. Eli slung on his own, and both of them bolted for the door, still buttoning their pants.

Fifteen minutes later Eli was in his jeep, steel pot on his head and pistol on his hip, zipping down the runway toward the pads where Charlie Company's seventeen M-60 tanks stood waiting amid the purposed frenzy. Jeeps and trucks crossed in all directions. Men from the battalion's seventy-two tanks scrambled for their vehicles.

Monthly alerts hit randomly, day or night, and no one ever knew whether this one might be the time the balloon goes up - war. The battalion's deployment during the Cuban Missile Crisis started just this way. For thirteen nerve-blistering days in October, the world moved toward nuclear Armageddon after American U-2 flights over Cuba discovered the installation of Soviet nuclear missiles aimed at the United States. President Kennedy threatened to knock them out. If war started, American Intelligence expected the Soviets to strike back in Germany where they held overwhelming numerical superiority.

On the fourth day of the crisis, the Sixteenth Armor and the rest of the Third Infantry Division deployed north of Wurzburg near the East German border, faced off against three Soviet divisions. Then, with an American naval blockade of Cuba in place, and the threat of an attack on the island, Khrushchev agreed to remove the Soviet missiles. In exchange, Kennedy pledged not to invade Cuba to overthrow Castro, then or in the future.

During those nine days in the field, action-induced spikes of adrenalin alternated with long hours of stupefying boredom. Yet as close as war was, at no time did Eli contemplate what it would be like to actually kill someone, no less the possibility he might die himself. All of his energy went into doing his job and doing it well. When it was over, he was relieved, of course. But it also felt like a ball game never played, or a canceled date with the town's loose redhead. It wasn't a total waste. His personal performance earned him his promotion from one of many platoon leaders in the battalion to Executive Officer of Charlie Company, second in command.

This alert and every alert began much the same as the Cuba alert. Radios squawked. Men scrambled up the noses of their tanks and into the turrets. Headlights came on as one tank after another started its engine, thundering diesel exhaust into the cold, clear pre-dawn darkness. Main guns swung from rear to front, ready to roll. The twinkling stars might have been called beautiful if Eli's mind wasn't focused on his urgent task.

The first job was to get the Charlie Company tanks off the runway, out the back gate, and into concealed positions in Kasper Forest. Tanks lined up on a runway made tempting targets for Soviet aircraft. If this time it was the real thing, the battalion would move out from the forest to planned positions, ready to block the Soviet invasion. The challenge was also to get Charlie Company out the gate first, just as they had done on every alert since Captain Symanski took over as company commander seven months earlier.

The taste of the diesel, the grind of gears, and the possibility of battle intoxicated Eli like a Spartan at Thermopylae. The inside of his gut churned, but ice water ran through his brain. Everything moved in slow motion; he could see one step ahead. Even an old war horse like Company First Sergeant Bill D. Pickett took comfort from his Executive Officer's clear eyed determination and commanding presence.

Eli's driver pulled the jeep up in front of the first platoon, next to Sergeant Pickett's jeep. The First Sergeant jumped out and hustled over. "The Old Man's not going to make it, sir," Pickett said in his Tennessee twang, referring to Captain Symanski. Eli nodded, unsurprised. Symanski no longer confined his weekend benders to weekends.

The headlights of sixteen of the company's seventeen tanks cut through the darkness. That meant each had a driver and at least one other crew member on board, ready to roll. "First and Third Platoons have checked in," Pickett hollered above the din of the engines. A cloud of icy breath belched from his mouth as he spoke.

Eli nodded. "Any other company out the gate yet?" Eli didn't want to finish second in this, his first chance to lead the company during an alert.

"No sir."

Eli keyed his radio handset. "Charlie Two Six, what's your status?"

Just then, the last tank's headlights came on. "This is Two Six. Ready to roll, over," Lieutenant Kaine crackled back, testosterone streaming through the speaker.

Eli keyed his handset again. "Hotel Six, this is Charlie Five. Ready to roll, over." He imagined Colonel Stratton on the other end, weighing the absence of Captain Symanski and whether to let Eli lead the battalion out without the Charlie Company commander.

Silence. Then, "Charlie Five, this is Hotel Six. Move out."

Tank treads clanked and ground. The earth shook. Charlie Company rumbled out the gate. God, I do love this, Eli thought.

He loved it all: the alerts, the maneuvers across the German countryside, mock tank battles, the pomp of the dress blues battalion parties, the golden horse cavalry scarves, the army lingo, and the implicit danger every minute of every day. Hell, he even liked creamed chip beef on toast - "shit on a shingle" - though he would never admit it. Ultimate orgasm came when the company's seventeen tanks lined up on the firing range at Grafenwehr, and opened fire simultaneously with their one-O-five millimeter cannons and machine guns, producing a noxious cocktail of gunpowder perfume, smoky haze, and ear-shattering explosions.

Two hours after Eli's phone rang, the battalion stood down, recalled. No war this time, but a reminder. Eli didn't look forward to going into Captain Symanski's office this morning when he returned to company headquarters. He never knew what he was going to find. He and Sergeant Pickett joined together as unacknowledged co-conspirators protecting their aging, battle worn company commander until he could retire next year. In Eli's eyes, Captain Ski had earned it.

The Captain joined the Army right before Pearl Harbor, landed with Patton in North Africa, and fought across Europe until VE day. When he was discharged, he drifted for a few years until the Army called him back to active duty during the Korean War. He was wounded twice.

First Sergeant Pickett, himself a decorated Korean War veteran, seemed to know everything about everyone. He confided in Eli that Captain Ski was divorced, estranged from his son and daughter, and just waiting to retire to a fishing boat in the Florida Keys. Two weeks ago he learned the Army had sent his son, a first lieutenant, to someplace called Vietnam as a military adviser. The Captain worried about him.

Eli appreciated Captain Symanski for plucking him from the crowd of platoon leaders to be his executive officer. He mentored Eli. He was a superb teacher, a compassionate leader, and a masterful tactician in tank warfare. Eli and every man in the company would gladly follow Captain Ski into battle, drunk or sober.

Eli held his breath and knocked softly on the closed door to the Captain's office. When he didn't answer, Eli opened the door slowly and found him asleep in his chair, head down on the desk, window shades half-drawn. A near-empty bottle of bourbon sat in the bottom desk drawer, visible to anyone who couldn't smell it.

Captain Symanski raised his head when he heard Eli enter, and brushed back his messy graying hair with his fingers. He nodded a greeting and then a forced a fake cough. He pulled a bottle of cough syrup from his breast pocket and offered it to Eli. Eli shook his head. The Captain took a short swig.

Eli reported on the alert, and the company's success. In response, Symanski told him to give the men the afternoon off as a reward. "You take a short day too," the old man said, struggling to keep from slurring his words. "You earned it."

He was about to leave the captain to sleep it off when he thought better of it. Hell, it's still his company, he thought. "Sir, Private Salyer's in trouble again. He was picked up by the MP's on Saturday night, drunk as a skunk and out after curfew. Sergeant Pickett had to go down and bail him out of the brig. Second time in a month. We have to do something."

At first his words didn't seem to register. Captain Symanski took another slug of cough syrup. His red-rimmed grey-blue eyes blinked and narrowed. He cleared his foggy throat before speaking. "Remember this, Lieutenant. These are young men who are in a strange country far from home, lonely, horny as hell, and under a tension day and night no nineteen year old should have to live with. They know what you know. Fifty kilometers from here, three Soviet armored divisions sit across the East German border, ready to roll. Against our one reinforced tank battalion. When the balloon goes up, we're not going to last very long."

It sounded to Eli like he was making excuses for every eight ball in the battalion. "So what do we do about Salyer?"

"They might act like little boys sometimes, but when the time comes, these young men will fight like hell."

"He's just going to do it again."

"Make him your jeep driver." Eli started to protest, but Symanski kept talking. "Salyer's just a scared kid, never been away from his momma before. Appeal to his pride. He'll know you're taking a chance on him. Turn him around and every enlisted man in the battalion will think you're some kind of god."

Eli nodded. It made some sense, worth a try. He could always court-martial Salyer later if he screwed up again.

He closed the door quietly on his way out. Every day he was running the company more and more, even making personnel assignments usually the sole prerogative of the company commander. Symanski approved each one without question. Eli looked to Sergeant Pickett for affirmation, uncertain of the rules. The veteran First Sergeant encouraged him to keep on going.

Lieutenant Richard Kaine, First Platoon Leader, lurked in the hallway when Eli tiptoed out of Captain Symanski's office. Eli knew what was coming.

"Is he drunk again?" Kaine demanded to know.

Eli pointed a finger at his chest. "Lieutenant, you are out of line."

"You can't keep covering for him. Hell, he's putting the whole company in danger."

"Get your ass down to the motor pool and check how maintenance is going," Eli ordered. "Now!" Kaine's face turned violet red. Tense muscles bulged in the necks of both men. Eli clinched his fists.

Kaine relaxed his shoulders and forced a synthetic smile onto his face. "C'mon Eli. If Ski goes down they're gonna make you company commander."

"Lieutenant, I gave you an order. Get down to the motor pool." He stared at Kaine hard enough to bore a hole between his eyes.

"Yes, sir," Kaine replied, giving him an unnecessary salute, almost mocking.

Kaine's message was clear. He was ready to tell Colonel Stratton and, as a reward, he expected to be made Executive Officer when Eli was promoted. Eli didn't want that honor over the dead body of a man he respected. But if the worst happened, one thing was for sure. He would fight like hell to keep Kaine from being named his XO.

"The Lieutenant might want to keep an eye on Lieutenant Kaine," Pickett cautioned him a couple of weeks earlier. "Some young men's ambitions are bigger than their britches."

Eli didn't like Kaine, not even a little. He took satisfaction whenever he overheard one of the enlisted men use the nickname they bestowed on Kaine: *Little Dick*, a sobriquet earned by his tiny penis and his martinet manner.

Before Eli arrived as XO of Charlie Company, Kaine had anointed himself *Senior* Platoon Leader, with power to haze the two very new platoon leaders as if they were fraternity pledges. He inspected their shoes daily, administered oral quizzes on obscure Army technical manuals, and sent them to the motor pool on scavenger hunts. Eli put a stop to it the minute Sergeant Pickett gave him a heads up, to the enormous gratitude of the two junior lieutenants.

Kaine was one of those good old boys from Alabama who relived the glories of the Confederacy every Friday during Happy Hour at the Officers' Club. He graduated from The Citadel in Charleston, South Carolina, finishing seventh in his class, and never tired of telling how Citadel cadets fired the first shots at Fort Sumter to open the War Between the States. Kaine applauded recently elected Alabama Governor Wallace when he declared in his inaugural speech, "segregation now, segregation tomorrow, segregation forever."

Surely some other Southern officers thought like Richard Kaine, but none bragged about it. Kaine's Second Platoon was the only platoon in the company that didn't have a single black tank commander. When the opportunity to appoint one occurred in December, he convinced Captain Symanski to assign a white buck sergeant rather than any of the more seasoned Negro, Puerto Rican, or Latino sergeants. Eli and Sergeant Pickett objected, but Symanski felt a commander at any level had the right to pick the people in command under him.

On duty, Kaine kept his prejudices to himself, but his exaggerated Southern accent often betrayed him. He said the word "*nigra*" in such a way that it came out close to "*nigger.*" He didn't pretend it was an accident. Every time he said it, Eli thought about Nate Owens and Roy Gooden, good buddies ever since their days together on the high school track team. He even dated Nate's younger sister Julia a couple of times. Then he thought that perhaps it wasn't such a good idea when, on their second date, she responded enthusiastically to his kiss goodnight.

Mid-morning Eli drove over to the tank pads to commend each of the crews for their performance during the alert. He joined in the easy, obscene banter with the Charlie 33 tank crew about their big guns ready to fire a load. He ordered the cooks to deliver hot coffee, hot chocolate, and donuts tank-side. He walked through the packed mess hall at lunch time. "Just like momma used to make," he told a couple of the cooks after sampling the pork chops and apple pie. He released the troops after lunch. By two o'clock he was dragging, ready to get back home, settle in, and graze on a peanut butter and jelly sandwich.

He parked his Volkswagen in his usual spot in front of his apartment and turned off the engine. Something brown on the floor on the passenger's side caught his eye. He leaned over and picked up Lara Kohler's beret. He remembered knocking it off her head Saturday night when he kissed her. She was in such a hurry to get out of the car she must have left it behind. I'll have Harry give it to Margot, he thought.

He threw the beret on the desk in the living room, and then went to change into civvies. When he came out of the bedroom, he walked over to the desk and picked up the beret. She looked so cute with it pulled halfway down over her ears. He raised the cap to his nose and smelled the eucalyptus of her hair. And he tasted the brown sugar when he kissed her full lips.

What the hell, he said to himself. He pulled on his overcoat, stuffed the beret in a pocket, and locked the door behind him.

SIX

Lara said she worked for a photographer around the corner from the *Rathaus*, on Kaiserstrasse. It was only a short walk from his apartment, across the park and down the street from the tower. The cold afternoon kept most people inside, but he passed one old man who gave him a nod, a mother pushing a baby carriage, and two older women who didn't look at him. Eli ignored them all.

She really is an interesting girl, he thought as he turned onto Kaiserstrasse. He had dated four German girls since he got here. Not one of them had read an American novel, listened to American jazz, or gorged on American movies. Besides, he had no better prospects at the moment. Maybe she was worth another shot or so. In two weeks he was heading to the field for seven days - maneuvers north of Schweinfurt. If he hadn't scored by then, he'd move on.

He spotted the shop near an elaborate eighteenth century fountain, just down the street from the Baroque, onion-turreted Lutheran church. He peered inside the big window with *Kaltenbach Fotographie* lettered straight across it. Lara was waiting on a sour pussed older woman and a stone faced older man. She held a picture from a stack in front of them. The woman stuck out her jaw and pursed her lips when she talked. Lara said something in return. Her Mona Lisa smile never left her lips. A ripple ran up Eli's leg.

He examined the contents in the show window, killing time, and waiting for the customers to leave. He recognized an Agfa camera, a new Leica M3, a light meter, and some telephoto lenses, but he didn't know what any of the camera paraphernalia did.

When the old couple finally finished and exited the shop, the properly dressed man gave Eli a nod and a formal "*guten tag.*" The dowdy women took a quick glance at Eli's telltale white sidewalled G.I. haircut and turned away without a word. Eli nodded and muttered "*guten tag.*"

"*Leutnant* Schneider. How nice it is to see you." Lara looked surprised when he walked in, but pleased.

"Eli," he responded. He pulled her brown beret from his coat pocket and handed it to her. "I found this in my car."

"Oh, yes. Thank you. I wondered what happened to it." She examined it too closely, perhaps embarrassed by the kiss and her hasty exit Saturday night.

Uncomfortable seconds passed. She offered a broader smile. He returned it. "You have a very nice shop," he said, glancing around at the numerous large black and white portraits on the walls, mostly of weddings, anniversaries, and first communions. Even an untrained eye like Eli's could recognize the artistry in each of them. "Did you take these pictures?"

"No, no. I cannot take such good pictures. These were all taken by *Herr* Kaltenbach. He took some of them before he came to Kronberg. That was several years ago. Look at this one," she said, pointing at one near the entrance, an up-close portrait of an old farmer in work clothes, his cratered face telling the story of his hard life. "That was taken in Silesia right after the war." But Eli fixed on the one next to it of a beautiful woman and an equally attractive teenage girl. The photograph gave off a mystical air.

Lara chattered aimlessly, too nervous to stop talking. She's adorable, Eli thought. "Would you like to have a cup of coffee," he finally interrupted.

She stopped talking, startled. "Now?"

"Yes, right now." He gave her his most charming smile.

"But I have much work to do."

Eli didn't know what to say. An older man's voice from the back room saved him. "Go have coffee."

"Thank you, *Herr* Kaltenbach," Lara answered. "I will return in thirty minutes." Eli glanced at his watch. Not much time to operate, he thought.

Lara bundled up for the cold. She already wore black woolen stockings, ankle high leather boots, and a bulky blue turtleneck. To that she added her tan loden coat, warm mittens, a scarf, and the brown beret. "At last I am ready," she smiled.

She led Eli to a coffee shop just around the corner, marching quick time against the cold. "They have very nice hot apple strudel and hot chocolate," she said. They ordered in the ground floor bakery, and then climbed the narrow staircase to the near-ly-empty small eating area on the second floor.

Their table looked out on the cobblestoned square across from the City Hall. Eli was very familiar with two streets running off the far end of the square, Schwietzergasse and Hermstrasse, together known to the troops as the Combat Zone. On one street white soldiers frequented the many bars, gasthauses, and restaurants; the other street was reserved for blacks. On duty, the Army operated with few integration problems, particularly in the combat units like the Sixteenth Armor. If you could fight, you were okay no matter your color. But off duty, mixing immediately exploded into violence.

The worst fights were over German women. Most Germans looked down on *frauleins* who dated white soldiers; those who dated black soldiers were shunned by both German men and white G.I.'s. Eli occasionally spotted a mulatto child in town, one of those left behind by a departing black soldier. There had been an entire black Military Police company stationed in Kronberg in the first years after the war, before the Army integrated. Those offspring and their mothers were usually outcasts. The Germans had their own ideas about the Master Race, but American racial prejudices surely didn't help.

The streetlights had not yet come on, but two Military Policemen already patrolled the entrance to the Combat Zone, pistols on their hips and nightsticks in their hands. Business should be light on a Monday night after an alert. Fridays were the worst. Sometimes Eli was called to bail one of the Charlie Company troopers out of the brig. That led to a Disciplinary Report. The number of Charlie Company's monthly DR's was growing the more drink dulled Captain Symanski's vigilance. Colonel Stratton had taken note of the deteriorating situation.

Lara chattered aimlessly about film speeds, lighting, and photo composition. Eli moved his concern about DR's to the back of his mind when the waitress brought them their hot apple strudel and hot chocolate in individual porcelain pots. Lara poured Eli's from his pot, and then poured her own.

They attacked their strudels. Then stopped and laughed when, after the first bites, they both realized they were holding their forks in their left hand - lefties in common. Eli held his fork up in salute. Then they went back on the attack, pausing only for gulps of hot chocolate. The strudels were quickly devoured.

"Did you like it?" Lara asked.

"Loved it."

Lara flipped her hair back behind her ear with her left hand. She licked her lips, tilted her head, and broadened her smile. Her brown eyes shimmered.

She's flirting with me, Eli said to himself. "Would you like to go out for dinner Saturday night?"

Her smile disappeared. She looked down into her lap, embarrassed. "I am sorry, but I am not free Saturday night."

Eli was crushed, irritated. A minute ago he didn't care much about her one way or the other. Now he wanted her. "Another date?" he asked, probing.

"Is that how you call it in English? A date?"

"Break it."

"I cannot." Lara tried to give him a sad look, but the small smile on the corners wouldn't go away. She nibbled on an already-chewed finger nail. Eli didn't know if she was thinking it over, or trying to extract herself from an uncomfortable situation. Then she lowered her hand from her mouth, an appealing plea in her smile. "Maybe we can have dinner together on Sunday night? Yah?"

He quietly breathed out. "*Das ist gute*," he said. That is good.

On the walk back to the apartment, Eli felt satisfied to have another shot at Lara. But he also felt an unreasonable jealousy. He wondered if his competition was German or American.

Harry provided no help in figuring out the identity of Lara's Saturday night date. But he did suggest a nice quiet restaurant for dinner called the Golden Kreuz in the nearby town of Iphofen.

Eli picked Lara up at the western side of the *Alte Brucke* at five o'clock on Sunday. When she crested the bridge and saw him waiting, she nearly broke into a trot. He was dying to know how her date went Saturday night, hoping it was a bust. During the short ride to Iphofen, he made several indirect references, encouraging her to talk a little about it. She didn't. It couldn't be too serious a relationship, he thought, or she wouldn't have agreed to go out with me the very next night. But it also might make her less willing to go where he wanted to go.

Iphofen was a typical Bavarian farm town, old and quaint. In the springtime, it reeked of unprocessed human feces used to fertilize the fields. Eli's suspension-free Volkswagen bounced across the uneven cobblestones. He apologized. "It is a very nice car," she said when he disparaged his pitiful vehicle.

He found the Golden Kreuz on the small town square right where Harry said it would be. "I have never eaten here," Lara said, as excited as a young girl on a school outing to the zoo. "Margot says it is very good."

They resumed their conversation from Monday's coffee as though they were old friends, comfortable with each other. She told him she was reading Gunter Grass's new book, *The Tin Drum*. "He is a German writer. We do not have so many good writers as in America."

"What's it about?"

"This is too difficult to explain. You will like it. We all learn something about Germans from it." She didn't need to say that what we needed to learn was how Hitler happened. Eli got the point. He promised to read it.

They both ordered the goulash soup Harry recommended, followed by sauerbraten with red cabbage and *spatzle*. Eli ordered a good bottle of local white Franken wine in its telltale oval green bottle. He intended to lubricate Lara's inhibitions.

When the main course arrived, they both attacked their plates like starving wolves - or a hungry child in a war torn town. They didn't stop to speak until Lara mopped up the last remnants on her plate with a piece of course black bread.

"Did you think I was out with a man?"

He was embarrassed, and didn't answer. Instead he reached in his pocket for his pack of cigarettes. He offered one to her.

"It was my sister Katrin. I promised her I would take her to the moving picture show."

He gave her a big grin. She reached across the table and touched his hand. A spark traveled up his arm and down to his groin. He relaxed. Maybe it was the wine or maybe it was the removal of an obstruction, but their conversation turned more personal after that. Every once in a while her deep dark eyes opened wide and she raised her fingers to her lips as though he had just said something marvelously interesting.

She told him she worked on her day off at an orphanage, tending to brown babies. "They are so cute. I feel so sorry for them not to have a father. Margot is almost an orphan. Did Harry tell you her father was killed in 1942 when she was just a baby? He was a sergeant in the Afrika Korps. Such a pity she never knew him. That is why they are so poor."

Eli shared her sympathy, but didn't tell her he was an orphan himself. Instead he told her his father was a butcher who owned his own store in Brooklyn. He told her that in high school he won the district wrestling championship in his weight class. And he told her he was the youngest executive officer in the Sixteenth Armor. She was impressed.

He learned she was Lutheran and went to the church down the street from the Kaltenbach Fotographie shop, but she didn't go often. He didn't offer that he was Jewish. Such a revelation could immediately foil his intentions. He quickly changed the subject by asking about her sister.

Lara obviously adored Katrin, and Katrin adored her. "I am the big sister. I have to be the serious one because Katrin is crazy as a cuckoo bird." She laughed. "Do you have any sisters or brothers?"

His dead sisters glanced off his mind. He lit another cigarette. "No." He took a long drag and exhaled slowly. "But I have my cousins Max and Rose. They are like a brother and a sister."

Lara noticed his change of mood and gave him a questioning look. He changed the subject, telling her funny stories about his foreign trips with Harry. She had never been outside of Germany, she said. In fact, she had never been further than Munich. She listened attentively as he regaled her with the charms of Rome, Paris, London, and Amsterdam. His enthusiasm for their history, culture, and beauty was genuine. She would love the people, he said, particularly the exuberant Italians and the proper British. For a minute, he was so lost in his story and in her that he envisioned taking her to each of those places as if it was the natural thing to do.

"And do you like Germany?" she asked when he slowed down.

He sobered. "I miss my home and my family." He flicked an ash in the near-full ashtray, and then took another sip of wine.

"But you help us here to keep away the Russians. They are criminals." She frowned.

"We do what we can." Then he changed the subject again, to one he knew would bring back a smile - her passion for photography.

She described some of the techniques *Herr* Kaltenbach taught her. Eli feigned great interest, but couldn't understand half of what she said. Clearly her mentor was her hero.

"Did I tell you he was from Silesia? That used to be the eastern part of Germany, for centuries. Then after the war the Russians gave it to Poland to pay them back for taking the eastern part of their country. They expelled all of the Germans from Silesia. *Herr* Kaltenbach's family had lived there for many hundreds of years."

"Does *Herr* Kaltenbach have a wife?"

"She died during the war. So did his daughter. It is very sad."

Eli sensed there was more to the story, something dark, but

Lara offered no more. He welcomed the relief when the waiter brought their dessert and coffee. Eli loved the *stollen,* a fruit cake with marzipan covered with icing. This time they ate their desserts slowly. He enjoyed watching her eat. And each time he looked in her eyes she looked back at him in the same thirsting way.

"I just got a new Dave Brubeck album," he said as the car approached Kronberg. "Want to come to the apartment and hear it? Maybe Harry and Margot will be there," though he knew full well they wouldn't be.

"I must go home now," she answered. But this time she really did sound disappointed, not frightened.

"Can I drive you home?"

"*Nein, danke.* My father."

He pulled over at the end of the bridge in a dark spot away from the street light, and turned off the engine. Lara pulled off her brown beret and shoved it in her pocket. She turned her lips to him. He kissed her, and she kissed him back. After a very long kiss, they stopped to catch their breath, and then kissed again. He moved his hand to her breast but could feel little through her heavy loden coat. When he again tried to unbutton it, she put her hand on his and pulled away.

She looked in his eyes and touched his cheek. "It has been a wonderful evening," she said. "Thank you for dinner." She kissed him lightly, and then opened the car door. This time he walked her halfway across the bridge. Before they parted, he asked if he could see her for coffee again on Wednesday, and go dancing on Saturday night at the Cave in Sulzfeld.

She nodded her head. "Yah."

"Both?"

"But of course, both." She ran her tongue over her upper lip and then smiled. "It is a date." She looked around to be sure no one would see them. Then she kissed him on the cheek.

He watched her hurry the rest of the way across the short bridge over the Main River, her boots clicking on the sidewalk. He wanted to hold her, to touch her, even if only on a dance floor. Now he had to figure out a way to get her back to his apartment. Time was running out. The following week the battalion headed to the field for seven days of maneuvers. He was in the hunt now, and he intended to have her. Then why was he feeling so selfish?

SEVEN

A locked door greeted Eli when he arrived at Kaltenbach Fotographie late Wednesday afternoon. A woman dressed in dark clothes swept the sidewalk two doors down in front of the *friseur* - the beauty parlor. She stopped to stare at him. Eli rapped lightly on the glass and waited. When no one came, he rapped again, louder this time. He peered in the window. An older man with bushy gray eyebrows scurried from the back room to unlock the door.

"I am so sorry," he said. "I am all alone in the shop." His accent was clearly German, but with a British twist.

"I am looking for Lara Kohler."

The German broke a smile. "Ah, you must be Lara's *leutnant*."

Eli liked the possessive sound of that - Lara's *leutnant*. "Yes I am."

"Please come in." He pointed with the pipe in his hand. "I sent Lara to the *pharmazie*. It is not far on her bicycle. She should return quickly. Can I offer you some tea while you wait?"

"No thank you. Please don't let me keep you from your work."

"It is no problem." *Herr* Kaltenbach replied. "I will enjoy a moment to talk with Lara's friend."

Eli liked him immediately. He had a kind countenance and the disposition of an artist. His bowtie hung loosely behind a cardigan sweater. Buttoned suspenders held up his baggy pants.

He smelled of strong pipe tobacco.

One particular portrait on the wall again caught Eli's eye. He gestured toward it. "Lara told me that is your wife and daughter," he said.

Herr Kaltenbach nodded. The smile melted into melancholy. They studied the portrait together. "My daughter was gentle as a little bird. Like Lara," *Herr* Kaltenbach said. "Please be careful, *Leutnant*. She is delicate."

He looked over at Eli. Eli could feel his ears burning. He continued to study the portrait. Lara is no child, he thought. She's twenty-four years old, the same as me, and just as able to take care of herself.

"Lara tells me your name is Schneider. *Ein Deutcher name,* yah?"

Eli heard this question often in Germany, and it never failed to grate on him. He thought if anyone should recognize a Jewish name when he heard it, it would be a German. They used to be good at sniffing out Jews. Eli usually enjoyed slinging it back at them: "*Nein Deutcher. Juden*" - a Jew. Not this time. He was not about to reveal his ancestry to Lara through this stranger he had just met. So he said, "Maybe German many years ago. Now it is American."

Herr Kaltenbach nodded, but he gave Eli's face a closer examination. Myth had it that Nazis could uncover Jews just by looking at them, particularly their beaked noses. Some Germans still maintained Jews smelled different.

"Do you speak German?" *Herr* Kaltenbach asked.

"Only a few words."

"The only Americans who speak good German are the Jews. They make Yiddish sound like German."

Just then Lara peddled up on her bicycle. She put down the kick stand, and then took a package from the basket on the handlebars. Her cheeks glowed rosy red from the still-biting March cold. When she walked in and saw Eli waiting, her dark eyes opened wide and her smile lit up. Eli wanted to grab her and kiss her, but he knew better than to do it in front of a proper German elder like *Herr* Kaltenbach.

When the two of them left for coffee, *Herr* Kaltenbach shook Eli's hand. "*Leutnant*, please call me Otto."

"And please call me Eli."

On the way to the coffee shop, Lara put her gloved hand through his arm, a bold, possessive gesture in public. "*Herr* Kaltenbach likes you," she said.

"And I liked him, very much," he replied. Eli had just passed an important test, and perhaps gained an important ally, someone she worshipped.

Saturday night they stopped at a small restaurant on their way to Sulzfeld for a quick bite to eat. They never seemed to run out of interesting things to talk about. But tonight Lara had something on her mind, something that raised Eli's defenses.

"Many famous Americans are from Germany," she said, sopping up the remaining gravy on her plate with a hunk of black bread. She glanced up at Eli. She shoved the bread in her mouth and talked while she chewed. "Did you know Albert Einstein was born in Germany?"

"Yes, of course. Everyone knows that."

"And Sigmund Freud? He is Austrian actually."

"Yes."

"And Robert Oppenheimer. His father was German." She looked up again from her bread mopping as if studying his reaction. She was probing for something, but he didn't know what.

"And Andre Previn. He was born in Berlin." This time she stared right in his eyes.

Then it smacked him in the ear. All of these people she mentioned were Jews, German Jews. Was this a question? Had she figured out he was Jewish? His investment in her could be lost the instant he confirmed her suspicion. He wasn't going to let that happen. He pulled out his pack of cigarettes and offered her one. She shook her head. He lit his and blew the smoke out the side of his mouth.

"I didn't know Previn was German," he said, trying to sound nonchalant. "Have you heard his jazz album, *My Fair Lady*?"

"No, I have not heard it."

"It's great. I have it. I'll play it for you some time."

Their buxom waitress interrupted, clearing empty plates away. She said something to Lara in German Eli didn't understand, but it provoked a smile in Lara. "She says we looked so hungry she thought we would swallow the silverware," Lara laughed when the waitress walked away.

Eli grabbed at any subject that would deflect her inquisition. "Tell me, how did you learn to ride a bicycle?"

She brightened - a new mood. "My father bought me a shiny new bicycle when I was eleven years old. He taught me how to ride it. Then I taught Margot. She did not have a bicycle so I let her borrow mine. She crashed it, and my father was very angry with me."

"My cousin Max taught me to ride. He taught me most things, like baseball and football." Also about girls and sex, drinking and smoking.

He relaxed again, satisfied he had dodged the sink hole for the time being, but uncertain he had done anything to dispel her doubts. It perturbed him to even think about it, but he remembered Patty Bruni. He lost his virginity at seventeen to Patty, a good Catholic girl from Berkinbury with whom he fell madly in love. She ruined it one night during an earnest intellectual conversation about religion.

"Don't you ever feel guilty?" Patty asked, truly perplexed.

"About what?"

"Because your people killed Christ."

Stunned, he offered a confused, lawyerly defense against an unjust charge. His passion for Patty withered that night.

He didn't know how much of an obstacle his Jewishness now presented in his quest to have Lara, or what to do about it. Did she care that much if he was Jewish? Probably; she was a German, after all? So he could lie about it, or face it head on. But maybe the best course was just to continue to dodge it for now.

That night at the Cave she cuddled close to him every time they danced, and held her hand to the back of his head. When they left and got in the car, she immediately turned her lips to him and invited a long kiss.

He reminded her he was departing on maneuvers Monday morning. He said it with the too-earnest drama of a soldier going off to war, and might never return.

"You are so brave," she responded. But it did nothing to advance his cause. He again tried to coax her back to his apartment. When she again declined, he decided this was getting much too frustrating. Time had run out.

But when they parked by the bridge, she said, "Do you like omelets? I can cook an omelet."

"I love omelets," he answered, unsure where this was going.

"Sometime I will come to your apartment and make you an omelet."

"Do you know how to cook?"

"I only know how to make the omelets," she laughed. "My mother has not taught me how to cook anything else."

"When I get back from maneuvers?" he pressed.

"Sometime. We will see."

He took that as a yes. The next morning when Harry asked him how it went, he answered, "I'm still only standing on first base, but we just went into extra innings." He began plotting how to turn an omelet into a visit to the bedroom.

The war games began the following Monday morning when the tanks rolled out the back gate of Holden Barracks. Dubbed March Storm, these were the biggest maneuvers since the Cuban Missile Crisis last October. The Third Infantry Division Commanding General led the Blue Force against a much larger Red Force simulating a Soviet invasion. Eli's battalion of the 16th Armor and two battalions of the 78th Infantry comprised the Blue Force.

The two opposing forces clogged the German roads and chewed up the countryside. Townspeople congregated to watch them rumble through, some to applaud, others to gape in disgust. Eli loved the competition of the games. "It's better than sex," Harry said one time. But that was before he met Margot.

Over the next seven days, Eli's single focus was on the battle at hand. But in quiet moments, thoughts of Lara sneaked in. Sure, he admitted, he failed to score before his deadline. But that smile of hers, and her willowy body, beguiled him. Her good heart and fine mind fascinated him. Was it worth another try?

A week after departing, the battalion returned home, passing through Kronberg on Hindenburg Strasse right by his apartment. A few people in the park and near the tower stopped to watch. He wished Lara could see him on top of his tank.

The Blue Force paid a price for its victory. An armored personnel carrier ran over a young rifleman from the 78th Infantry one night and killed him. The only casualties in the 16th Armor this time were the two chickens crushed under the treads of an

Alpha Company tank. Eli didn't envy the company's executive officer, who would be buried with paperwork and a time-wasting investigation. Abundant compensation would ultimately flow to the farmer for the two chickens, as well as obscene compensation for the chickens' unborn offspring for generations yet to come.

A call came over the radio for Eli while he was still directing the bedding down of the company's tanks and equipment. Colonel Stratton wanted to see him immediately. Eli's antenna shot up. The battalion commander didn't frequently ask to see a junior company executive officer.

Eli's mind went right to Richard Kaine. Two days earlier, Sergeant Picket warned him, Kaine interrogated the medics about Charlie Company's excessive use of cough syrup. By the time he marched through the doors of Battalion Headquarters, Eli had already invented a plausible explanation for the abundant medicinal consumption.

The Colonel glanced up from behind his desk when Eli entered his office, his limp fatigues still covered with a layer of dust from the maneuvers. Stratton radiated the natural force of a daring cavalry commander, a modern day incarnation of General George Patton. Many in the battalion, officers and enlisted men alike, felt they bore the burden of his self-serving pursuit of a general's gold star. They resented it. But nobody could deny that the 16th Armor was a superb fighting force, as bold as their magnetic leader.

Eli stood at attention in front of the desk until Stratton ordered him to stand "at ease." The Colonel's hard tone and icy expression revealed nothing. "Schneider, I need you to do something for me." Eli's stomach puckered, fearing what was coming next. "I got a call from Chaplain Kaplan just before we left for the field. Can you guess what that was about?"

At least it wasn't about Symanski and cough syrup. Eli exhaled, relieved. Major Kaplan was the Division's Jewish chaplain. He called Eli three times the previous month, virtually commanding him to attend Friday night Sabbath services. Eli refused, and explained that he wasn't religious.

He never felt very Jewish growing up, even though he was circumcised at birth, had his bar mitzvah at thirteen, and lived surrounded by Jews. But he hadn't even known he was Jewish until he was eight years old and came to America. In Russia, Auntie Via raised him as a Christian, and had him worship in the Russian Orthodox Church to hide his identity from the Germans. In America, he tried being a good Jew, but the religious part didn't take, only the pride.

He could be defiant when insulted by Gentiles about being Jewish, but equally repelled when too tightly embraced by his brethren. He was most comfortable when he visited cousins Max and Rose in Berkinbury, which he did each summer for a month or two all the way through high school. In that small mill town, his religion seldom mattered. Max's and Rose's friends were all Gentiles, and Eli dated only Gentile girls while there. He only rarely encountered one whose father wouldn't let her date Jews.

"I'm not religious, sir," Eli now asserted again to Colonel Stratton. He could have explained further, but resented the need to do so.

"You've got a J on your dog tags, don't you?" Colonel Stratton responded sharply.

The colonel pointed out that Eli was the highest ranking Jew in the battalion, and needed to set an example for the Jewish enlisted men. He warned that Chaplain Kaplan was hot under the collar about a lieutenant defying him. He threatened to carry his beef up the line to General Mildren, the Division Commander, if Eli continued to resist. That would mean trouble for both Eli and the colonel.

When Eli didn't respond, an exaggerated smile cracked Stratton's stony face. "Tell you what, Lieutenant. You attend Friday night's service just this once. Then I'll go to bat for you after that. Okay?"

"Yes sir." It was a fair trade, even if it smelled more like an order than an offer. It could have been worse, Eli thought.

He took a step back and came to attention, prepared to leave. Stratton stopped him. "How are things going down in Charlie Company?" He tried making it sound like a casual question. Eli knew better. Captain Ski had been mostly sober throughout the war games, but Kaine may have squealed about the cough syrup after all.

"Everything is fine," Eli said. "I'm learning a lot from Captain Symanski."

"You'd make a good company commander, Lieutenant. You're ready. Of course I'd need you to extend your tour beyond November. What do you think about that?"

"I really appreciate it, sir. Let me think it over." You don't dismiss a colonel's offer without due consideration, but Eli had no intention of staying in Germany one minute longer than was required.

Colonel Stratton leaned forward, his elbows on the desk, fingers interlaced. "Don't think too long," he warned, his eyes glaring again.

Eli didn't know what to make of Stratton's offer. He was flattered, though he feared this had more to do with Captain Symanski than himself. What could he do about Symanski anyway? The only thing he knew for sure was that he planned spending Friday night at Chaplain Kaplan's Sabbath service in

Wurzburg. Once that was over with, Colonel Stratton would owe him one.

Then he began to fantasize about Saturday night, Lara, and an omelet.

EIGHT

"I cannot make an omelet this weekend," Lara replied to Eli's too-eager invitation. She fiddled with the handle of her coffee cup, her untouched apple strudel in front of her. In the middle of the afternoon, they were the only two in the coffee shop, except for the nosey waitress, a grim, wide-bodied older woman who kept looking over at them.

"I don't get it. You said you'd come to the apartment when I got back." He threw his fork on the table. Lara jumped. "Well, I'm back."

The waitress waddled over, wearing a severe Prussian-like expression. She must have asked Lara if anything was wrong. Lara shook her head and answered in German. The woman withdrew but kept a watchful eye on the obnoxious American.

Lara nibbled on her fingernail. "My father, he is suspicious."

"So tell him. It's time I met your father and mother anyway. Are you ashamed of me?" She's figured out I'm Jewish, Eli suspected. Now she doesn't know what to do about it.

"Oh no. I can never be ashamed of you," she protested. "But my father asks me many questions."

He didn't ask her out for Saturday night when they separated that afternoon. Her disappointment showed enough to rub Eli's conscience. But he had had enough of this. She was more trouble than she was worth, and he was too old for adolescent games.

When he got back to the apartment, Eli vented his frustration onto Harry. "My god, you'd think she was a virgin."

Harry slung a leg over the arm of his easy chair and admired the drifting smoke rings he blew toward the ceiling. "Maybe she is," he replied. His teasing tone left no doubt he thought it highly unlikely.

Eli took him seriously. "That can't be. She's twenty-four years old, for chrissake." Yet when he put it together, it made some sense: affection one minute and distance the next.

"I think this girl is getting to you, my friend."

"Bullshit," Eli snapped back.

"You haven't called her a Kraut in ages." Harry couldn't wipe the smirk off of his face. He was enjoying his friend's unexpected distress.

Eli grabbed two beers from the refrigerator and ambled back into the living room. He handed a bottle to Harry. "Ask Margot," he said.

"Ask her what?"

"If Lara's a virgin."

Harry took a swig from the bottle. "Ask your friend Willy," he responded, the smirk dissipated. "He knows everything that goes on in Kronberg, especially about things like that."

Lara was starting to drive Eli nuts, and he didn't like it one bit. Yet she was the most appealing woman he had met since he left Brooklyn, and he wasn't about to give up the chase so easily. Maybe he was missing something. A talk with his one German friend, Willy Speer, sounded like a good idea.

Willy was a columnist and assistant editor of his father's newspaper, *Kronberg Zeitung*. He stuck his nose into everything in town. The two of them usually met once a week for a beer when Eli wasn't in the field. He missed a few weeks since he started seeing Lara.

Their friendship was the remnant of the quintet Harry put together that included Eli, Willy and two of Willy's friends. The three young German men and the two Americans met every Thursday for beer and bratwurst, drinking, and rowdy singing. Harry was sure if Eli got to know some Germans his own age, he would lose his bad attitude. He didn't. Harry was the life of the party, but once Margot beguiled him, he stopped coming. Then two of the young Germans stopped coming too, bored with always-sulking Eli and the too-serious Willy.

One night it ended up just Eli and Willy at the Schutzenhaus gasthaus, an unglamorous bar, restaurant, and boarding house a block down from Eli's apartment. For a while the two of them sat nursing their steins of beer, awkward and solemn, searching for something to talk about. Their acquaintance might have ended that night if Eli hadn't accidentally made an offhand remark about Germany's economic miracle - the astonishing rebirth of its economy. That set Willy off on a track that was part history lesson and part indictment of his own people.

"You know, of course, that right after the war the Allies wanted to make Germany an agrarian society." he said. "Can you see that? Turn a nation of engineers, mathematicians, and scientists into a nation of farmers? We would have died." He flicked the ash of his cigarette into the big green ashtray on the plank table and glanced up at Eli, wondering if he should continue.

Eli didn't know whether to leave or listen, so he just said, "How did you stop it from happening?"

"We? We did not stop it. The Russians stopped it. America needed to keep Germany out of the Soviet orbit. An economic miracle to prove how democratic capitalism is very much better than communism. So the Marshall Plan."

It sounded as though Willy was discounting American generosity. "Then the United States didn't contribute much?" Eli said sarcastically, pointedly sticking out his lower lip.

"No, no. You misunderstand me. We would not have survived without America. After the war we were hungry all the time, only twelve hundred calories a day for adults. Even less for children. But freeing the industrial leaders sent to the jails after the war, that should not have happened. They were all released in 1951, a fraction of the time they should have spent in jail. Big men in our top companies. Siemens, Krupp, Daimler, Bayer. Others. Not killers perhaps, but supporters of Hitler nevertheless. Who do you think built the crematoriums and provided the gas? Who do you think used the slave labor in their factories? And who built the armaments? But some people in high places said we needed these businessmen again to make the economic miracle. So they were released."

Willy's face was turning red, contorted in frustration. He grabbed a big pretzel from the basket on the table and took a vicious bite. Eli had never had a frank conversation with a German before, and he was gripped by it. He commented or asked a question now and then only to keep Willy talking.

"Everyone wants to forget," Willy sneered, the cynic. "When the Allied occupation ended in 1955, everyone had a job and enough to eat. Now look at us. Some grown too fat. It is a modest prosperity, but maybe enough so a person can buy a small car. Maybe a washing machine or a television set."

Willy looked at Eli as if assessing him for the first time. He must have liked what he saw. He tore off another chunk of pretzel and nibbled at the end. "You yourself also eat as though you once knew what it was like to be hungry."

"Me?" Eli smiled a forced smile. "Never. I'm American. A chicken in every pot."

Willy didn't respond, but his look said he wasn't sure he believed that. He changed subjects. "Most children are happy, yes? We run around and play. But, you see, our parents, they all walked around with their heads down in those first years after the war."

"Maybe they were ashamed." They had much to be ashamed about, Eli thought.

"No, not ashamed. Afraid. Afraid someone would look them in the eye and see something. Recognize someone. Turn them in to the American authorities. Afraid to say how they really felt about Nazis and about losing the war. When you are defeated and occupied, you lose your dignity. Then after 1949 we were a democracy. Respectable. We had our own Deutsche Mark. We stopped big inflation and the black market. An ally now, not an enemy. America now a guest, no longer only an occupier. Our protector. And when we could have our own army again and join NATO, we could have our respect back." Willy lit a cigarette and blew the smoke out the side of his mouth. He chuckled. "But not a very good army I am told. Yah? Imagine, Germans who are not good soldiers. We thought it was in our blood."

Eli hesitated before asking. "And the Nuremberg Trials?"

"Some thought they cleansed the blood from our hands. Many thought they were simply victor's justice. German war crimes were no worse than Russian war crimes, they said. Or American war crimes for that matter."

"And what do you think?"

"I think Germany had much to pay for, and is not done paying yet. We have washed some of the blood away, but not all of it. We have much more to do to redeem ourselves with the Jewish people. We may never be able to do enough to wipe that away."

The more Willy talked, the more Eli liked him, someone eager to make things right. Someone maybe even a little vulnerable, like him. "Do you know I am Jewish?" he asked, perhaps challenging Willy to defend himself.

"That is funny. You do not look Jewish." When he first said it, he looked so serious. Then a small smile crept into the corners of his mouth. When Eli smiled back, Willy laughed. Then Eli laughed. "Of course I know you are Jewish. From the beginning. How? The name. It could be German, of course, but more likely Yiddish." He laughed again, more genuine now, more at ease. "Actually, you do not look German, so I imagine your name is Yiddish. Russian perhaps?"

Eli smiled, more at ease himself. "My parents were both born in Russia." With that, Willy assumed the role of the journalist, now asking Eli questions about his growing up in Brooklyn, and what America was like. Eli told him a lot, but managed to avoid revealing anything that happened before he was eight years old.

They talked until nearly closing time, nursing their beers and filling the ashtray with cigarette butts. They arranged to meet again for beer and bratwurst at the Schutzenhaus the next Thursday.

Willy and Eli would probably have remained just drinking buddies if it weren't for the big argument Willy had with his father some weeks later. Willy wrote one too many columns critical of people like his father who remained silent during Hitler's rise to power. When his father saw the raw copy, he exploded, accusing his son of gross ingratitude. That night Willy recounted the incident to Eli, blow by blow. By the third liter of beer, they were both in their cups.

"He said I did not know what it was like to be hungry and afraid. Of course I know. Does he not realize how afraid I was the night my mother died?" It just spilled out, an uncontrollable hurt across his face.

That startled Eli, even in his modestly inebriated state. "Dead? Your mother is dead? But I thought..."

"That's my stepmother. My real mother died of cancer when I was nine."

Willy then described his mother withering before his eyes, his feelings of panic, helplessness, and disgust. "The last thing she said to me was to be a good boy for my father." A year later his father re-married, a young wife to help raise Willy and his younger brother. She was not unkind, but she was strict, unlike his warm and gentle mother.

Willy pulled his handkerchief from his coat pocket and blew his nose, covering his eyes so Eli wouldn't see the welling tears. Eli put a hand on his friend's shoulder. "I lost my mother and father when I was two," he said softly. Willy gave Eli as startled a look as Eli had given Willy. This time it was Eli's turn to sniffle and turn his head away.

A few minutes later, Eli asked, "Do you still miss her?"

Willy nodded. "Every day."

"I didn't know my mother. I was too young. But I miss her." Eli didn't mention how his mother and father died, and Willy didn't ask. He sensed it was too sensitive for discussion.

After another beer and more sharing of personal morsels, they embraced and said goodnight, drunk as skunks. They were now bound by a shared sorrow more powerful than history. To Eli, it didn't make any sense that he would have a German friend, so he tried not to think of Willy as a German. Now he looked forward to every meeting with Willy.

The night after his talk with Harry about Lara's virginity, Eli headed off to meet Willy at the Schutzenhaus. Mostly German working men frequented this pre-war Bavarian gasthaus. Eli often felt uncomfortable when he was the only American there, and wondered what they would do if they knew he was a Jew. The men were friendly enough, but many of them looked just the right age to have goose-stepped across Europe with the Wehrmacht or the SS.

When one of them recognized him as an American soldier, which wasn't hard to do with his American clothes and army haircut, the man would assert that he had fought on the Eastern Front against the Ruskies. "You would think we were on the same side back then," Eli once said to Willy. "In their minds, we should have been," Willy snorted, "fighting Communists and Jews together."

Willy judged Germans more harshly than even Eli, and Eli liked him for it. His columns in the *Kronberg Zeitung* condemned Germans of his parents' generation for following Hitler so obediently then and refusing to atone now. He likewise criticized his own generation for ignoring it. As a result, he was none-too-popular in town. Willy translated a few of his columns for Eli. "You're lucky they haven't thrown you off the *Alte Brucke*," Eli joked. "I run too fast," Willy answered back without a smile.

He did not exempt his own father from his harsh criticism. His father resented Willy for his conceit. "Then why does he let you write those columns?" Eli asked after one of their particularly bitter family arguments. "Guilt," Willy answered. "And he knows I'm right. If we don't admit what we did and make amends, we will be condemned for all time."

Willy was usually direct and unemotional, even where emotion was appropriate. When presenting his case, he sounded like a dispassionate, aggressive prosecutor. So Eli was unprepared when he walked into the gasthaus to find Willy at the bar engaged in a shouting match with a muscular middle-aged man in grimy work clothes. Willy's anger turned his face white; the other man sprayed spit when he yelled.

Eli understood only enough German to make out words like

dummkopf, Jude killor, Nazi, and *arschlecker.* A few of the other men in the bar shouted encouragement to Willy's brawny adversary. They all looked like they worked on road construction crews or in a factory, and hadn't shaved or bathed in a few days. Willy, on the other hand, looked like he had stepped out of the German edition of GQ Magazine with his tight fitting gray sweater, black pants pegged at the bottom, and pointy-toed black shoes. He was the only one in the place who could pass for a stereotypical Aryan, tall and slender with blond hair so pure it was almost white. His gold rimmed glasses embellished his stern professorial facade.

Captain Symanski taught Eli that sometimes retreat is better than annihilation. Outnumbered, outflanked, and outgunned, that seemed to be the situation right now. So Eli pushed his way between two angry men. He pulled at Willy's sleeve. His friend looked relieved when he saw reinforcements had arrived. "Let's get out of here," Eli urged. Willy nodded. He grabbed his gray tweed overcoat from a clothes tree near the door, and then flung one more barb at the man he had been arguing with. The man yelled something back, and gave him the universal digital gesture of contempt.

Willy led the way past the furniture store toward a wine bar down the street, his shoulders hunched and his hands shoved deep in his coat pockets. His feet moved so rapidly on the sidewalk Eli had to go into forced-march mode to keep up. German sounds spewed from Willy's mouth like verbal sewage.

"Hey, slow down," Eli begged. When Willy did slow down a little, Eli asked what the argument was about.

Willy kept walking. Then he stopped abruptly just as they got to the wine bar. "Those shitheads did not like my column in the newspaper today."

"That's no surprise. Who did you attack this time?" Eli kidded Willy, but he admired him. Willy was one of the rare few who prodded German conscience about the war and the Holocaust.

When they entered the bar, the two young men found a spot away from the door. Only a half dozen tables were occupied. Sometimes a stray American soldier wandered in, but tonight the men and women were all sedate locals. When the plump, pigtailed waitress came over, they each ordered a plum brandy. The waitress gave Willy a covetous look, but Willy ignored her.

"Judgment is coming and they do not like it," Willy continued, rapping his knuckled fist on the table. "They deny they even knew what was going on... the murders... the Jews. They go on justifying what they did. They say they were only German patriots doing what they had to do to defend their country. You think we did not have our own Nazis right here in Kronberg? They were everywhere." Two older businessmen at a nearby table stole a look over when Willy raised his voice and hammered the table. He stared them down until they looked away, and then continued.

"Trials for the Auschwitz murders begin in Frankfurt in May. It is the first time, you see, when Germans will be trying other Germans for these crimes - these war atrocities. Then the children are going to start asking their parents what they did during the war. And the children are not going to be satisfied with the answers." Eli let his friend ramble. He wasn't going to be able to talk about anything else until he got this out of his system.

"And you?" Eli finally interjected. "What are you going to ask?"

"I do not need to ask. I already know. My father did nothing. He just kept publishing his newspaper, printing whatever Goebbels told him to print."

"What else could he do?"

"That's what they all say: I had no choice. I did not know." Willy pulled out his pack of HB cigarettes and struck a match. The smell of burnt rope drifted up Eli's nose. "My father, he maintained his neutrality. He says he never supported Hitler before he came to power. Then it was too late."

Eli wanted to tell Willy not to feel so guilty, but he wasn't in the habit of relieving Germans of their guilt, even a friend.

Willy's mood changed when the large waitress with the pronounced cleavage set their glasses of plum brandy down in front of them. She said something to Willy in German that sounded like a bawdy invitation. He laughed, and then took a deep gulp of his brandy. Eli sipped his.

"So, something is on your mind?" Willy asked, brighter now. "Have you been getting in trouble?"

"Maybe. Do you know a girl named Lara Kohler?"

"Lara Kohler?" Willy raised his eyebrows, surprised. He set his brandy down on the table. "Are you getting into Lara Kohler?"

"What can you tell me about her?"

For a long moment, Willy studied the glowing end of his cigarette, and then took a puff. "I did not really know her so well. She was a year younger and lived on the other side of the river. The Kohlers were hungry like everyone else after the war, but at least Lara did not have to carry around her father's guilt like the rest of us did. They say Herr Kohler spent time in a concentration camp for opposing Hitler. There was no mistake she was proud of her father, and maybe more confident because of it. The other children envied her a little, but did not resent it because she was so nice."

Willy twisted his cigarette in his fingers, watched the smoke rise, then took another puff. "For Lara it was good. The rest of us understood our fathers and mothers had something to hide, something we did not understand. Something our parents only whispered about if they spoke of it at all."

"That's all you know about her?" Eli asked, disappointed by the skimpy information.

"Not all. Maybe a little bit more. You see we went to *gymnasium* together. That is like your high school, for kids who will go on to university. Lara was very smart and very nice. She was in the middle of everything. How do you say it? Very popular. Everyone wanted to be her friend, boys and girls. The boys, of course, wanted more than to be friends. Then something happened." Willy pushed his glasses back up his nose and frowned.

Eli leaned forward, more interested. "What do you mean, something happened?"

Willy stroked his chin, as though reflecting, hesitant to continue. "I don't know what. It was in the winter of my last year at *gymnasium*. It seems Lara got very sick and was gone from school for more than a month. I heard from someone she had an illness and they took her to Munich to be treated in a hospital there. I do not know why our hospital in Wurzburg wasn't good enough. When she came back, she was different. She kept to herself and was very quiet. She used to be at all the parties, surrounded by boys eager to be with her. But now I never saw her any more. The next year I went to the university in Wurzburg and did not think anything more about her."

"What was wrong with her?"

"I do not know. Nobody said." Willy looked away, fixed on a vacant spot on the far wall.

Eli waited a moment. When he was sure nothing more was coming, he went on. "Did you ever date her?"

Willy snickered, relieved. "Me? No, no. But I am surprised she would see you."

"And what's wrong with me?"

"Someone like Lara would never date an American. You know Germans do not think much of girls who see soldiers. On top of that, I do not think Lara goes on a date with many boys after her illness, German or American."

Eli wanted to know more about this illness. It seemed important, but Willy didn't know anything more. So Eli switched subjects. "What do you know about her father? He doesn't seem to like Americans."

"He is Headmaster at the *gymnasium* now, an important and respected man in Kronberg. That is only in the last five years. He was still teaching in Wurzburg when Lara and I were in school."

"Do you like him?"

"I do not know him, but those who do know him say he is very stern."

"And?"

"You want to know if he had anything to do with the Nazi Party? Is that what you are asking? They say he was in a concentration camp. But I do not know. My father has doubts. Rumors are always going around. If everyone was guilty, at least a little, then no one was guilty. I can find out more information about him if you would like. I am acquainted with someone who has access to the old Nazi files every day. I can ask."

"It doesn't matter. I probably won't see her again." Then why did he want to know everything he could about her?

At the end of the evening, Willy walked Eli to his apartment, the two friends mellow from a second glass of plum brandy. They shook hands to say goodbye. Eli turned toward the apartment entrance. Willy stopped. "Eli, do you believe it is in our blood, German blood? This evilness?"

Eli turned around. "I don't know, Willy. Harry says no, for whatever that's worth. He says it would make it too easy on the ones who committed the worst crimes. They could argue it was in their blood. So it's not their fault. They're not responsible."

"A good argument." Willy walked away. "Thank you," he said without looking back.

Harry at the time had gone on to admonish Eli that if evil can be in all Germans' blood, then certain prejudicial characteristics could be in all Jews' blood too: Unscrupulous, conniving, money grubbing, rude, and pushy. "Well I don't believe it," Harry insisted. "I don't believe it is in German blood, and I don't believe it is in Jewish blood." Eli was not ready to concede the point as far as Germans went. That would be too convenient. Besides, how then could he justify his loathing of all Germans?

He lay awake half the night asking why he was so caught up with this girl. He chewed over what Willy told him concerning Lara's abrupt change of personality when she was seventeen, after she was so sick. It was curious, maybe even important. But so what? She was still a Kraut like all the rest of them. If all I want is a woman to take to bed, he told himself, call Greta, Trudi or Sonja. They were always ready and willing. Greta would try anything, but she could barely speak a few words of English. Trudi was fat, and Sonja smelled like a barnyard. And all three of them were dull as cardboard.

Lawrence of Arabia was playing at the Holden Post movie theater Friday night. It wouldn't hurt to give Lara one more try.

NINE

The Saturday night Lara came to Eli's apartment to make him an omelet did not go at all according to plan.

The previous evening he took her to the movies at Holden Barracks. Every horny nineteen year old enlisted man without a Friday night pass ogled Lara as they stood in line to buy tickets. Just before the lights went down and the show began, Lara reached into her purse and pulled out a pair of black rimmed eyeglasses. She put them on and turned to Eli for his inspection.

"I cannot see so well from far away." She smiled an embarrassed smile.

"You look cute," he said. She wrinkled her nose and squeezed his hand.

On the way out, they bumped into Captain Johnson, the Battalion Adjutant. The Captain was a West Pointer, ram-rod straight and serious even when off-duty in civvies. He gave Lara the once-over and a pleasant hello when Eli introduced them. But Mrs. Johnson ground her teeth and turned her back without even a grunt, staring at the poster for next week's main attraction.

Lara stuffed her hands deep in her coat pockets when they walked away, scowling. "They all think we're whores, the girls who go out with G.I.'s. The American wives think so, and so do the German mothers."

Eli put his arm around her and kissed the top of her head. "*Macht nichts.* Who cares," she said, shaking off the bad taste of

Mrs. Johnson.

That night while they were making out in his car by the bridge, she surprised him. "Tomorrow I make you an omelet. Yah? We close the shop on Saturday at two o'clock. You can meet me there and we will go buy eggs." That night she also let him squeeze her tit on the outside of her blouse, but that was all, and only for a few seconds. It was enough for the moment.

Perseverance pays off, Eli said to himself after she disappeared over the bridge. He just won a skirmish; now it was time for a major assault. Without coaxing, Harry volunteered to stay away from the apartment all of Saturday night.

No detail was too small to ignore in Eli's planning. After dinner, he would move her to the sofa in the living room. He picked out three record albums. Open with Dave Brubeck because he knew she liked him. Then romantic Chet Baker when they started making out. The tough call was the music for the money play. Should it be Johnny Mathis, a proven winner? Or Frank Sinatra, who Lara liked? He decided on Sinatra's *In the Wee Small Hours*.

Next question: should he leave the light on over the desk? The one on the end table by the sofa might be better. When things got really going, he could reach up and click it off.

Before he went to pick her up, he checked the apartment one more time. Fortunately, the cleaning woman had just been there the day before. When *Frau* Gielser first rented to the two bachelors, she was sufficiently wary to insist on having a cleaning woman under her supervision come in every week. That was fine with Eli because Harry was something of a slob. His side of the bedroom and the closet were mountains of sloth. Discarded dirty shirts, unhung pants, and fashionable sweaters littered the floor. Eli's side, on the other hand, always looked like it was ready for Saturday morning inspection.

He hid the best seller he was reading, *The Rise and Fall of the Third Reich*, in the bookcase. On their first date Lara recommended he read *The Tin Drum* by a German author, so he placed that on the desk in the living room where she was sure to see it. Then he thought better of it and put *The Rise And Fall* back on the desk alongside it.

Lara was waiting for him when he walked into the shop, as excited as a child on the way to Coney Island. She kissed *Herr* Kaltenbach on the cheek before they left. Otto told them to enjoy their omelets. He seemed to be rooting for them, but his expression warned Eli to be careful with her.

The sun warmed this late March Saturday, herald of an early end to one of the worst German winters in a hundred years. They strolled around the market square and down narrow side streets, arm in arm, both of them giggling like little children at the silliest things. Eli forgot for the moment where he was. He just enjoyed being with this woman.

They stopped at different stores to buy eggs, lettuce and tomatoes for a salad, a bottle of white Franken wine, a loaf of black bread, a hunk of Emmentaler cheese, and *stollen* from their favorite bakery. As they were ready to head back to the apartment, Eli grabbed a bunch of field flowers from a cart in front of the flower shop. Lara broke off a purple one and put it in her hair.

She sashayed up the concrete steps to the entrance of his apartment building and entered as though she lived there. On the way up the stairs, they passed *Frau* Giesler coming down. Usually the landlady tried to be friendly with Eli when she saw him, and sometimes they exchanged a few words. Not this time. She took one look at Lara and shook her head. Lara lowered hers, embarrassed. Shaming by his landlady was not a good way to start the evening.

"Eva Braun," Lara muttered under her breath. Eli started laughing. Then Lara started laughing. Eli unlocked the door to his apartment and ushered her in.

Lara looked around the small place - the kitchen, the bathroom, the living room - admiring everything she saw: Eli's Utrillo Paris poster, Harry's cuckoo clock, and most of all the small gas water heaters over the tub in the bathroom and the sink in the kitchen. "You are fortunate to have hot water," she said. "Many German homes are not so fortunate." She noticed every other detail. But she refused to even glance in the direction of the open door into the bedroom.

Eli had never really watched anyone preparing dinner before. Now he couldn't take his eyes off of her. She fascinated him with the way she cracked the eggs and whipped them, a happy smile on the corners of her mouth; he almost hacked off his finger cutting up the tomatoes for the salad. She looked like she belonged in his kitchen. She was impossibly adorable, a towel tied around her tiny waist as a makeshift apron. He liked this feeling. He kissed her on the back of the neck. She turned around and gave him a firm kiss on the lips, then cut it off. "Time to cook the omelet," she said, poking him playfully with the flat whisk she brought in her purse.

They attacked their omelets and gulped the wine as though they didn't know where their next meal might be coming from. Between bites he managed to repeat "this is delicious" several times.

She swallowed and said, "My mother told me you catch a husband with love, but you keep him with food." As soon as the words were out of her mouth, she turned bright red. She jammed another bite in her mouth. He loved to watch the passion with which she devoured food.

Over coffee and cake, they slowed down and resumed their conversation about last night's show, *Lawrence of Arabia.* "In the film maybe Peter O'Toole likes boys better than he likes girls," she said.

"What a pity." Eli lit two cigarettes and handed one to her.

"I think Omar Sharif is much better looking," she said, her dark eyes teasing. "He looks like you." She ran her tongue over her upper lip.

"But I thought I looked like Paul Newman."

She looked down at her lap, feigned bashfulness. "Margot was not supposed to tell you that."

They made small talk for a few minutes. He asked her about her photography. She asked him about life in the Army.

"Do you like to shoot the big guns?" she asked.

"Harry says it's better than sex."

She laughed. "That cannot be so. Not with Margot." She flipped her hair back behind her left ear.

This is it, Eli said to himself, now or never. Out loud he said, "Leave the dishes. I'll wash them later."

He turned off the light in the kitchen and moved into the living room. He put the Chet Baker record on the stereo. Lara stopped to scrutinize the two books on his desk. She said nothing about them. Instead she asked who he liked better, Duke Ellington or Count Basie. When he said Count Basie, she launched into a vigorous and learned argument that Ellington was the more important musician. Next it was an academic discussion of Dave Brubeck, and then Gerry Mulligan. She knew more about jazz than he ever bothered to know. All he cared about was the sounds they made.

She curled up on the couch and took off her shoes. When he sat down next to her, she snuggled up to him but went on talking. He forgot to turn out either the light over the desk or the one next to the couch.

She turned her head to him and waited for his lips to come to hers. She ran her hand over his chest. He ran his hand over her chest, lingering on her breast. She pressed herself against him. He could hear her lungs filling and emptying. He unbuttoned the top two buttons of her blouse, and put his hand inside. She let his fingers explore for only a moment before she pulled away, gasping.

"We must not go so fast," she said.

"You've got to be kidding." He wanted to scream. His groin ached.

She sat up and re-buttoned her blouse. "Please do not be disappointed with me," she pleaded. He sulked. She touched his cheek when he wouldn't answer. "Give me time."

He forced a smile. "Like the omelet?"

"Yes, like the omelet."

She kissed him. He kissed her back, more cautious this time, more tender. Pressing himself on her wasn't in him. He thought about what Otto Kaltenbach said: "Please be careful, *Leutnant*. She is a delicate girl." So this time he was the one who paused.

He reached for his pack of Pall Malls on the end table and took out two. He lit them. She took one and leaned her head on his shoulder. She took the conversation down a new path. "Have you finished reading *The Tin Drum*?" she asked.

"I'm still working on it. You have to explain it to me."

"There is nothing to explain," she said. "It is about Germans and Nazis and the war." But then they spent the next half hour talking about it. He asked serious, thoughtful questions, and she gave serious, well considered answers. He had had no intention of starting a discussion about Nazis, but one thing seemed to lead to another.

The conversation hit a dead spot. The music stopped. Laugh-

ter and unintelligible shouting from outside filled the quiet inside, the noise probably from the Schutzenhaus down the street.
Drunken German men always sounded threatening to Eli, like
they were preparing to ignite a *pogrom*.

"You want to know if my father was a Nazi, yes?" she asked.

"I hadn't thought about it," he lied.

"My father was not a Nazi. He opposed the Nazis right from
the beginning. During the war they put him in a concentration
camp. He did not come home until one year after it ended.
Momma and I were living alone here in Kronberg. We almost
starved."

"I would like to meet your father and your mother."

"Not yet," she answered quickly. Then she grabbed his hand
and held it, massaging it with her fingers. He liked the feeling.

"Why does he hate Americans so much?" His tone might
have sounded too much like an accusation.

"He does not hate Americans. But he wants to protect his
daughters, especially me."

"Then let me convince him I will not dishonor you." As soon
as he said it, Eli wanted to take it back. He had every intention
of deflowering her if given the chance. He just wanted her to
want it too.

"You are sweet," she said. Her brief smile quickly dissolved.
"Most German men my father's age feel humiliated. First they
were defeated in the war. Then they could not feed their families. And now they cannot protect their women from sleeping
with Americans, particularly the black men. And then there are
the children, the mixed ones particularly. No one wants them
and no one wants their mothers. I feel so sorry for them."

"Is that why you work at the orphanage on your day off?"

She nodded her head, and then brushed the corner of her eye.
"But my father says we must be proud to be Germans. He says

the Nazis were the ones who committed the crimes, not ordinary Germans. He says we suffered enough for the war. The bombings, the hunger, the destruction of our cities, the rape of our women by the Russians. We were fortunate we were here in Kronberg, in the American zone. My mother was a very attractive woman. Many men would like to have her, I am sure."

She presented her father's arguments as if by rote, without conviction, Eli noticed. But nonetheless, he understood her respect for her father precluded criticism if he ever wanted a shot at her. So he just let her continue.

"My father says the Allies did not need to fire bomb Dresden. Germany had already lost the war. And he says the Americans dropping atomic bombs on Japan was an atrocity too. He does not like these trials that are starting soon in Frankfurt. The Auschwitz trials. He said in the end the Americans will go home and leave us to blame each other."

By the time she finished, Eli decided he didn't like her father very much. Some of his disgust dripped onto Lara. "And what do you think?" he asked to know.

"I think my father is wrong. I am ashamed for my country. We are guilty and must live with what we have done. No excuses. We must prove to the world we can again be moral people." Eli was glad to hear her say it, but the speech sounded a little too rehearsed, telling him what he wanted to hear. He scrutinized the Utrillo poster pinned to the wall across the room.

Lara's eyes pleaded with him. "I do not want you to think we are all monsters."

He relaxed his tense shoulders, and reached his hand to her cheek. "I could never think you are a monster." He kissed her gently.

"I would die if I thought my father had anything to do with killing Jews." She said it softly.

She's guessed I'm a Jew, he thought. A touch of concern rippled through, and then he felt offended by it. If she didn't like it, tough cookies. But he wasn't ready to admit anything just yet, so he let her go on.

"There were many Jews in Kronberg before the war, before *Kristallnacht*. Over three hundred. Most of them left after that night, but some of them were killed by the Nazis later. Their synagogue, the one with onions on top of the two towers, it is still there by the river, empty. The mobs ransacked it and destroyed their holy scrolls. What do they call them? Torah? It is a pity. Maybe someday Jews will come back to Kronberg and open the synagogue again."

He swallowed and said nothing, afraid he would give himself away. This is not fun, he thought. He fumbled for something to change the subject just when Lara jumped up from the couch, wearing a fresh smile. "Come; let me help you clean up the dishes. I insist on it," she said.

She tied the towel around her waist again. She washed and he dried. It felt like they were playing house, and he liked it. Every so often they stopped to kiss. He ran his hand up and down the outside of her blouse. She let him. Now that he had touched her breasts, he felt possessive about them.

He walked her halfway across the bridge that night. "One day soon, I must walk the rest of the way across the bridge," he said.

"One day soon," she answered.

She looked around to make sure no one was looking and then kissed him hard on the lips.

"You made a wonderful omelet," he said.

In spite of some dark conversation, Eli couldn't remember the last time he had such a good time without having sex. Lara seemed so at home in his kitchen, like she belonged there. She was the most interesting girl he had met in a long time. He did get to first base, and she didn't say "never." She just said they had to go slow. That was encouraging. And when he did get to the Promised Land, how much sweeter a prize she would be.

Wow, she's smart. She knows about so much. But her father is a problem. Maybe he did oppose the Nazis, and Eli did have to give him points for spending time in a concentration camp. That was a big deal. But for someone imprisoned by them, he didn't sound too upset with them. All that talk about Nazis sure killed the romance of the evening, he thought. But he was relieved to know she hated them almost as much as Willy. And she felt compassion for Jews.

When Eli related to Harry how they talked about Nazis half the night, Harry laughed and told him that was the dumbest way to try to get laid he had ever heard of. He teased Eli for his new-found chivalrous behavior.

Eli was only half-listening. While they talked, he picked up the tasseled throw pillow from the sofa and held it to his nose. He could still smell Lara's eucalyptus on it. He would take whatever came next as it came.

TEN

The cornflowers, chamomile, and crocuses bloomed early that April. The tulips in the park across the street from the apartment poked their heads up, and the linden trees budded. The farmers plowed the fields with teams of oxen. Cars again competed for space on the roads with ox carts, slow moving tractors, and tiny three wheeled trucks. The stench of manure drenched the villages surrounding Kronberg. And Lara substituted a royal blue raincoat for her heavy winter loden coat.

Lara and Eli now took for granted they would see each other every Friday and Saturday night. Eli snuck away early for coffee at least twice a week, often arriving at Otto's shop still in his fatigues. If Lara was busy or out running an errand, he talked to Otto and looked at the voluminous private collection of his photos. Eli could not visit the shop without stopping for a moment to stare at the portrait by the door of Otto's wife and daughter.

Lara was still too modest to show Eli her work; one day Otto did. "She has extraordinary talent," Otto said, "but she must build her confidence." Her photos astonished Eli the first time he saw them. Otto's work was mostly studio portraits. Lara's captured the humanity of people leading their lives: a farmer and his weather-beaten wife on an ox cart, a teacher in her classroom, little schoolgirls playing hopscotch in their uniforms, a woman in a stall selling fish.

For the first time since he arrived in Germany, Eli felt part of a family beyond that of the Army. There was Lara, of course, but also Harry, Margot, Otto, and Willy. Maybe even his landlady, *Frau* Giesler. She grunted a *"guten abend"* to Lara when they passed again on the stairway up to Eli's apartment.

Still, a single spear of cold German conceit from *Herr Ober*, the headwaiter at the Officers Club, reminded Eli he lived in a nest of werewolves who only a few years ago murdered his family. Many of them would have gladly done the same to him, even now.

His friend Willy kept his animosity toward Nazis boiling. He shared a beer with Willy a few days after Willy excoriated his neighbors again in his latest column in the *Kronberg Zeitung*. He wrote that Germans now sincerely hated Hitler, but they hated him because he lost the war, and then killed himself while they were left to suffer the consequences. Their outrage was one born of self pity, not moral outrage or remorse for what they themselves did, or what was done in their name. *It was not just the criminal Nazis, the madmen who did this,* Willy wrote. *It was the decent people who cheered Hitler on and followed him. There are a few exceptions, but the whole German nation has blood on its hands.*

"Apparently *Herr* Kohler was one of those exceptions," Eli said to Willy in the back corner of the Gasthaus Zum Stern. Willy was no longer welcome in the Schutzenhaus.

"Maybe not an exception," his friend responded.

Eli gave him a quizzical look. "What about his time in a concentration camp?"

"Then you are still seeing Lara?" Willy's voice carried just a hint of jealousy, or maybe resentment at yet another American stealing a desirable German girl.

"I keep asking to meet her father, but she keeps saying 'not yet'."

"He doesn't like Jews," Willy said. He took a long gulp from his stein, examining the suds at the bottom.

Eli prepared to question or argue, but didn't really want to hear any more. So he let the dark words float on a cloud of cigarette smoke. Then he buried the conversation lest it disturb the springtime Lara brought to him.

Eli awoke each morning so full of energy he beat Harry to the bathroom. He raced to the base often in time for morning calisthenics, and then raced to the photo shop in the afternoon. Only rarely did anything other than Lara or Charlie Company distract him. He read in *Stars and Stripes* about Buddhist monk protests in Vietnam, police dogs in Birmingham attacking Negro and white Freedom Riders, and Sandy Koufax pitching a no hitter against the Giants. But that all seemed like an imaginary world unrelated to his own.

He thought Lara was going to cry when he told her he and Harry received orders to attend a five day course on Nuclear-Biological-Chemical Warfare at the Army Training Center in Vilseck. It was only a hundred seventy five kilometers away, near the Czech border, but it might as well have been at the end of the earth. Eli didn't have the heart to tell her that on May 10th the whole battalion would depart for fifteen days at Grafenwehr.

While he was at Vilseck, an alert was called. He phoned Sergeant Pickett as soon as he could to find out if Captain Symanski was sober. "The Old Man was clear as the water in a mountain stream," Pickett answered. "Led us out the gate, first again." That didn't stop Kaine from giving Eli an earful when he got back.

"The man's a drunk," Kaine charged. "Do you want to wait until he gets someone killed? It'll be on your head."

"You keep up talk like that and I'll charge you with insubordination," Eli shot back. But he worried Kaine might be right. What if someone did die because of Symanski and he had done nothing? At least for now the Old Man had his drinking under control. All Eli could do was keep an eye on him, and fill in as best he could.

The night Eli and Harry returned, Lara and Margot charged up the steps to the apartment, eager to see their men. After small talk and a beer, Harry and Margot retreated to the bedroom and closed the door. Eli hoped the raucous grunts, groans, Margot's yells, and rocking furniture would turn Lara on. Instead she turned into a tree trunk, unresponsive even when he unbuttoned her blouse and slid his hands in. She broke off during one deep kiss to look at her watch. A while later Margot opened the door to the bedroom, still adjusting her clothes. Harry came out satisfied.

"I must go home now," Lara said, rising from the sofa, as if she had been waiting for the two other lovers to finish. Eli was perplexed and frustrated, not new feelings when it came to Lara. Why was she tropically hot one minute and arctic frozen the next? Fear of her father? The mysterious disease when she was seventeen? Maybe religion - hers or his?

It was fruitless to speculate about what was going on in her head. But he had promised to go slowly, and so he would, until he couldn't go slowly any more. Whatever it was, his patience neared bottom. The frustration was beginning to feel too much like high school. If things didn't change soon, the Grafenwehr trip would be a good time to end it.

Her next two visits to the apartment went better. The first time, she let him explore more, though still no home run. The second time he was sure this was it. She groaned when his fingers probed under her skirt, and pressed herself against him. Then she slammed on the brakes. No guy could ever exert the willpower she did when she stopped short of culmination. Nonetheless, it was progress. For a girl like Lara, it showed how much she cared for him beyond what any words could say. But when she broke her embrace, she looked terrified.

When he told her he was leaving in mid-May for fifteen days, he was sure she would break into tears. It irritated him when instead she responded cheerfully. "You will do very well when you shoot the big guns," she teased. Then more serious, "You will telephone me, yah?"

He told her he would be busy all of the time, but would call the first chance he got. And he would send her post cards or a letter.

"Send them to the shop," she asked. Her father remained a shadowy presence.

Eli had to tell someone back home about Lara. On the first of May he sat down to write his cousin Max a letter, but he knew all Max would care about was the sex. And Lara was no longer just about that. So instead he wrote his cousin Rose. Five years older, she had been like his big sister ever since he came to America. Now she was married and still living in Berkinbury with her husband and two infant boys. If anyone would understand, it would be Rose. He didn't hide his feelings.

She's amazing. We see each other all of the time, and I have gotten to know her very well. We are so comfortable to-gether it's like we are two old friends. She's as smart as any girl I know. She's good looking and graceful as a ballerina. She's totally Americanized and would fit right into Berkinbury. She hates Nazis, of course, and feels very guilty about everything. You will like her.

Rose's airmail letter came flying back. It arrived the day the battalion departed for Grafenwehr. He read it on the train ride up. In keeping with her blunt personality, Rose's reply was as subtle as a prickly pear.

Are you crazy! Pull your pants up and think with your brain. You'll be coming home in six months. Wait for a nice Jewish girl, or at least an American. You can't bring back a Nazi. It would kill your Grandpa Avi and Grandma Sara.

Eli churned until the train pulled into Grafenwehr's stations, and the busied unloading of the tanks from the flatbed railcars began. That night he sought out Harry at the makeshift Officers Club in a field tent big enough to serve as a combat surgery center. The two friends went outside with their steins of beer and sat down on the dry ground under a tree. Eli told Harry about Rose's letter.

"She's right, you know," Harry said.

"But what about you and Margot? You must be thinking about taking her home."

"Can you just see Mother introducing Margot to her women's bridge club in Scarsdale? Or Father introducing her to his Wall Street associates? It's not going to happen. Margot knew that from the beginning. I'm going home alone when November comes around, and so are you."

Eli liked Margot in spite of her sluttish ways. She was devoted to Harry, and together they had a closeness Eli only dreamed about. However clear Harry made it at the beginning of their relationship, Eli couldn't imagine Margot's heartbreak when Harry left. Rose upset him the first time he read her letter, but now he was glad he wrote her. She was right, of course, and he couldn't ever forget that.

Harry offered wise counsel too. But Harry couldn't even predict his own future, no less foresee someone else's.

ELEVEN

The intensity of the tank gunnery training consumed every moment of Eli's days and nights. He telephoned Lara at the shop on the third day he was at Grafenwehr, but only had time to tell her he missed her. "I am going to give you such a big welcome when you come home," she promised. He liked the sound of that, but lost the thought in the thundering of the guns in the night firing a couple of hours later.

Eli didn't even notice Harry was gone until the thirteenth day. "He went back to Kronberg a few days ago," a Bravo Company platoon leader told him when he came looking. The platoon leader suggested it had to be something important because Colonel Stratton went back too. Stratton returned the next morning. Harry didn't. Eli tried to call him at the apartment but no one answered. He sniffed around, but had little time, and no one knew anything anyway, not even Sergeant Pickett, who usually knew all the scuttlebutt.

Eli supervised the unloading of the tanks at the Kronberg rail station, a few blocks from his apartment. He had his jeep driver drop him off at home without returning first to Holden Barracks like he usually did.

When he burst through the door, Harry was in the living room loading his souvenirs into a cardboard box. He didn't even look up when he heard Eli come in. A half dozen sealed boxes surrounded him, along with his footlocker. Two leather suitcases stood in the hallway.

"Harry! What the hell is going on?"

Harry's ever-present smile was nowhere in sight. He looked exhausted. "Eli, you're not going to believe this."

"Tell me."

"Margot and I are getting married."

"Married? What the hell! You said...."

"I know what I said. But she's pregnant."

A lungful of air escaped from Eli as if he had been hit in the gut with a rifle butt. "How in the hell did this happen?"

"The way it usually happens." Harry smiled just a little, and then it disappeared again. He wiped his fingers across his freckled forehead. "I received an order to report back to Battalion HQ in Kronberg. I thought I was being sent home to be the duty officer until the battalion got back. But when I walked in the door, Colonel Stratton was waiting for me, along with Chaplain Dorland, and the Burgermeister, Margot's Uncle Erich. You know her uncle is the one who got her the job at the PX, right?

Eli pulled a cigarette from the breast pocket of his rumpled, dust covered fatigues and lit up. Then he plopped down on the edge of the couch. Harry took a seat on the footlocker and resumed the story.

"Anyway, Colonel Stratton laid it out to me - the need to keep good relations between the Germans and the American Army, and all of that bullcrap. Then he told me I had two choices: marry Margot or take an assignment in Africa in a place worse than my worst nightmare where no one would ever find me, followed by a less than honorable discharge. Chaplain Dorland then offered a few words of encouragement about Christ, love, and duty. Burgermeister Steinbach, my beloved future Uncle Erich, just glared at me as if he wanted to shoot me. He's the one who complained to Stratton."

"Wait a second, Harry. You're getting railroaded." Eli

slammed his fist down on the end table, shaking the lamp so hard it nearly toppled. "They can't make you do this. Fight it. I'll help you. Damn it, you can just pay her off. How much do you think it would take?"

"Eli, stop. Stop. Listen to me. I want to marry her." Harry could read the disbelief on Eli's face. He took a breath waiting for his friend to hear what he just said. "She loves me more than anyone's ever loved me. She'll make a good wife and a good mother. I know she will."

Eli blinked, unsure what to say next. "But do you love her?"

"Yes, I really think I do. I didn't realize it until now. Imagine, Eli. I'm going to be a daddy. And I'm going to try to be a good one, not like my father. And I'm going to be a good husband."

"But Harry, she's been around."

"She told me everything I need to know a long time ago. She's been a one-guy girl ever since she met me. That's all I care about."

"And you can live with that?"

"If she really loves me. And I know she does."

Eli could think of a million reasons to object, but it would do no good, so he offered only one. "Have you told your parents yet?"

"I called them. Got about what you'd expect. Father disowned me and said he never wanted to hear from me again. Mother cried." He snuffed out his cigarette, and then clasped his hands together. "You know, for the first time I feel free. I don't have to live my life anymore to satisfy their narrow minds."

"So what are you going to do?" Eli asked.

"For now we're going to live with Margot's mother and grandmother till we get our own apartment. I'm going to stay in the Army for a while. Hell, it's the only thing I've ever been any good at, aside from getting in trouble." He smiled a forlorn smile. "I've already extended. Another year in Germany. Then if I decide to stay in, maybe a tour as an adviser in Vietnam. Colonel Stratton said he could swing it. It's not much, but it's the only war we have. A chance to earn those Captain's bars early."

Eli wanted to say something profound to his friend, something hopeful and comforting. But he could think of nothing to say. The Army demanded its young officers in Germany grow up in a hurry, all the way up. But this seemed like asking too much.

Harry's big grin reappeared. "Hey, man. Lara's going to be Margot's witness. How about if you be mine? The wedding's Saturday at the City Hall. Twelve hundred hours sharp. The Germans wait for no one."

"You got it, man." Eli slapped his friend on the back and gave him the biggest smile he could muster.

Eli helped Harry pack the rest of his things, and then haul them out to Harry's white convertible. The roar of tank engines and clank of tracks across the park on Hindenburg Strasse interrupted their farewell. They stopped to watch Bravo Company coming from the train station, guns facing to the rear, and tank commanders' heads poking up from the turrets. The seventeen tanks and following support vehicles headed for the *Neue Brucke* across the Main River, then on to the back gate of Holden Barracks.

"They're keeping tight formation," Harry mused, approving. He turned for one last look at the gray stone apartment building. Clouds of diesel exhaust drifted across the park. Rain sprinkles began to fall.

"I'm going to miss you." Eli said.

Harry clapped Eli on the back, perhaps embarrassed by the unmanly show of affection. "Hell, I'm still going to be here." But they both knew things could never be the same. Eli waited until the car vanished in the direction of the furniture store before scurrying back to the apartment, wet.

Eli hadn't felt so alone since the day he met Harry. Now he was abandoned again, just like what happened every time he loved someone. He thought about the day Grandpa Avi told him how his real mother and father had died, murdered by Germans. And here he was in the middle of them, at the moment hating every single one.

The dark rain began to fall harder, splattering against the living room window and running down the rain pipes. He made himself a peanut butter and jelly sandwich, and opened a bottle of beer. The apartment was so bare without Harry's collection of German junk. His absent cuckoo clock left an open hole on the wall. When the hour came, Eli listened for the annoying cuckoo bird, but it didn't come.

He walked into the bedroom. The mattress on which Harry and Margot conceived their child was bare, unmade. The room, without Harry's clutter, was too neat to bear. So Eli threw his own dirty laundry on the floor, and crawled into bed.

He couldn't wait to get out of this country. And he was in no hurry to see Lara.

TWELVE

The June sun shined on Harry and Margot the Saturday they were married. By the end of the day, neither Eli nor Lara knew if any of that sunshine was meant for them.

The old city hall, the pride of Kronberg, stood with dignity since the sixteenth century. Now the *Rathaus* marked the edge of the Combat Zone where, in a few hours, horny young American soldiers would swarm the bars and restaurants. Middle aged prostitutes from out of town would crowd the two narrow streets, eager to earn some American dollars.

Harry paced the hall outside the Great Room on the second floor. Eli peaked inside. Columns of hand painted Italian ceramic tiles intermixed with polished oak paneled walls. Several aisles of green leathered oak chairs stood in formation before a tile-covered fireplace; the large leaded and stained glass windows lining the far end brightened the room. An elderly custodian unfolded a green felt cloth bearing the Kronberg town seal and spread it on the ceremonial table. Harry and Margot would soon take their wedding vows in front of that table.

Harry and Eli arrived at eleven thirty. Twelve o'clock drew close, and the women still hadn't appeared. Harry lit his third cigarette. The magistrate arrived wearing a black renaissance robe and hat, accompanied by the Burgermeister - Uncle Erich. Harry checked his watch one more time. German punctuality waited for no one, man or woman.

Just then Otto Kaltenbach hurried into the room carrying his favorite Leica camera. "The girls will be here in one moment," he announced as formally as a court herald. "They have been at the *friseur* - the hairdresser." Harry relaxed. He put out his cigarette. Then he saw Margot coming up the stairs and hurried towards her.

Margot lent proof to the truth that every bride is beautiful on her wedding day. Her modest white dress covered her below her knees and down to her elbows. Every hair was in place. She carried a bouquet of red roses. Her mother, her grandmother, and Lara trailed behind. Her mother wore a common flower-print cotton dress; Grandma dressed in black, her only attire since losing her son in the war twenty years earlier.

Eli didn't spot Lara until she reached the landing and turned the corner into the Great Room. When he did, tingling ran up his legs and landed in his heart. She looked like a nymph he had only dreamed about - maybe a little like Audrey Hepburn. She had cut her blondish hair above her shoulders and pulled it back behind her ears, with a thin hair braid across the crown. The cinched waist of her sleeveless soft blue dress enhanced her tiny waist and modest breasts. The lapels and big buttons added style. She looked gorgeous, sexy, and adorable all at the same time. Eli didn't know whether to put her on a pedestal and admire her, or throw her on the table and ravage her. When she raised her arms to embrace him, he saw she shaved her underarms, an intimate detail meant just for him.

"My god, you are beautiful," he said, for the first of many times that day.

He hugged her, and she kissed his cheek. "And you are so handsome in your nice suit."

The magistrate recounted the history of Kronberg in a solemn tone, but he brightened when he began the marriage vows. Every so often he stopped and asked Margot a question. She answered "Yah." Then he asked Harry, and Harry answered "Yah." He couldn't really understand the German; later Margot kidded him that the magistrate was asking him if he wanted to buy a pig farm. After the magistrate prattled on awhile, she finally whispered in Harry's ear that "we are married now."

Harry kissed her, not a sexy kiss and not a dutiful one, but one that said "I love this woman, now and forever." Eli envied Harry. He had someone who loved him and would never leave him, someone to whom he was the most important person in the world. Every so often before, during, and after the ceremony, Lara looked at Eli with those beguiling dark eyes and smiled a smile that said "I can give this to you too." She glowed in the sunlight coming through the ancient glass windows.

After the ceremony, Otto took pictures, many of the bride and groom, and some of their little wedding party. He stopped Eli and Lara, and made them pose for one. After he snapped it, they relaxed and turned toward each other, ready for a kiss. That's when he snapped the second one, the one he gave Eli in a silver frame a couple of weeks later.

On the walk to Greifensteiner Restaurant for the wedding lunch, Lara clung to his hand and wouldn't let go until he yanked it away so he could put his arm around her waist and pull her to him. She grasped his other hand and snuggled into his shoulder, oblivious to the older German women who clucked their disapproval as they passed by. One said something that could be interpreted as "whore." Lara ignored them, as lost in Eli as he was in her.

He climbed the stairway to the second floor of the restaurant behind her. When they got to the top, she spun around and kissed him. "I have wanted to do that all day," she said.

Lara sat on one side of Margot, and Harry on the other. Eli sat next to Lara on the near end. Grandma, Margot's mother,

Uncle Burgermeister, and Otto sat on the other side of the table. Lara and Eli kept rubbing legs and touching hands under the table. He ran his fingers from her knee to her thigh and back again. She gave him a peck on the cheek when he did. Grandma gave them a stern look and mumbled something in German Eli didn't understand. Lara snickered and put her hand to her mouth. Margot interpreted: "She says you are a bull in heat and that someone better tie up your balls with a belt."

The waiters filled their glasses with Franken wine from traditional *Bocksbeutel* bottles. Eli gave a warm, heartfelt toast to Harry and Margot. Then he raised his glass and called out "*prosit!*" Margot liked his toast so much she got up and gave him a kiss on the cheek. Harry feigned jealousy. Uncle Burgermeister, substituting in the father's role, gave an apparently sentimental toast which left Margot's mother misty eyed. He finished it with another *prosit!*

Like a moth to a flame, Eli touched Lara once too often, and flew too close to her big, dark, burning eyes. He felt his stomach shake, about to detonate. Then it rumbled. What the hell was going on? All he knew was he had to get out of there, fast! He stood up in a hurry, ran down the steps, and out the door. He leaned against the half-timbered stucco wall and wretched; only a teaspoon of bile came out from his near-empty stomach. Sweat covered his forehead. Uncontrolled rapid gulps of air warned of another eruption.

Harry ran after him when he saw his friend in distress. "Are you okay?" he asked when he caught up to him. "You're white."

Obviously he was not okay, but he answered, "Yeah." He tried to smile but couldn't. "For a minute there it felt like a convoy of two-and-a-half ton trucks drove through my gut."

"Something you ate?"

Eli shook his head slowly, and closed his eyes as if in pain.

"Harry, I'm falling in love with her." The words were out of his mouth before he could shut it.

"Anyone with half a brain can see that. So what's the problem?"

"For god's sake, Harry. This can't happen." Harry pulled a pack of cigarettes from his suit pocket and offered one to Eli. He took it, then yanked his handkerchief from his back pocket and blew his nose. "What am I going to do?"

"You're going to go back in there and enjoy my wedding day," Harry answered. "Then, whatever you decide, be kind to her. Or I'll kill you."

When they returned, Lara looked worried. "Are you alright darling?" She touched the palm of her hand to his cheek. "You feel warm."

He nodded. He kissed her hand, then put his hand to the back of her head and kissed her ever so gently on the lips. She called him darling, he realized. And she said it with such tenderness he thought his heart would melt.

He couldn't eat the venison, potato dumplings, and vinegar beets even though they looked delicious. He pushed them around on his plate. Lara ate all of hers, and then reached over and skewered a dumpling from his plate. An hour later Harry and Margot mounted the white Chevy Impala chariot and left on a three day honeymoon at a nice spa hotel in Bad Homburg, just north of Frankfurt.

When the party broke up, Grandma said something to Lara which made her blush. She bent over and kissed Grandma on the cheek.

"What did she say?" Eli asked when they were out of earshot.

"I can't tell you." She blushed again.

Eli didn't need to persuade Lara to come back to his apartment this time. She clung to him and he to her all of the way.

They passed the tower and crossed the street to the park. Eli looked around to see who might be watching. Lara didn't seem to care.

The sun had not yet set when they climbed the steps. As soon as they got in the door, they grabbed each other. Eli pulled and Lara pushed them toward the living room. He undid his tie, pulled off his jacket and threw them on the floor without letting go of her. She kicked off her shoes. They collapsed in each others' arms on the couch. Their tongues probed, first in her mouth, then in his.

She didn't stop him when he touched his hand to her knee under her dress. She squeaked and pressed herself against him when his hand moved up the inside of her milky thigh. She let his fingers probe beneath her underpants, her breaths short and deep. She squirmed. He fumbled urgently inside his pants pocket for the condom. Where the hell was it?

She shivered, and then froze, rigid. "Stop. Please stop." She bolted upright. "You're messing up my dress," she gasped, throaty, shaking.

"So take it off," he grunted.

She raised her forearm between them when he reached for her again. "We must talk first." Lara struggled to catch her breath, laboring to inhale and exhale. She held her hand to her chest. Eli had never before known any healthy young woman who could exert such control at such a moment.

"Talk? What is there to possibly talk about?" he demanded. He rose from the couch. "I have to go to the toilette."

He ran cold water over his face until it hurt, and then studied his distraught face in the mirror. "What am I going to do?" he pleaded.

If she wanted to talk, that's what they would do. He was ready. It was time to tell her the truth - more than she wanted to hear. Maybe it would finish this whole bewildering thing once and for all.

When he returned, she was leaning against the bookcase looking through his record albums. She had straightened her dress and her hair. Her lipstick, always minimal, was gone. Her vulnerability weakened his resentment.

"There is something I must tell to you," she said. He patted the couch for her to join him, but she stayed on her side of the living room, leaning against the bookcase. She lowered her chin, avoiding his eyes.

"Let me go first," he cut in. Before she could respond, he blurted out "I'm Jewish," daring her. Then he waited.

She raised her head and fixed on him. "Do you think that matters to me, that you are Jewish? I thought so from the beginning. *Herr* Kaltenbach thought so too. But you should know it would not matter."

"I didn't know what you might think," he answered sharply, suddenly offended. Her words reminded him for an instant that Otto was of the German generation who thought they could pick out Jews by their looks and their smell.

"I am not one of those Germans," she shot back. "Do you think I am?"

"I do wonder about your father. How he will feel if he ever meets me."

"Father does not like Jews, but he is not me." Lara stood at attention, as though Eli were judging her, and not the other way around.

He relaxed, relieved of a burden. An enormous dark secret he had been carrying around since he met her lifted from his shoulders. When she saw him relax, she relaxed a little too. But she stayed on her side of the room.

Now unbridled, he kept going, but he kept watch for her reaction. He revealed another dark secret: he was born in the Ukraine and only came to America when he was eight years old. She looked surprised, but nothing more. He didn't tell her he came as an orphan, or that Germans killed his mother, father, sisters, grandmother, and grandfather. His omission left her believing Kira and Jake were his real mother and father.

"Your big secret, it is not so bad," she said. "Is that all?"

He nodded. Only a little lie. Then he patted the cushion again, inviting her to join him on the sofa. He felt giddy, ready to move on, to pick up where they left off. But something still troubled her, and he didn't know what else he could say. Maybe mention that he was not religious? He shouldn't have to say that. After all, he wasn't pressing her about her religion.

She moved over to the desk and leaned against it, keeping a safe distance. Then she sat down on the desk chair, composing her thoughts, deciding. She examined the polished nubs of her chewed fingernails.

"I am afraid I have something terrible to tell you." She said it slowly, her tone like one announcing a death in the family. He could see her hand shaking. "When I was seventeen, I went out with an American boy. Not an officer. A Private." She hesitated, uncertain whether to continue.

Is she trying to tell me she screwed him? Eli said to himself. She was twenty-four years old now. He wanted to tell her he wasn't expecting a virgin. "That's it?" he said. She didn't answer. "C'mon, whatever you did, it's not so terrible?"

The smell of *Frau* Giesler's roasting rump roast seeped in through the cracks between the floor boards. Children playing at dusk in the park across the street called out to each other, a game that sounded like Red Light-Green Light. Eli reached for his pack of cigarettes. He stopped when Lara began to speak again.

"There is more to tell. Worse." She took a deep breath, glanced up, then back down when she caught him studying her. He could barely make out her next words. "I became pregnant," she said quietly.

Eli tried to mask his astonishment behind an indifferent expression. Suddenly his revelation that he was Jewish didn't seem so big. She waited for her words to stop ringing. She squeezed her fingers together so hard they turned white, and then raised her eyes to meet his.

"My mother would have nothing to do with me." She gulped. "So my father took me to Munich to my aunt's to stay until the baby was born. He took care of me."

Eli's heart fibrillated so hard he thought he might have a cardiac arrest. Where he came from, respectable girls didn't get pregnant at seventeen. "And you had the baby there?" It was the only thing he could think to say.

She shook her head. "No. I had a miscarriage a week later." She looked relieved to have finally said the words she had been dreading. Now she waited for the executioner's decision.

When she first started talking, Eli thought he was ready to hear anything, but he never expected this. Yet befuddled as he was, he knew the next thing he said mattered as much as anything he ever said in his life. "You poor thing," was what came out. "You must have been scared to death." And he meant it.

She almost smiled. "I was very frightened."

"What about the father? That American Private." That son-of-a-bitch.

"He wanted nothing more to do with me. He went back home to the States in a little while."

Eli forced himself to look her in the eye. "Did you love him?" he asked.

"I thought I did at the time, but no. I did not love him. I was just a young girl who one night had too much to drink, a foolish mistake. I never let him touch me again. Or anyone else until you."

"This is why you had to go slow with me?"

"Yes, I had to be sure."

"It's not such a big mistake." But he found himself feeling jealous, a strange reaction for him. And why not? This day had been full of strange reactions.

She looked directly at him, pleading. "It will make a difference about how you feel with me?"

"No, absolutely not." He sounded decidedly more certain than he felt. "But it will take some getting used to."

"You will tell me if it ever does make a difference, yes?"

"It won't." He was not as sure as he tried to sound. Compassion. Lust. Disgust. Tenderness. Disgrace. Love. They all banged around his brain too quickly to take root. What he knew was he had to have her, and not just for his physical pleasure. It was now more than that, another new feeling. He wanted to protect her.

She smiled for the first time since they started talking. A tingling ran up his leg again and landed in his heart, the same feeling as when he first saw her today. "Spend the night," he said, his voice breathy.

She came over and sat down next to him. "I cannot, not here. I want you to think about what I have told you. For a few days. Then, if you still want, we will go away for the weekend. Yes?"

"Where?"

"Nuremberg. It is a nice city, and it is not far." She had apparently been thinking about this, and had a different plan than his more immediate one.

Eli was suddenly famished. "Are you hungry? There's not

much in the house. Just some C-Rations."

"Let us look." Lara took him by the hand and led him into the kitchen.

She chose the ham and lima beans, he the turkey loaf. He heated them on the two-burner gas stove while she set the table. He popped open two bottles of Kulmbacher beer. She waved off his offer of a glass and drank right from the bottle. C-Rations never tasted so good.

"This is delicious," she said as she slowly savored each bite. He hardly ate, unable to take his eyes off of her. Her smile had changed, more sure now, more intimate, more just for him.

When they were washing the dishes, she said "You were upset *Herr* Kaltenbach guessed you are Jewish. Yes?"

"I didn't think *Herr* Kaltenbach made such distinctions."

"Let me tell you why." She put the plate she was drying down on the counter top. "*Herr* Kaltenbach was married to a Jewess, long before the Nuremberg Laws made it illegal for any new marriages between Jew and Gentile. He and Adriana were married twenty-one years and very much in love. She worked with him in his photographic studio in Silesia. They had a beautiful daughter named Sophie. You have seen their picture."

After Lara's earlier revelation, neither this nor anything else could surprise him. But it explained a lot about Otto, and about Lara.

She sniffled and blew into a napkin. "They thought for a long time they would be protected because *Herr* Kaltenbach was a Gentile. He even had his church minister write a letter. But finally in 1942 they had rounded up all of the other Jews, so they came for the ones married to Gentiles. The Gestapo pounded on their door one night and took Adriana and Sophie away. He never knew what happened to them until a few years after the war when the concentration camp records were made open to everyone. They died at Auschwitz, Sophie eleven months after they arrived, and Adriana a month later." Lara blew her nose again.

"Why didn't they get out when they could?" Eli wanted to scream. But that would sound like he was judging the victims, both the Kaltenbachs and the Schneiders. His smothered frustration was more toward his own mother and father than the Kaltenbachs.

They talked and talked far into the night about every piece of their lives, mostly the good things, but some of the bad. They talked no more of the war or Nazis.

He snuggled with her on the couch, curiously content, her head resting on his shoulder, her eucalyptus hair brushing his nose. Every so often she raised her head and offered her lips for him to kiss. Ella Fitzgerald serenaded them on the record player. When Ella finished, Lara picked out an Anita O'Day album, then Johnny Mathis.

She told him about playing the flute when she was in junior high school, and about her first boyfriend, a trombone player named Wolfgang. Eli confessed to her his one serious relationship, with Jeannette Easton, a Carlyle townie. They fell in love early in his junior year in college. He told Lara they broke up over their religious differences. He didn't tell her Jeannette would do anything for him, but the more love she gave him the more a sense of impending doom grew inside of him, the fear she would abandon him. He kept raising the stakes, torturing the poor girl with one unreasonable demand after another until he made his fear come true. When she broke it off, Jeannette was devastated; he was relieved.

The more they talked the more they revealed. At the end of the evening Eli realized he had told her things about himself he never told anyone, not even Harry or his cousin Max. Nevertheless, occasional jealousy intruded, a shard from the G.I. who got her pregnant. He also found something new inside of himself - a determination to shield her from anyone who would hurt her. He didn't know where this was going, but he didn't want to even think about that right now.

This was a day neither of them ever wanted to end. When he kissed her goodnight on the bridge, she wouldn't let go.

"Next weekend we go to Nuremberg," he said as they touched hands.

"Yes. Nuremberg next weekend."

He wanted to tell her he loved her, but he couldn't. He was going home in five months. Alone. He wouldn't stay in Germany a minute longer than he had to, not for anyone. She knew that from the beginning. He would be good to her in the time they had together. And he would make no promises he couldn't keep. She had not asked for any, even for Nuremberg.

So everything should have been settled. But first Eli had to learn that if the Army wanted you to have a girlfriend they would have issued you one.

THIRTEEN

Something should have warned Eli this was not a routine alert. For one thing, Captain Symanski was stone cold sober when, at two o'clock in the morning, he led the company out the back gate and into the dense cover of Kasper Forest. But Eli's mind was too much on Lara, Nuremberg - and what came with it.

Everyone anticipated the usual return to base, maybe with time to catch a few more winks before reveille. Eli wanted to get home and finish packing for their trip. Then Colonel Stratton summoned all of the company commanders to his location. When half an hour passed with no news, Eli checked in with Sergeant Pickett; the First Sergeant hadn't heard any scuttlebutt. The longer they remained in position in the forest, the more this began to feel like trouble.

Normally Eli would be out in the ink-black night checking on each of the tank crews. This time he hung back at the company command post waiting, as tense and impatient as everyone else. Finally Captain Symanski brought word down from Headquarters. The battalion was headed out for war games. He didn't say for how long. In a flash, Eli's fantasies of Nuremberg vanished, destroyed by the damn Army, and he was furious about it. How many months had he been working on Lara? Too many. And this time his frustration wasn't her fault.

At first sunlight, the relentless column of 16th Armor tanks crossed the Main River at Volkach, swung north at Prosselheim, and ran a long stretch through small, stinky farm towns. The Cuban Missile Crisis seven months earlier began in the same way. So this time, trigger fingers itched, and radios bristled with too much traffic, voices high pitched and charged. When the column paused outside of Bergtheim, Captain Symanski sent word through Sergeant Pickett and Eli that this was an extended three-day training exercise, nothing more, and to keep the radio traffic down.

Combat fever and anxiety diminished. But every time his jeep hit a pothole, Eli cursed the Army and his bad luck. If he and Lara had gone away to Nuremberg together, he would have scored for sure. Now she had time to reconsider, and she could very well change her mind. Why not? Her last experience with an American hadn't exactly been a jar full of jelly. That image carried the bitter taste of jealousy, and maybe a little questioning of Lara, though he resisted faulting her. He warned himself he must lock that thought in the same box where he buried other dark thoughts.

At Poppenhausen, the seventy-two tanks swung back east toward Dittelbron, finally deploying by mid afternoon in a forest just north of Schweinfurt. Eli didn't want to be there.

That night he lay awake in his sleeping bag on the hard ground. He missed Lara already, though he refused to put those words to his feelings. He could taste her heated kisses when his fingers touched between her legs. Then he replayed every detail of their conversations Saturday night, from serious to funny and back again. He told her more about himself than he ever exposed to anyone, and it had felt good. No one could blame him for holding back his last big secret: Germans murdered his family. How could he ever tell her that? She might think he was blaming her.

She told him so much about herself, things she hadn't even told Margot, and that felt good too. He really knew her now. It never occurred to him that she might have her own secrets, as dark to her as his were to him.

His last thought before he fell asleep was that Lara was a vulnerable butterfly, scared and ashamed. She was older than seventeen now, and maybe wiser, but no more experienced. His job was to make sure she was not hurt again, at least not by him.

Late the next afternoon, Captain Symanski assembled his officers and NCOs to brief them. That night the entire battalion was ordered to cross the Main River south of Bergrheinfeld on a pontoon bridge the 3rd Infantry Division combat engineers hastily assembled. This was a tricky movement the battalion attempted only once before.

During the briefing, Captain Symanski pointed out checkpoints on a field map using a twig from a tree branch as a pointer. His right hand shook so much that at one point he had to grab it with his left. Everyone noticed, but Richard Kaine fixed his prickly stare on Eli as though to say "this man isn't fit to command." Eli concentrated on the map and Charlie Company's tactical objective.

Symanski finished and asked for questions. Kaine thickened his drawl. "This is gonna' be as much fun as wearin' a white sheet at a watermelon eatin' contest, if you know what I mean." No one laughed but Kaine. Captain Ski blinked his eyes twice, frowned, shook his head, and then said, "Dismissed."

Like a good coach, the Captain taught, inspired, and directed his team. Eli commanded the lead tank across the narrow, shaky pontoon bridge, inch by inch in the pitch black, the treads hanging over the edge. The river rushed by only a couple of feet below. He held his breath until the company's seventeen tanks cleared the far side.

In spite of Symanski's sound performance, rumors continued to circulate about large quantities of cough syrup being dispensed by the medics to Charlie Company - unusual for June.

While the battalion was in the field, Pope John XXIII died. He had been good for Jews. Eli wished he could thank the Pope. He would have also loved the opportunity to enlighten Patty Bruni, his high school truelove; her dead Pope had declared Jews should not be blamed for killing her Christ.

The Pope wasn't the only one who died that June. A white racist gunned down Medgar Evers, the black civil rights leader. That same week Governor George Wallace blocked the entrance to the University of Alabama to prevent the first two black students from enrolling. President Kennedy nationalized the Alabama National Guard and forced the integration. Eli said nothing to Richard Kaine when he saw him the next morning, but whistled The Battle Hymn of The Republic loud enough for him to resent.

Armed Forces Network and *Stars and Stripes* also reported that a Buddhist monk burned himself alive in Saigon to protest President Ngo Dinh Diem's persecution of Buddhists. The ghastly photos of this man on fire set off a blaze of condemnation around the world. Eli thought about Harry's intention to seek combat experience in Vietnam, and wondered if Diem was the man we should be sending our troops to protect.

FOURTEEN

Eli saw Lara twice that week after the Schweinfurt exercise. He was afraid to bring up Nuremberg, but she twice declared her intention to carry through with it. The first mention was firm, the second one he had to interpret through her half-German half-English mumbles, made while chewing on her fingernails.

The early Friday afternoon traffic moved as slow as molasses flowing sideways. A workman driving a powerless tiny three-wheeled pickup backed cars up a dozen deep until they could pass. When Eli finally got around him, he ran into an Army convoy of six two-and-a-half-ton trucks loaded with supplies. Eli let out a few choice curses when next a farmer walking his oxen down the middle of Highway 8 stopped everything. Opels and Volkswagens driven by Germans waited patiently. The Fords, Chevys, and DeSotos driven by Americans beeped their horns like a herd of impatient geese. At last the impediments dissolved, and Eli pressed his old Volkswagen to its modest limits. He apologized to Lara for his foul language.

Neither Lara nor Eli said much from the time he picked her up at the shop. He smoked one cigarette after another; Lara kept pace until the inside of the car looked like an artillery smokescreen. He turned the radio dial until he locked onto Radio Luxembourg. American hit tunes filled the nervous quiet. Lara stared ahead. She occasionally glanced over at him, then quickly away. For two weeks Eli's pants palpitated every time he thought about spending the night with Lara. He didn't want to mess this up by saying the wrong thing now that he was so close. He wanted her to be willing, not obligated.

"I only reserved one room," he finally said when they were about a half hour outside Nuremberg.

"But of course. It is much less expensive that way," she answered, as though expense was the only consideration. She concentrated on the jeep in front of them. Then she looked at him with her adorable eyes, and laughed out loud. She touched her hand to his thigh. He jumped, then glanced over at her quickly, and laughed too.

"I am not a foolish schoolgirl anymore," she said. After that, they had no trouble finding things to say.

Eli carried their suitcases into the Grand Hotel across the square from the neo-gothic domed central train station. The square bustled with streetcars, bicycles, autos, plump business men in dark suits carrying briefcases, and dumpy *hausfraus* lugging cloth shopping bags. The tower of the medieval city wall on the opposite street corner marked the entrance to the Old Town.

The hotel was indeed grand, the favorite of Hitler and the Nazi elite during their day, and then the center of activity for the generals and high ranking officers of the American occupation forces. Now the annex of the Grand Hotel was reserved for American soldiers. Even lieutenants had no difficulty reserving a room for three dollars a night.

It had one other advantage: this American-run hotel did not require couples to produce proof they were married. Many of the better German hotels turned away unmarrieds. Nonetheless, the elderly German clerk at the front desk frowned as he examined the military identification card Eli handed him and the passport Lara handed him. Lara frowned right back at him, and snatched her passport out of his hand when he finished recording the necessary information. The clerk reached into one of the pigeon holes behind him, withdrew a room key attached to a brass weight, and placed it on the counter in front of Eli. "Nazi," Lara muttered as they walked away, loud enough for the clerk to hear.

They clacked across the rich marble floor following after the bellboy carrying their luggage. Even the elevator was covered in marble and stunning oak panels with gleaming brass railings. Lara looked at Eli, and took his hand. "I have never stayed in such a handsome hotel," she said.

"*Danke schoen, Leutnant* Schneider," the bellboy said when Eli tipped him. Then turning to Lara, "Is there anything else I can do for you, *Frau* Schneider?" Eli flinched.

"No thank you," she answered. The upturned corners of her lips hinted at a shy smile.

The door closed, and they were all alone. Now that he had her where he had been trying so hard to get her these past months, he was suddenly awkward. So was she. They unpacked trying not to look at each other, he rapidly and she purposefully. He averted his eyes when she took her slip, underwear, and nightgown from the suitcase and put them in the top bureau drawer.

While Lara finished up, Eli stood at the window, absorbed by the people on the cobblestoned street below leading into the Old Town. He didn't know what to do next. Lara hugged him from behind. He turned and wrapped his arms around her.

"We will go slowly," he said.

"I am here because I want to be here," she answered. But she kissed him lightly with a touch that said "be patient with me."

They both looked outside for a few minutes, arms around each other's waist. "Are you hungry?" he asked.

"Not yet. Let's walk."

The warm June sun still stood high, but the Old Town already swarmed with enlisted men in shined shoes and pressed Army greens on overnight passes. Word had it that the Combat Zone in Nuremberg was wild. Professionals gathered every Friday night from every small town within fifty miles, ready to satisfy for only a few marks and a beer. Lara had never even been in the Combat Zone in Kronberg; the scene amused her as though it were a French movie. "Horizontal collaboration, yah?" she quipped.

When Eli stopped to light a cigarette, Lara glanced in a jewelry store window. A young American soldier grinning like a hyena saddled up to her, a couple of his buddies nearby lending encouragement. "Hey *schatzie, was ist los*? - Hey sweetie, what's up?" Eli charged like a bull. "Get lost Private," he growled in the soldier's face. The young man backed off. "Sorry Sir. I didn't realize," he stammered, then hurried off, his friends' laughter chasing him.

"You protect me," Lara said as they walked away. She put her arm in his.

"I'm sorry about that," he replied, embarrassed by his fellow Americans.

"It is nothing."

Next it was her turn to suffer embarrassment when they passed two professionals in telltale brown leather skirts cut so far above their knees their private parts almost showed. They passed two more cruising the streets searching for early customers. Eli tried not to look at them; it was hard. Lara pretended not to see.

Eli stared when they passed a nice looking, well dressed German girl with her arm tight around the waist of a black G.I. It was still a strange sight to him, something he rarely saw back home, even in New York City. Lara caught his stare. "Some German girls give themselves to dark American men to say they denounce their own people," she explained. "The girls hate their parents for their Nazi past. They know older people have prejudice." When Eli didn't respond, she went on. "I am one of the lucky ones. My father opposed Hitler so I do not live with shame."

When they came to the river, Eli checked his watch for the hundredth time willing it to go faster, and thinking about the bed waiting for them back in the hotel. "It is only five minutes since last time you looked," she said. How can she be so calm about it when she knows what's coming, he asked himself?

He felt as juvenile and impatient as he had on Senior Prom night in high school when he couldn't wait for the dance to be over so he could seduce his date, Suzie Grossman, under the gymnasium bleachers. He hoped tonight he would have better luck than he had back then.

When he asked again if Lara was hungry for dinner, this time she said yes. The Gasthaus auf der Konigstrasse across the street from their hotel was an authentic German pub with dark wooden half timbers and wainscoting. The man behind the bar sported lederhosen; their waitress wore pigtails and a pink apron. "We must have the bratwurst," Lara said with enthusiasm. "Nuremberg is famous for it." She ordered nine of the little sausages, and a half liter of beer. Eli followed her lead.

As soon as the waitress put the plates in front of them, Lara speared a chunk of bratwurst, scooped up a gob of sauerkraut on her fork, and dunked it in brown mustard and the smooth horseradish. She kept going, putting down her knife now and then to take a quick bite of a giant soft pretzel, or a slurp of beer. Watching her chew and swallow gave him a soft erection, a stupid and odd reaction, he thought. When she finished, she burped. They both laughed. He appreciated the bratwurst, but couldn't wait to swallow the last bite, pay the check, and head back to their room.

The June sun refused to set, still brightening the early evening. "We will go to the hotel now," Lara announced with purpose, as though willing herself to take the next step. When Eli asked the clerk at the front desk for the key, the pathetic little man again presented it with a disapproving frown. "Nazi," Eli whispered this time.

On the ride up on the elevator, Eli asked one last time if satisfying himself was worth taking this gentle woman's last bit of innocence. Then he told himself it was no longer just for his gratification. It was something more than that, much more, but he didn't want to name just what that something was.

He put the key on the bureau, but didn't turn on the light. Then he closed the curtains to cut out the golden glow from the dimming sun. Lara stood by the bed, hands at her sides like a young deer waiting for the wolf to attack. Eli walked over to her and ran the back of his hand over her cheek. She bent to it.

"We can go slowly," he said. "We have all weekend. It doesn't have to be now." But he didn't mean it. He wanted her.

She kissed his hand, and then turned around, her back to him. She pulled her hair up. "Help me unbutton my dress," she said with quiet resolve. "I am ready."

When she turned around, he kissed her. She pressed herself against him, and felt him against her. She inhaled. He helped her pull her slip over her head. She turned the bed down while he tore off his shirt and pulled off his pants. She reached behind and unhooked her bra, and then turned around slowly so he could appreciate the whiteness of her bare breasts. "My god, you are beautiful." He smiled. She looked serious, determined.

They groped at each other as eager and clumsy as two virgins. He couldn't find his way; Lara had to guide him. She moaned and tensed, then began moving. She kissed him violently and clasped him with the grip of Samson. He tried to savor each movement, but each time she groaned in his ear it brought him closer. Her noises came more urgently. She thrust more rapidly. Then a little cry, and a louder one. She gripped him. With his last tremor, he felt a release, a warmth, a pleasure he had never felt before.

They lay like that, catching their breath, touching and kissing, but more tender now. Their sweat ran together. She looked at him, her dark eyes so close he could see right inside her. "Are you okay?" he asked, panting.

"*Wunderbar.*" Wonderful.

"Next time it won't have to be so fast."

"I liked it just the way it was."

They nestled in each others' arms. He ran his fingers down her spine and over her cheeks. She kissed the top of his nose and snuggled into his shoulder, her hair tickling him. He could feel her heart beating. They lay like that until the gray outside turned into night, silent and comfortable. He didn't want to ever let go.

He was drifting off when she said, "I love you."

Needles poked him all over. He had to say something fast, something that meant something. Something true. But he couldn't say *that*. Not yet. Maybe never. So instead he whispered, "You are my *schatzie*."

That was enough. "I am your *schatzie*?" She sounded astonished, happy. "I am your sweetheart?"

"You are my sweetheart."

She purred and snuggled deeper in his arms. He thought she had fallen asleep. "I do not expect any promises," she said quietly.

He wanted to protest, but what could he say? He was going home in five months, period. Guilt jabbed him again. He had just taken her virtue with no more commitment than her first

American G.I. That one had nearly destroyed her.

He pretended to be asleep.

When he came out of the bathroom the next morning, he didn't expect the sunshine to be pouring through partially-opened curtains. Lara lay sprawled on the bed wearing nothing at all but a big, mischievous smile and her black rimmed eyeglasses. Her blond-brown hair flowed across the plump pillow, one arm dangling over her head. The featherbed gathered at the foot of the bed.

She touched her glasses and looked hard at him. "I want to see you better," she giggled.

He admired every inch of her from the hair on her head to her belly button to her painted toenails. She held out her arms and legs welcoming him, and then wound herself around him.

The intimacy of her hearty morning breath took him to a different place. This time was slow and sure and tender. And when they both finished, sated and satisfied, they teased and played. She startled him when she asked, "Am I good piece of ass?"

"What? Where did you learn that?"

"Margot. She says she is the best piece of ass."

"You are not a piece of ass. Don't ever say that."

"What does it mean, a piece of ass?"

"A girl who does what we just did."

"But I was good? Yah?"

"Spectacular!"

That seemed to satisfy her. She wound herself around him again, her small breasts resting against his chest. His heart swelled. He kissed her and then hugged her, her ear close to his lips. "I love you," he said.

And for the first time in his life, he no longer felt alone.

"Have you ever taken a bath with anyone?" Eli asked as he cradled her in the warm water of the tub.

She splashed him. "Only my little sister."

They washed each other's backs, and then the fronts. Gently. Intimately. After they toweled each other off, he kissed every inch of her, and she kissed every inch of him. She smelled like honey and tasted like jasmine.

After a lazy breakfast of wurst, cheese, black bread, and coffee, they wandered the Old Town arm in arm. Every so often they stopped to kiss, Lara unconscious of the disapproving clucks of the watchful *hausfraus.*

She nearly hopped out of her shoes when she spotted a street stall with a red and white striped awning. "We must have some *lebkuchen*." She ran over and, before he could reach for his wallet, pulled a few marks from her purse and purchased a big round cookie covered with sugar icing. "You call it gingerbread," she said. "Nuremberg is famous for gingerbread." She broke off a hunk and held it to his mouth. He chewed off a piece. She stuffed the remainder in her own mouth, and then kissed him, mixing crumbs.

They crossed the bridge over the Main River and wandered past the Beautiful Fountain, on the way to the Albrecht Durerhaus and the Kaiserburg, the imperial castle on the hill. Eli paused in front of the Frauenkirche. He had not set foot in a German church since he arrived, no matter how famous it might be. And he wasn't about to now.

"I will wait out here if you want to go in and see it." He tried to sound as indifferent as he could.

"No," she replied. "I do not go to church so often."

He held her hand as they walked away. "Does it bother you that I am Jewish?"

She stopped, turned toward him, and took his other hand in

hers. "Never. I am proud to be with you." Did he detect just a little catch in her voice? Apologetic? Sympathetic? He let it drop, and soon they were laughing and kissing again.

Every so often Lara paused to take a picture with her sophisticated-looking Agfa camera, capturing a landmark or a close up of Eli until he begged off. At the bridge on the way back from the castle, she stopped a kindly older man with a mustache and asked him to take a picture of them together. She directed the man to frame the Helig Geist Spital, a gothic hospice overhanging the water, in the background. She gestured toward the sun and had him move two steps to the left. Her theatrics amused the man. "*Sehr gut. Vielen Dank*," she said after he clicked a third picture.

The old man with the mustache tipped his hat, smiled, and said something in German. "What did he say?" Eli asked.

"He said we make a cute couple." She put her one arm through his and squeezed his hand with the other.

Just past the bridge, they stopped to watch a puppet show. Fifteen cute, well-behaved schoolchildren sat on benches in front of the puppet theater, their two attentive teachers nearby. The children must have been eleven or twelve years old, the boys in coats, ties, and short pants, the girls in dresses and high white socks. A jolly older man with a concertina provided the musical accompaniment. Part way through, the puppets and the children broke into song, swaying back and forth. Lara joined in, clapping like one of the children when they finished. Eli asked Lara what the words to the song meant.

"The woman says please not to break her heart in two, and the man says he must go away for a year but he will be true to her. And when he comes back if she still loves him they will marry. It is a good song, no?"

"Yes, it is a good song." He tried to tell her with his eyes that he wouldn't break her heart, but it would be a lie.

Eli wanted to buy her something. At first she refused. When he found a silver heart on a chain in a jewelry store, she allowed herself to be persuaded. The rest of the afternoon she kept touching it, checked it out in her reflection in store windows, and stopped at the one mirror they passed. "I will never take it off," she said.

They spent the rest of the afternoon at the Nuremberg Zoo looking at lions, a pacing polar bear, a partially submerged hippopotamus, and other exotic mammals. At the monkey cage, they caught a pair of chimpanzees copulating.

"She is a good piece of ass, yah?" Lara whispered in Eli's ear.

"Not as good as you," he leered. She punched him playfully in the ribs.

That evening they ate the same bratwurst in the same gasthaus across the street from the Grand Hotel. The waitress in the pink apron, now like an old friend, asked them if they were on their honeymoon. The question didn't embarrass either one of them.

A different clerk manned the hotel front desk, one with a friendly twinkle. This time Eli didn't flinch when he referred to them as *Leutnant* and *Frau* Schneider.

On the way to the elevator, some old black and white photos hanging on a hallway wall beckoned Lara. One depicted the elegant Old Town as it was in 1938. Another as it looked in 1945, a pile of bombed out rubble. The last as it stood today, rebuilt as an exact replica of the 1938 Old Town.

"My father brought me here when it was all rubble. Just he and I," Lara said, her eyes darting from picture to picture, and back. "I was only a little girl. He said he wanted me to see what the Americans and British did to us, and to not forget it."

"And what did you say?"

"I said we must have done something very bad to be punished like this."

That night there was no hesitation, no awkwardness, only tenderness spiced with seductive teasing.

When they finished, she rested her head on his chest, and stroked his stomach as though petting a cat. He ran his hand through her hair and down her glistening back.

This has been the best day of my life, he thought. Then he said it out loud.

Lara squeezed him. "I have never been so happy," she purred.

Eli felt complete for the first time, no longer alone. He couldn't be hurt as long as he held her in his arms. To hell with Nazis, he wanted to shout. I'm tired of it. I love her. That's it! That's all that matters.

They fell asleep with arms and legs entwined, contented by the sweet scent of their sex.

The high-low wail of police sirens shocked him awake with the sun just peaking through the curtains. Still in a haze, fear churned through him of the Gestapo coming to arrest him and take him away. He got out of bed and looked out the window. Two police cars stopped across the street, their red lights spinning on top.

Maybe it was the Gestapo scare that set Eli off, but before they left Nuremberg for home, he insisted they stop at Soldiers Field, the old Nazi Party rally grounds. This was the gigantic stadium with the marble reviewing stands where the Nazis held their primitive torchlight rallies, Hitler saluting the thousands of massed troops from high on the rostrum.

Lara picked up on his changed mood from the second she

woke up. She asked him if she had done something wrong. He assured her she hadn't. The touch of her hand comforted him, but couldn't drive out the darkness.

This was how he felt last August when he visited the Dachau concentration camp just outside of Munich. Then he had choked up, frightened, mindful he had been in a place of death much like that one. Only the audacity of his Grandpa Lieb and Auntie Via saved him. He wanted to scream and run. But he had to bear witness to Dachau, to the ghastly extermination chambers, the ovens, and the rooms where Nazi doctors conducted horrific experiments on human guinea pigs - Jews and gypsies. He looked out the barbed wire fence and saw how close the camp stood to the edge of the town. How could Germans deny they knew what was going on inside? They could peer right through the barbed wire and see it with their own eyes. They could smell the burning carcasses of dead prisoners going up the ovens' chimneys. They could see the steady stream of trucks and trains bringing in more and more and more prisoners. But the trucks and trains always left empty.

A visitor to the death camp had carved an inscription on a barracks wall: "Perhaps a people deserve the leader they get." Not since his arrival had he hated Germans so much as he did that day, all of them.

Eli didn't say much driving home. Lara tried to get him to talk. She offered tenderness, and condemnation of the horror of it all. Eli turned on Radio Luxembourg. Peter, Paul, and Mary sang about this land - America - being "made for you and me." And he couldn't wait to get back there, far away from this dark place.

Lara reached over and switched off the radio. "What the German people did was awful. What do you want me to do? You say what and I will do it." She spoke evenly, without a hint of resentment. "I will do penance. We will go together the next time you go to your synagogue."

"I don't go to synagogue."

Neither of them spoke. He pressed the accelerator harder. "You think the evil is in our blood? In the blood of all German people?"

"Not in you. Never."

"Yes, me too. I am German." She yanked one of her fowl smelling HB cigarettes from her purse. She shook her head when he offered one of his Pall Malls. "I have done evil things too."

"Getting pregnant as a teenager isn't evil," Eli answered. "He took advantage."

"You don't know."

Eli didn't want to believe there was something corrupt in German blood, but if there was, he needed to know it was not in Lara. "I want to meet your father and mother." He paused. When she didn't reply, he continued. "Are you afraid they won't like me? Because I'm an American? Or because I'm a Jew?"

"No, no. It is not that," she snuffed out her cigarette and threw it out the open car window. "It is because I am afraid you will not like them. And then you will not like me."

"Why won't I like them?"

"My family is difficult." She stared out the front windshield at the hay wagon up ahead. "My mother does not care what goes on in my life. She does not ask. She has not spoken to me much in eight years. Since my mistake. She thinks I am filthy."

"And your father?"

"He watches me close. He wants to know every small thing. But he wants to know nothing about my little sister Katrin. He does not talk to her since she was a baby."

"Why doesn't he talk to her?"

"Maybe because she was not convenient. She was born soon after he came home from the war. We did not have much money then or much to eat."

Eli thought about his own sprawling family - aunts, uncles, cousins, his mother and father, Grandma Sara and Grandpa Avi. He could not imagine such unkindness in a family.

"You will meet them soon." She reached over and caressed his upper arm.

He pulled off to the side the first chance he got, onto a dirt road on the edge of a small wood. He brushed his lips on her forehead and then kissed her. "I should not punish you for what others did."

"It is possible I deserve to be punished."

"I love you," he said. "Nothing will ever change that."

"I do love you too, more than is possible."

This time she didn't stop him when he insisted on dropping her off in front of her house.

For Eli, this had been a weekend of unimagined love, intense hate, and unanswerable questions about blood guilt. Right now he needed above all to talk to Grandpa Avi. He was the only person who could make sense out of confusion when it sought to drown the young man. But his grandfather was beyond reach. So now what?

FIFTEEN

Everything changed in Nuremberg. And nothing changed. Love and Nazis still didn't mix, especially if you're a Jew whose family was killed by Nazis. Honey and arsenic.

Late that next Monday afternoon, Eli cut out early and drove to Kaltenbach Fotographie. The "Closed" sign hung in the window as he knew it would on a Monday. He rapped lightly on the window and waited, then rapped again. At last Otto came out from the back room behind the counter, wearing his usual rumpled white shirt and gray cardigan sweater, even on a warm June day. He looked puzzled when he saw it was Eli, but hurried to unlock the door.

"Come in, come in," he beckoned. "Lara is not here. It is her day off."

"Oh, I forgot." Both knew that wasn't true.

"Please, come have some tea." He nodded toward the back room. "I need a distraction."

Eli stopped, as always, to admire the portrait of Otto's wife and daughter. He looked in their eyes, and they looked back at him. Each visit he got to know them better.

After a moment's quiet, he followed Otto into the back room, and sat down at the bruised gray work table. He put his pillbox fatigue hat on the work counter behind him. The chemical smell from the adjoining darkroom drifted in. Otto filled a small kettle with water and placed it on an electric hot plate.

"They were both so beautiful," Eli said.

"That is why you came? To talk about Adriana and Sophie?"

"Maybe." Eli tried to conceal his agitation, but it showed in his too-controlled tone. "I need to understand. How do you live with these people who murdered your wife and daughter?"

Otto pulled two flowered china cups and saucers from an overhead cabinet, and placed them on the table in front of Eli. He stared over Eli's head at the blank wall. "You are asking about you and Lara," he said. "So I must tell you this. Lara loved you from the time she met you. When I saw her after your first date, she asked me the same question. You see, she guessed right from the beginning you were Jewish. It did not bother her, but she wanted to know how I lived with what the Nazis - my own people - did to Adriana and Sophie."

"She knew right from the start?"

"She knew."

"And she saw me again anyway." Eli said it more to himself than to Otto. The kettle whistled. Otto took it from the stove and measured in the tea leaves to steep.

"You see, we cannot always choose who we love, or when and where. When Adriana and I fell in love it was a different time and a different Germany from the one at the end. We had many happy times. We were married nine years when Sophie was born. Adriana had two miscarriages, and we didn't think we would ever have a child. Then we had this beautiful daughter, beautiful in every way, like her mother."

Otto poured the tea through a strainer into the two cups, and placed one in front of Eli. Eli took a sip of the bitter brew, and then added a teaspoon of sugar. He waited for Otto to go on.

"I lived among Jews all of my married life, you see. I went to synagogue sometimes with Adriana. We had Passover Seder. I let her raise Sophie as a Jew. Why not? I was not so religious. But we lived among Germans too. Good people. My family loved Adriana. My friends loved Adriana. They would not harm a hair on her head. There were many prominent Jewish families in Germany. This was my home, and this was Adriana's home. We loved our country. Both of us. And when our country was in trouble after the first war, we suffered with our country. We wanted to do what we could to make it better. For ourselves, of course, but more for our daughter.

"By the time Hitler came, the people were starving, desperate. Pride was long since gone. Now there was only hunger, fear, shame, panic. We were a great people who had fallen into despair, with no one to help us. Then the Nazis, a pit of snakes. It was like a plague, a disease, sweeping away the doubt and the goodness of a whole nation. At first, even Adriana's brother thought there might be some good in Hitler. Only a few were wise enough and strong enough to resist."

Otto stopped to light his pipe. When Eli lit a cigarette, a choking haze fogged the small room. An army truck lumbered by outside. Women's laughter muffled through the wall of the shop next door. Eli pondered and Otto waited.

"I don't understand," Eli said.

"How I can go on living? Because the last thing Adriana said to me is that I have an obligation. An obligation to go on living for her and for Sophie. And so I try. And this is where I do my penance, my atonement. In Germany. Where would be better? Israel maybe. But I am too old now. And I did not earn it. Adriana did not want to leave even when we knew Jews were in danger. It was our home. I should have forced her to go. So, you see, it is my fault too. I have much to atone for. My blindness that my countrymen would ever do such things."

"Do you forgive them?"

"Many have acknowledged their guilt. The good ones. They do what they can to make up for what they did. Many of those who do the most good now are not the ones who did the worst things then. They are the ones whose biggest crime was that they tolerated the beasts in their midst. But the shame is so great, the immorality so immense you cannot imagine it if you have not lived through it."

"I have," Eli said.

"I know."

"Lara told you?"

"She did not have to tell me. It is written on your face."

"I cannot forget."

"But we must forget if we are to go on living."

Eli finished his tea and pushed the cup away. He lit another cigarette. "You haven't answered the biggest question."

"Is this evil in our blood - the German blood? This is your question?"

"Yes."

"Such nonsense. That would be the simple answer. A whole people evil? It is what Hitler said about the Jews, and now Jews say about Germans. No. It is not so. Each person is responsible for his own actions." Otto's tone hardened. "Look at the good people around you, the children. Look at Lara. How can you think for even one moment there can be anything evil in such a girl?"

"I don't." And he meant it. He took a last puff and snuffed out the remains of his cigarette in the big glass ashtray. "You sound like my Grandpa Avi. He always says you must judge each person one by one. Some are mostly good, some mostly bad, and a few truly evil."

"Yes, it is so. But sometimes the evil ones are in charge, at least for a while. I make no excuses for them."

Before Eli left, Otto handed him a small brown manila envelope. "For you," he said.

Eli opened it and pulled out the picture of Lara and him at

the wedding, the second one where they were not posing. He caught his breath. It had the same aura as the picture of Adriana and Sophie, taken by the same hand. "Lara is so beautiful," he said.

"And you are so handsome. It is a picture of two people who love each other very much." He hesitated, uncertain if he should say what he wanted to say. Then he went on. "Now Lara gives me comfort. She is like a granddaughter. She does not receive encouragement or so much affection from her father or mother. You must know that. I have met them. They are unpleasant people. That is why she is cautious about trusting love."

Outside, Eli leaned against his forlorn blue Volkswagen for a few moments, looking down Kaiserstrasse toward the church and the *Alte Brucke*. He could feel Otto's hurt torturing his own heart. The old man lived his loss all over again in the telling, but he had to say to Eli what he said. Eli had seen the same anguish in Grandpa Avi when he told him about the murder of his family in Uman.

Hard as it was, Otto's words helped. He made it sound so plausible, Eli thought. Forgive and forget. If he can do it, so can I. He lost a woman he loved deeply, the joy of his life. And he lost his cherished child. I lost parents, sisters, and grandparents I never knew and cannot remember.

Eli never felt so complete as he did when he held Lara in his arms. He could never give her up, no matter what blood flowed through her. He must live as though he and Lara were the only two people in the world, the only two who counted. This evil, whatever it was, did not exist in Lara, and it did not exist in Otto, of that he was sure.

It was time he wrote someone in his family and told them how he felt about Lara. But who to write? Max wouldn't take him seriously, and Rose would lecture him again. Mother Kira and Father Jake wouldn't understand. And he could see Auntie Esther saying, "Go ahead, marry your Nazi, may she rot in hell." It had to be Grandpa Avi. He would say, "If you love her and she loves you, it will work out."

Then he had to confront her father, a puzzling man who hated Americans and Jews, but resisted Hitler and protected his daughter. He also had to figure out this mother who sounded heartless as a hammer. She must have a soft spot somewhere.

First thing, he had to talk to Willy to gather a bit of local intelligence. His German friend surely knew something about this mysterious *Herr* Kohler and his heartless *frau*. Forewarned, Eli could construct a workable battle plan.

SIXTEEN

That June, the sun shined on Bavaria every day, or at least on Lara and Eli. Monday through Thursday, Eli snuck out for lunch with Lara, duties neglected. His company clerk, Specialist Pierce, covered for him. Eli told him zilch about his destination, and let Pierce assume it was nothing more than a regular *fraulein* quickie.

The two lovers spent every Friday night, and most of Saturday and Sunday, together, always ending the day at the apartment. Eli pushed the twin beds together making one gigantic nest. He had his side and Lara hers. The first time she spent the night wasn't planned; in the morning she had to borrow Eli's toothbrush. The next time she brought her own, and left it. Then she left a nightgown, a fresh set of underwear, and a woman's personal necessities.

The cream porcelain vase Lara brought over softened the male edge of the place. She always brought flowers to fill it, sometimes handpicked and sometimes bought at the stall on the market square. On a day trip to Marienberg Castle in Wurzburg, Eli purchased a watercolor for his wall. And in the ancient tourist town of Rothenberg, he bought a cuckoo clock to hang in the spot where Harry's used to hang. When Lara changed the curtains in the living room from plastic to warm burnt orange, the apartment started to feel like a home - their home. Eli's favorite object in the whole place, and Lara's too, was the picture Otto took of them at the wedding. It sat on the desk next to the one of Grandma Sara and Grandpa Avi, framed in silver.

Eli began a mail order course to learn to speak better German. Lara now bathed every day, and shaved whenever necessary. They took long baths together most weekend mornings, but sometimes he enjoyed just sitting on the sink watching her, and she enjoyed his appreciation. He got to know every inch of her body, envying every freckle, every mole, and every toe. She explored him as though he were a new toy to play with, marveling at the parts boys had that girls didn't. She put on a little welcomed weight around her hips, breasts, and fanny - just the right amount in just the right places. She could still pass for a willowy ballerina, but no longer looked like a malnourished teenager.

They laughed a lot, about the silliest things. She refused to remove the silver heart necklace he bought her in Nuremberg even during their lovemaking. The most she would do was turn it when she was on top so it hung down her back.

The landlady, *Frau* Giesler, smiled at Lara one day when they met on the steps. They exchanged a few words in German. A few minutes later *Frau* Giesler appeared at the door with two big slices of German chocolate cake she had baked. The next weekend Lara returned the favor with a small bag of spice cookies she bought at their favorite bakery on the market square.

Lara tried to cook something besides eggs. She didn't do badly with the knockwurst on a roll with roast potatoes and a green salad. But the Wiener schnitzel came out a little on the rare side. The liver with onions was a different story. Eli took a bite and began to chew the overcooked meat, forcing it down. Lara took her first bite, smiled, and shrugged her shoulders. "This liver will made good soles for your combat shoes," she laughed. That night they ate American peanut butter and grape jelly on white bread from the base Commissary.

The quiet times together in the apartment were the best. They listened to some Dave Brubeck or Dizzy Gillespie, talked or read, content to be alone with each other. A few times Lara took Eli's copy of *The Rise and Fall of the Third Reich* from the bookcase and studied a few chapters. Sometimes she asked Eli to interpret a word or a passage. The book put her in a dark, troubled mood.

"How could people do such terrible things?" she asked one night.

"God knows."

She returned the book to the bookcase, her back still to Eli. "Do you think what they say is true? That it is in the German blood?"

"Don't say such a thing. The answer is no."

"Maybe yes."

"It's not in your blood. That's all I care about."

"You don't know me."

All the more reason to meet your mother and father, Eli thought. But Lara procrastinated.

On Sundays they joined the parade of Germans who went for a mid-day stroll through the cobblestoned streets of town - men, women, and children. Sometimes the love birds packed a picnic lunch and bicycled out to a grassy spot hidden by thick bushes on the riverbank near the close-by town of Mainbrunn. Lara made his favorite wurst sandwiches on dark bread with a slice of Emmentaler cheese and hot mustard. Eli brought apples and beer.

On their three-mile journey, he liked to drop behind her and watch her pump her bicycle peddles, her blue striped sundress climbing above her knees, her muscular legs moving in rhythm. Her pony-tailed hair turned blonder in the June sun, and her skin more bronzed. Most of the time Eli had difficulty keeping his hands off of her long enough to eat. One day he looked around to be sure no one had discovered them, and then slid his hand under her dress. She let him go for a few minutes, but when she started squirming, she stopped him. "No, not here," she said, catching her breath. They jumped on their bicycles and made it back to the apartment in Olympic time.

The day Eli visited her at the orphanage, where she volunteered one day a week, he gazed deep into her heart. She didn't see him when he peaked in. She had five or six big-eyed four-year-olds gathered around her in a semi-circle as she read them a Grimm's fairy tale. A little brown skinned boy with kinky light hair nestled in her lap - one of the brown babies left behind when his black American father rotated home.

When she finished the story, she gave the boy a hug and a long kiss on the cheek. He looked at her with adoring eyes, and reached up and touched her nose. Lara told Eli later that the little boy's mother was only a child herself and couldn't handle him. Nobody would adopt him, so he ended up in the orphanage. "He is such a nice little boy," she said. "I wish I could keep him." She did not say it idly.

Toward the end of June, Harry and Margot invited them to their new apartment for dinner. It looked much like their old bachelor pad only smaller. The sofa, stuffed chair, and desk were the same army-issue; Harry's German souvenirs littered the bookcase, table tops, and walls. Margot added doilies, flowered curtains, and miniature etchings.

Lara and Eli took the sofa, Eli's arm draped over her shoulder. Margot brought them all bottles of beer, and then sat on Harry's lap on the stuffed chair. Her tummy bulge was beginning to show in her tight skirt. Her already-full breasts ballooned, stretching her low cut sleeveless top. Harry's hand rested possessively on her stomach.

While the girls fixed dinner in the kitchen, Eli and Harry sipped their beers in the living room. Two days before, President John F. Kennedy visited Berlin and delivered a memorable speech to an adoring crowd of 450,000 Berliners, broadcast live on German national television and Armed Forces Network. All of Germany seemed enthralled by the young American president and what he said. Strangers stopped Eli on the street to shake his hand and thank him, as though he knew Kennedy personally. Lara was so excited she slept over on a Thursday night.

"So what do you think about this *ich bin ein Berliner* speech?" Eli asked.

"I think our president just tweaked Khrushchev's nose. He sure let him know we're not leaving Berlin." Harry, a Republican by birthright, showed decidedly more enthusiasm for the President than he normally did. Usually that was Eli's job.

"But two years later and the wall's still there. So in the end, do you think it means anything?"

"It does to the Germans," Harry answered. "It means we're all family now."

"Yeah, right. Family."

"That war's over, Eli. In the next one, we're on the same side."

"So now we have to love them?" Eli responded with a dose of sarcasm. He took a long gulp from his beer bottle.

"Only one at a time," Harry laughed.

Eli leaned forward and lowered his voice to a whisper. "You know, Harry, Americans want the Germans as allies against the Soviets. But Jews aren't the only ones who hate the Germans. So does most of Europe. That's not going to change any time soon."

Harry in turn leaned toward Eli and lowered his voice too. "And the Germans aren't always so fond of Americans. Hell, their country still isn't their own. American tanks chew up their streets, clog their roads, and churn up their countryside. Packs of G.I.'s with their bananas hanging out troll the town eyeing anyone in a skirt, insulting their daughters and their wives."

"We're the only card they have to play, you know. Without us they'd already be Soviet slaves."

"So even after her," he said motioning toward Lara in the kitchen. "You still think they're all just a bunch of Krauts."

"No, no. I love her, Harry. And she knows it. It's just taking me time to make sense out of it." Lara's head turned when she heard the word love, but she went on cutting up the cucumbers on the counter in the kitchen.

"Well you better sort it out soon, my friend. It's almost July, and you're going home in four months."

"I know."

Eli didn't let go of Lara's hand all of the way home. "They are very happy," Lara said.

I need what they have, he wanted to say. Not to be alone anymore, or ever again. But was it even possible with someone like Lara, someone with the blood of Nazis running through her veins. Yes, he thought. I can do this. Then why do I keep asking the same question?

He didn't use a condom that night as he usually did at this time of month. Maybe it was just for his own pleasure, or maybe he was playing Russian roulette, hoping for an accident like Harry's to resolve everything. In the morning, Eli apologized to Lara over breakfast. She let his words hang in the air as if waiting for a commitment that he would marry her if she got pregnant.

When he didn't speak, she did. "Do not worry. It is probably not necessary for a condom. Since my mistake, my miscarriage, the doctor says I may not be able to have babies."

He put a hand to his lips, then dropped it. He hadn't seen that coming.

"It is not your worry." She wiped the frown from her brow, and gave him a weak smile. "Come. It is a nice day out. We will go for a ride to Bamberg to see the castle and the Old Town. It is very historic."

One minute he was praying she wasn't pregnant. The next minute he felt great loss. She is supposed to want children, he thought. And so am I. How can she dismiss it as though it were little more than an inconvenience? But she was not about to discuss it at the moment. That was a conversation for another time. What other surprises lie in wait? But why should she tell all of her secrets when he still held back a secret of his own.

Throughout June and past the July Fourth celebration, the Sixteenth Armor remained close to home, healing its vehicles, equipment, and troops from the continuous field exercises endured since the past October. Lara and Eli had time to get to know each other better, more intimately, more completely than they had ever known anyone before.

When the time came for the battalion to take to the field again, they told each other it was only for eight days. But they caught a glimpse of what separation might be like when Eli rotated home in November. He pushed that thought out of his mind and tried to concentrate on the business at hand.

Captain Symanski stayed sober, but Harry warned Eli rumors were floating around Battalion Headquarters. A few of the enlisted men were giving odds Symanski would be gone by Labor Day. Kaine's insinuations to Eli were more subtle, but just as frequent.

Eli caught the captain alone at twilight of the next to last day of the war games. He urged him to have Kaine transferred. He knew it wouldn't solve Symanski's drinking problem, but it might make for a dignified exit. The last thing Eli wanted right now was to have the whole business fall on him when he wanted his freedom to spend every possible moment with Lara.

"Kaine might be a good officer some day," Symanski said when Eli finished his pitch. He gave Eli a look that said he knew what was going on and didn't care. "Just has to learn to curb his ambitions." He paused and scrunched his lips. "Otherwise he might get himself shot in the back. It happens."

Twenty-four hours later Eli plodded up the stairs, eager to take a bath and wash off eight days' worth of sweat and filth before he saw Lara. But there she was sitting on the landing outside his apartment door, a bundle of food by her side. When she heard him coming, she bounced down the steps and threw herself into his arms, nearly knocking him down the stairs backwards.

"How did you know I was back?"

"I heard the tanks passing on Hindenburg Strasse," she said between kisses. "I could not wait any more."

"I'm all dirty. I smell."

"Come, I will bathe you." She took him by the hand and led him up the stairs.

She stripped down to her underwear so she wouldn't get her dress wet. When the tub was full of warm water, Eli crawled in. She soaped up the washcloth and began at the top of his neck, down his back, and all over until she was satisfied. She let out some of the dirty water and while fresh water poured in, she scrubbed his face, and then shampooed his hair.

She held out a big bath towel, wrapped it around him, and dried him carefully, stopping to kiss his shoulders and his stomach. She stroked him a few times until he couldn't stand it any longer.

He lifted her up and carried her to the bedroom, urgent now, feeling her warm breath close to his mouth, then kissing frantically. But it was Lara who took possession of him. She swung the silver heart to the back and climbed on top. Her wide brown eyes didn't blink until they finished. For a moment, all shadows went away.

"I missed that," he said, running his fingers through her hair and down her back.

"Me also." She bit his ear, and laughed.

She lazed on top, snuggled in, until the noise of Alpha Company tanks on Hindenburg Strasse roused them. He glanced at the alarm clock on the nightstand next to the bed. "They're late," he said.

Eli didn't want to spend even a minute away from Lara if he could help it. But weeks had gone by since he last saw Willy, and now Willy insisted they get together. So they met for dinner at a non-descript place so close to the *bahnhof* the tables rattled when an express train roared past the station.

They talked about the political problems of West German Chancellor Konrad Adenauer, the election of the new pope, and the Buddhist monks in Vietnam who immolated themselves. When they finished with their dinner, they turned to the place good friends always turned - the opposite sex. Willy was seeing a new girl.

"We'll have to meet her," Eli said. "See if we approve."

"We? You mean you and Lara Kohler?"

"Yes. Didn't I tell you I was still seeing her?"

"You did not need to. All of Kronberg knows. I saw you in town one day with your hands all over each other." He laughed the laugh of a lecher.

"I didn't think we were so obvious."

"What does her father have to say about it?" Willy took a drag on his cigarette, more serious now.

"I haven't met him yet."

Willy raised his eyebrows. "No? Why not?"

"I don't know. Lara's not eager for me to meet her parents."

Willy flicked an ash into the ashtray. "My father says there is something unusual about *Herr* Kohler."

"Like what?" Eli's ears perked up, defensive but curious.

"I am not sure. *Herr* Kohler claims he was imprisoned by the Nazis for opposing Hitler. But he came home from the war many months after all of the other Germans. And he lost two fingers. Frostbite maybe? Many soldiers on the Eastern Front lost fingers and toes to frostbite."

"So what's that got to do with me? Or Lara for that matter?"

"I have a good friend at the big Munich news magazine, *Rundschau*. We went to university together. He has access to all of the old Nazi records. Party membership files they kept on little index cards. They tried to destroy them at the end, but the allies came too fast. Let me ask him what he can find out about *Herr* Kohler. I will not tell him why I ask."

"Don't bother. I don't give a damn about *Herr* Kohler."

But he did give a damn. He questioned how Lara could still deny their relationship to her father and mother. They surely knew she was not staying overnight with Margot so often. And according to Willy, everyone in Kronberg saw them together in town.

The next day he asked her how much her parents knew about him.

"We play a game," she answered. "They pretend not to know, and I pretend not to tell them. It is easier that way."

"I must meet them now. It is time. No more pretending."

She noticed his new urgency. It said he would no longer be

put off. "Why does it matter so much to meet my father and mother? You will be going home soon." She studied the trough in his furrowed forehead.

"Maybe not."

But before he crossed such a big bridge, he had to know more about where her German blood came from.

SEVENTEEN

Of all the days to pour, it had to be this one Sunday afternoon. At least I'm not in the field slogging through the mud, Eli thought as he parked his car in front of the Kohler house. It looked like every other house on Schwarzacker Strasse, neither rich nor poor, big nor small. Gray field stone framed the front entry arch and the window sills. Dark gray slate tiles on the sharply slanted roof provided little contrast with the gray stucco walls, black shutters and black front door.

Here goes, he said to himself, ready or not. He collapsed his umbrella, took a deep breath, and knocked lightly. Lara opened the door so quickly she must have been waiting. She gave him a formal hug and chaste kiss on the cheek, but a big smile. "Poppa and *Mutti* are so excited to meet you," she said. "Come in, come in." She hung his umbrella and raincoat on a wooden clothes tree in the entryway.

Lara turned when she heard her sister Katrin behind her. "Katrin, this is *Leutnant* Schneider."

"Please call me Eli."

"I am pleased to meet you Eli." Katrin stuck out her hand for a strong, formal handshake.

"This is for you." Eli handed her a box of Whitman chocolates.

Lara guided him into the living room just as *Frau* Kohler entered, removing her apron from around her straight navy skirt. Again the introductions, the quick handshake, and Eli's delivery of a bouquet of multicolored mini daisies.

The three Kohler women looked astonishingly alike, except Katrin was rounder and better padded than Lara, her thick, long braid a shade darker. Inge Kohler dressed decidedly more stylish than the typical *hausfrau*, appealing, but her hard years were stamped on her unsmiling face.

"Please, will you have a seat," *Frau* Kohler gestured to Eli. She thanked him for the bouquet, and then handed it to Katrin, issuing her a gentle command.

Eli settled on the edge of a paisley covered French provincial chair opposite a stuffed mustard colored pre-war sofa. Embroidered lace doilies protected the arms and headrests. A large framed map of Europe hung on the opposite wall. Flowered Rosenthal china knick-knacks cluttered every available space. Only one lamp burned on this dark day, and the windows let in little light. The house smelled of dampness and brewing coffee.

Katrin filled the uncomfortable air with running questions about America. Did he know Elvis Presley? Was Audrey Hepburn really so pretty? How high was the tallest building he had ever been in? *Frau* Kohler said nearly nothing. Lara fidgeted like she was about to start chewing her nails again.

Eli waited anxiously for Herr Kohler, the father, to make his appearance. Five days earlier, Lara told her parents everything, even that Eli was Jewish. "They were okay with it?" he asked.

"Father does not say much ever. And Mother cannot stop saying what a disappointment I am to her. Only Katrin can do no wrong in Mother's eyes. But they want to meet you, to see this American Jew their daughter has fallen in love with." Eli wanted to meet them much more than they wanted to meet him. He had already commanded himself to like them, and wanted desperately for them to like him, for Lara's sake.

When the grandmother clock finished its second bong, the smack of leather shoes on a wooden floor sounded from the hall.

Herr Kohler stopped in the doorway and surveyed the scene, as erect as a Prussian general at attention. All he needed was a swagger stick and a monocle to go with his dark gray suit and vest. Eli rose from his chair when he heard him coming. Rudolph Kohler strode toward him and stopped abruptly when suitably close, and may have clicked his heels.

A blurred, panicky recognition seized Eli as forcefully as if the Gestapo had burst in the house to arrest him.

The deep scar running through *Herr* Kohler's left eyebrow would have scared anyone, but in Eli it produced terrified confusion, as though he knew this man from some other time, some other place, yet he was certain he had never met him. It left Eli with a wide open mouth, and *Herr* Kohler with a puzzled look. He gathered himself sufficiently to return *Herr* Kohler's abrupt handshake, and hand him a bottle of Chivas Regal. *Herr* Kohler examined it, and then nodded. He said something in German more elaborate than "thank you," but otherwise cold as an ice cube.

Only Eli seemed to be aware of the awkward tension when they all sat down around the big table in the dining room for coffee and *kuchen*. *Herr* Kohler commanded - glum, mechanical, and erect. He understood English, but wouldn't speak it. It hardly mattered. He said almost nothing anyway except to Lara. She interpreted when the headmaster directed a rare question or comment toward Eli.

Lara filled the conversation voids with exaggerations of Eli's military prowess, academic brilliance, and athletic accomplishment. Eli complimented *Frau* Kohler on the loveliness of her home and the delicious *kuchen*. He tried to ask enlightened questions of *Herr* Kohler, but the most he received back was a one word answer in German. Lara pretended not to notice, happy just to have the man she loved together at last in her home with her parents and sister. Katrin tried to help out her big sister by telling childhood stories about Lara, most of them flattering or funny, but a few embarrassing, like when she dated pimply faced Helmut Schmidt. Katrin laughed often and genuinely. Lara's laughs were eager and exaggerated.

Whenever *Herr* Kohler brought his coffee cup to his lips, he used his left hand. And when he did, Eli fixed on the missing ring finger and pinky, as well as the deep, ugly white scar running through his eyebrow.

When they finished, Eli and Lara's father adjourned to the living room while the women cleaned up. *Herr* Kohler poured some *schnapps* into two small crystal glasses from a cut-glass decanter on the carved walnut sideboard. He handed one to Eli and said *prosit* - cheers - without expression. Then he tilted his head back and downed it in one big gulp. Eli tried to do the same but nearly choked. It tasted like kerosene and went down his throat like barbed wire on fire. He thought he saw just a little smile on the corners of *Herr* Kohler's lips, amused at Eli's discomfort.

The two men sat on their chairs in silence, listening to the sound of rain running off the roof. After a few minutes, *Herr* Kohler said something Eli did not understand other than the word *panzer* - tank. He treated it as a question, replying that he was second in command of a company of seventeen tanks. *Herr* Kohler said something more in German, repeating the word *panzer*, then indicating with sign language and sounds that at least one tank had rumbled down the street in front of his house; the scar over his eye throbbed. His expression said he wasn't happy about it. The 16th Armor usually avoided this narrow street so, if that's what happened, it probably happened before Eli arrived in Kronberg.

From the kitchen, Eli heard someone say the word *Juden* -

Jewish. He thought he heard *Frau* Kohler answer, *es macht nichts. Herr* Kohler must have wondered why Eli was smiling. He wanted to jump up and hug *Frau* Kohler. If he understood correctly, either Katrin or Lara mentioned that Eli was a Jew. And *Frau* Kohler said "it doesn't matter." This whole uncomfortable day was worth it just to hear that.

On his way home the next day, Eli met Harry for a beer in the Officers Club, both still in their fatigues. Several weeks earlier Harry had taken over as Executive Officer of Bravo Company. This was the first chance they had to mark the event. Harry was eager to hear and Eli was eager to tell about the encounter with the Kohler family. They found a table in the corner of the near-empty bar.

Eli described the Kohler's' typical German house, and related the awkward silences, the severe parents, the cute little sister, and at the end, Lara's delight. "I really think she didn't see it," Eli said. "My guess is this is what passes for an enthusiastic reception in the Kohler household."

"Margot says the father's a strange bird, and the mother's not much better."

"The mother's not so bad. She seems okay with the idea her daughter's seeing a Jew."

"Lara's doing a lot more than just 'seeing'," Harry snorted.

"You know what I mean."

Three American schoolteachers came in the entrance to the bar with two young lieutenants in hot pursuit. The girls let them buy a round of drinks. One of the girls put a coin in the big, colorful juke box. Ray Charles' *Born to Lose* ended the early quiet. Soon the bar would be full. Another schoolteacher laughed too eagerly at something one of the lieutenants said. Harry and Eli watched the entertainment for a couple of minutes, and then turned back to their own conversation.

"What's this about a scar on her father's face?" Harry asked. "Margot says it scared the piss out of her first time she saw it."

"Scared the piss out of me, too," Eli said, his tone serious. "Looks like someone hit him with a shovel. Maybe he got it in prison."

"Prison? Margot never said anything about prison."

"You know what the strangest thing was? The father paid no attention to Katrin, and the mother hardly talked to Lara except to snarl at her. The parents never talked to each other, and neither of them smiled even once." Eli laughed a sarcastic laugh. "You know what her father calls Lara?"

"No. What?"

"Bonbon."

"Bonbon?"

"Yeah, because she's so sweet." Eli drained his stein. Harry did the same.

"So where does that leave you?" Harry asked.

"Well, I'm not going to call them Mom and Dad, that's for sure," he laughed. "But how would you like to help me pick out an engagement ring?"

That night the bad dreams started.

EIGHTEEN

Lara and Eli knew right away the visit to the Kohler house marked a passage of significance. Eli hinted at the end of the week maybe he wouldn't go home in November as he had planned, and that commanding a tank company tempted him. Lara offered that she would like to see America, and meet his family.

Eli was giddy at the thought. "They will love you. And you will love them. Grandpa Avi and Grandma Sara will spoil you. Mom and Dad too. Wait till you meet my cousins Max and Rose. They're crazy. "

"I will love them. I know it."

In spite of the sweet glow, every morning that week Eli awoke up with a strong feeling something horrible happened during the night. The realization it was only a dream didn't help him shake it off; the darkness hung around all day long. He willed himself to remember the dream, but he couldn't. So he willed himself to forget it.

Friday night they made love and fell asleep wrapped around each other, like usual. A few hours later Lara shook Eli hard. "Eli! Wake up! Wake up! You are having a nightmare."

"What... what?" He tried to clear his head.

"You keep yelling *'nyet, nyet.'*"

He was shaking with the sweats. "It's not a dream," he cried out through breathless gulps. "It really happened. The German major!"

The terror was that of a little boy. It frightened her. She drew him to her like a mother comforting her sick child, his head resting on her breast. She rocked him back and forth until his beating heart slowed and his tears stopped. "Please tell me," she begged.

He sat up and took a deep breath, staring at the blank wall across the room, arms linked around his bent knees. He started talking and didn't stop until there was nothing left to tell. First he told her the big secret - the horror - he had been keeping, about how his real mother and father, sisters, grandpa and grandma died - murdered by Nazis. Germans shot them and threw them into a pit in a ravine called Sukhi Yar on the edge of Uman in the Ukraine, along with all of the other Jews in his town. Then he told her how he was rescued and raised by a Gentile family friend, Valerya Shumenko - Auntie Via. Finally he told her how Valerya died walking him across Eastern Europe to a refugee camp in Austria, from which he was sent to America, a war orphan. By the time he finished, he was shaking again, exhausted and white.

"Oh my darling, my darling." Lara soothed him with her soft words and gentle strokes. "I am so sorry." His body racked with sobs again until finally hers did too.

Then he told her the rest of his secret, the one he just learned when he discovered his nightmare was real, an unearthed memory from when he was a five year old boy called Ilya. He told her everything except the vital names - Bonbon and Rudy.

When the German major come to visit, he always brought something nice to eat like canned ham, jam, or a loaf of fresh bread. Now and then he brought warm clothes for the two women or a toy for Ilya. Sometimes he let Ilya play with the lightning bolts on his uniform collar. After a couple of shots of vodka, he wagged his finger at Ilya's young, dark haired

Auntie Zoya and said "Kommen, Bonbon."

Auntie Zoya would follow him down the hall to the bedroom not saying a word, her head bent to her toes. The door closed, and remained closed, until in a little while Ilya heard the pounding of the bed and the major's urgent voice shouting "Bonbon, Bonbon." Then in just a minute longer he yelled "kommen, kommen." Sometimes Ilya heard Auntie Zoya squeak like a piglet, "Rudy, Rudy. Kommen."

On warm days Auntie Via took little Ilya outside until they were finished, but on wintry days they stayed inside and Auntie Via read him stories until the door to the bedroom opened and the major came out buckling his belt, satisfaction smeared across his face. Auntie Zoya always looked like a whipped criminal.

Ilya would never know for sure, but he later figured out Auntie Zoya was Auntie Via's daughter-in-law, the wife of her dead son. Ilya loved Auntie Zoya. She was very pretty and he hated to see her sad. So when the major left, Ilya took her calloused hand in his little hand, or crawled on her lap. He made funny faces and imitated animal sounds until she smiled. Her reward was a hug and a kiss on her cheek.

Then one March day Ilya heard big guns booming in the distance. Every day after, the sound came closer and closer. A flight of airplanes flew overhead and dropped loud bombs nearby. That day the major wasn't smiling when he drove up in his scout car.

He told Zoya he was leaving and demanded she go with him. She refused, so he begged her. The Nazi grew more agitated with each thunder of the approaching Russian guns. He warned her about what the Russians would do to her when they found out she had been collaborating with a German SS officer. But Auntie Zoya dug in her heels. She locked her arms across her chest and refused to budge. Ilya huddled in Auntie Via's arms in a corner by the wood-planked kitchen table.

"You whore," the major screamed right before he smashed Zoya in the face with the back of his hand. She staggered back against the wall by the fireplace nearly toppling over, terror scribbled all over her face. He clinched his fist and went after her again.

Ilya wanted to do something to stop the ugly man from hurting Auntie Zoya. But what could he do? He was only five years old, and he was very scared. So he closed his eyes and covered his ears with his hands. Auntie Via sheltered him with her body. When he heard Auntie Zoya scream, he opened his eyes and dropped his hands from his ears. She lifted the hot poker from the fireplace and struck the German major over the left eye so hard he fell to his knees, blood squirting out like a burst tomato. Auntie Zoya froze, the poker arched over her head, ready to swing again. The major drew his pistol from its holster and fired once, striking her in the heart. She looked surprised, and then she pitched forward like a dead log onto the plank floor.

The major swung the gun toward the little boy, red goop flowing between his fingers as he tried to stem the gush from his wounded eye socket. Ilya stood up and walked over to Auntie Zoya's body, blood running from her chest wound and from her nose. He bent down and picked up her hand in his. He looked over at Auntie Via, still on the floor by the table, and said, "She is dead."

Auntie Via turned to the major: "Spare him. He is only a little boy." She must have expected him to shoot her too. Instead he holstered his gun and left.

Two days later the Russian Army liberated Uman.

Lara knew her love, her Eli, was hemorrhaging and she did everything she could to save him. She cooked for him every evening and she stayed with him every night, cuddling him until he fell asleep. She condemned only the Nazis at first, then she cursed all Germans of that age, not even exempting her own mother and father. She tried to smile, but she couldn't. She started biting her fingernails again, and smoked too many cigarettes. Their lovemaking was desperate, nearly violent, a savage release for both of them.

She said "I am sorry," apologizing for the whole German nation, until Eli begged her to stop. "You did nothing," he said. "I love you." Then he tried to lighten the gloom. "You are my *schatzie*." That brought a small smile to the corners of her lips. But over the next few days, as the poison drained from Eli, it seemed to infect Lara.

One Saturday morning, she insisted they visit the derelict synagogue by the river, the one ransacked in 1938 during *Kristallnacht*. Even in its misery, the old building with its twin minaret-like steeples possessed a familiar Eastern mystique that drew Eli to it. A sign declared entry was forbidden. Plywood boards covered broken windows.

Lara tried the carved blue front door; it was locked. She stood in front of it willing it to open. When it didn't, she placed the flat of her hand on its scarred and weathered surface as though she were touching the Torah.

"Pray with me," she pleaded.

"I can't. I haven't talked to God in years."

"He will listen to you."

She grabbed his forearm and pulled him down with her to their knees. Then she closed her eyes and clasped her hands in front of her, squeezing her fingers together so hard they turned white. He watched her pain for a moment, then put his arm around her and closed his eyes.

"Dear God," he prayed, "spare this good woman. She has suffered enough."

After, they sat on a bench near the river, behind the synagogue. A barge chugged by, the black exhaust of its diesel engine wafting over them.

"You didn't do it," Eli said to her. "Your father didn't do it. You can't hold yourself responsible for everything Germany did. I can live with it, and so can you."

She held his hand and clutched his arm. "You don't understand," she said.

"No, you don't understand. You don't understand how much I love you. And that's all that matters."

In the following days, Lara found some relief in the photography shop, burying herself in the labors of developing and mounting photos. She obsessed with taking pictures of the orphans - one a little boy about five years old sitting alone at a school desk with an uneaten sandwich in front of him, his big dark eyes looking dreadfully sad.

Eli found his relief on the Holden Barracks post. He did calisthenics early mornings with the troops, and spent afternoons on the tank pads inspecting and drilling the Charlie Company crews. One day a Yellow Scarf practice exercise summoned the First Platoon to protect the nuclear weapons stored in a bunker in a far corner of the base. Eli mounted one of the tanks and sped down the tank runway and across the open field. The five tanks formed a protective circle around the ammo dump, their main guns and machine guns covering the compass. Eli really would have liked to open fire on someone, anyone. Instead, after about thirty minutes they stood down, and returned to their tank pads.

Now that he knew the full truth, Eli wanted to share everything with Lara. But he could not inflict his suspicions on her,
not when his conclusions seemed so illogical, so preposterously
coincidental. Yet there was the deep scar over *Herr* Kohler's left
eye and the missing fingers, possibly from frostbite common to
German soldiers on the Eastern Front. And then there were the
names. Auntie Zoya called her assailant Rudy, and he called her
Bonbon, just as he called Lara. Another coincidence?

He could forgive anything in Lara, but Eli had to remove his
darkest doubts about her father before doing what he intended to
do. He could only think of one way to remove those doubts, and
that was through his friend Willy Speer.

NINETEEN

Shared pain and selfless compassion bound Lara and Eli in ways nothing else could. She smiled again, they laughed, and they made love slowly and tenderly. She moved more of her clothes into his apartment, and no longer made any pretense with her parents about where she was spending her nights. Now and then *Frau* Kohler sent along a cooked roast or a German chocolate cake with Lara. Eli dragged his feet about seeking out Willy Speer's help, unwilling to disrupt their healing.

Two weeks later, the battalion road marched to Hohenfels, the old Wehrmacht training area southwest of Nuremberg, for joint maneuvers with units of the German Army. While he was gone, Lara spent her nights at her parents' house or with Margot.

Those eight blistering late August days away from Lara exhausted Eli. He would have liked to curl up in a corner and let the Army go to hell. But Captain Symanski's behavior bordered on schizophrenia. Most days the Captain was the veteran combat commander, leading his troops and training the junior officers. Then one afternoon he rode off by himself in his jeep and got lost for two hours until he radioed for help. Another day he missed Colonel Stratton's morning briefing; Eli had to rush over in his place. Stratton scowled when he saw Eli walk in the command tent. Symanski increasingly served as the butt of the enlisted men's jokes. They always stopped abruptly when Eli or Sergeant Pickett walked by, but the Captain was losing control of his company, and Eli didn't have the energy to resist.

Richard Kaine just bided his time, knowing he held a winning hand. With Eli's date for rotation home now little more than two months off, Kaine fantasized about bypassing the requisite stint as Company Executive Officer and jumping right to Company Commander when Symanski finally crumbled.

"Over my dead body," Eli told Harry when he related what was going on.

"You can't protect the Old Man forever," Harry responded.

By the time Eli rushed up the apartment steps to Lara's embrace, he knew what he had to do. First, Willy, then he would propose to Lara. He already composed in his mind the letter he would write to his father and mother to tell them of his coming engagement.

"You are serious about this, yes?" Willy said when Eli phoned to ask him if he could get his hands on any information about *Herr* Kohler's wartime service.

"I need to know if he fought on the Eastern Front, in a town called Uman in the Ukraine."

"My friend at the Munich *Rundschau* can get it. He owes me a large favor. He has access to all of the old Nazi and Wehrmacht files. They kept such good records, you know. But why such a hurry?"

"Because I'm going to marry his daughter." When Eli said it out loud, he did not sound as elated as he should have.

Willy didn't respond at once. Eli thought maybe they had been disconnected. When he spoke, he spoke quietly and deliberately. "These inquiries, sometimes they do not turn out to be so pleasant? I know. It has happened to friends who made inquiries about their parents."

"It won't change my mind about Lara, but I must know. She must know."

Ten days passed before Willy could get back to Eli with any

useful information about *Herr* Kohler. By then, the children finished their month's break and returned to school, and the days
ticked down until Eli rotated home. Willy's phone call came in
the middle of the morning. He sounded urgent. He offered to
drive over right away and meet Eli in the parking lot of the Officers Club just outside the main gate to the base.

Willy was waiting in his new lime-green Opel when Eli
pulled up and parked alongside him in the far back corner where
no one ever parked. Eli jumped in Willy's front seat, his heart
rushing. It was still too early for lunch so the lot was nearly
empty.

"My friend, sometimes it is best to let sleeping animals
sleep," Willy said. He didn't smile. A clasped manila envelope
lay on his lap. He offered it to Eli, but Eli let Willy's hand hang
in the air.

"Tell me what it says."

Willy raised a clinched fist to his lips and held it there for a
moment. Then he lowered it. "Do you know anything about the
Einsatzgruppen?"

"Some." Eli swallowed, tasting his own bile. Willy's question
already provided the answer about *Herr* Kohler. He felt pin-
pricks all over, and throbbing in his temples. He rolled down the
window and lit a cigarette.

"These were Heinrich Himmler's death squads," Willy began,
"directly supervised by Reinhard Heydrich. When Germany in-
vaded the Soviet Union in 1941, these units followed closely
behind the front-line Wehrmacht troops. Their job was to exe-
cute all of the Jews, Communist leaders, and gypsies they could
get their hands on. They did a good job. They killed one million
three hundred thousand Jews and about seven hundred thousand
of the others. There were four groups of these special
kommando units, with two thousand men in total. But they had

the full cooperation and logistical support of the Wehrmacht - drivers, radio operators, and supplies. They also received much assistance, even in the killings, from the Ukraine and Belarus auxiliary police. The *Einsatzgruppen* could not have been so successful in their mission if not for this help from the local people."

A car pulled up in the far end of the parking lot. Two young officers got out and marched toward the front steps of the Officers Club without noticing Willy's Opel. Unappetizing odors of roasting meats and frying potatoes from the club's kitchen invited themselves inside of the hot car baking under the mid-day sun.

"What does the *Einsatzgruppen* have to do with *Herr* Kohler?" Eli demanded to know, apprehension in his question.

Sweat stained the underarms of Willy's short sleeved blue shirt. "He was one of them," he said. "An SS major."

"In Uman?"

"No, not in Uman. As far as the records say, and the Nazi records are meticulous, he was never near the Ukraine, and certainly not near Uman."

"But he was knee deep in the killings?" Eli interrogated Willy as though Willy was the guilty party.

"Maybe not knee deep. He was an adjutant, a desk job, mostly back in Berlin. But he was part of Heydrich's staff. He provided the administration and logistical coordination. There was at least one action in Belarus in which he participated directly. Maybe as many as four."

"It's impossible. *Herr* Kohler is an educated man, a headmaster. Everybody respects him." Eli felt oddly defensive. Much as he resisted the thought, there was no denying Lara was bound to her father.

"Major Kohler's bosses were highly educated too." Willy put

the emphasis on the word *major* as if to contradict the very idea Major Kohler could now be a respected headmaster. "Three of the four *Einsatzgruppen* commanders held doctorate degrees from good German universities. So did others in the death squads. That must tell you something about the extent of the poison in the German blood at the time."

"But what about him being in a Nazi prison camp during the war?" Eli challenged, grasping at a straw.

"All a lie. He was a good liar, like many of that generation of Germans. Yes, he was in prison, but it was an American prison after the war, not a Nazi prison. The Americans held him until 1947 while they decided whether to put him on trial for war crimes. They did have a trial, but finally only for the twenty-four highest ranking *Einsatzgruppen* commanders. Kohler wasn't important enough. The twenty-four were all found guilty. Fourteen of them were ordered to be hanged, but in the end, only four hung. Too bad."

"God damn him!" Eli punched the dashboard with his balled fist. Then he stared out the windshield at the lush green trees at the edge of the parking lot. His head ached. His breaths labored. "What am I going to tell Lara?" This information could destroy her. Maybe he wouldn't tell her at all. But how could he live with a father-in-law who killed Jews?

"One more thing. How old is Katrin?" Willy asked.

"She's sixteen."

"This is what I thought. It means she was born in 1947. *Herr* Kohler didn't return to Kronberg until late in 1947, after the trials in Nuremberg began."

Eli turned his gaze toward Willy. "Are you saying...?"

Willy nodded his head. Katrin could not have been *Herr* Kohler's child.

At that moment Eli hated Willy and regretted he ever asked

for his help. Look at him, Eli said to himself. He's is wallowing in self-righteousness and false sympathy. But he himself is one of those blond haired, blue eyed Aryans Hitler loved so much.

"I am sorry I ever offered to obtain this information for you." Willy said. He leaned back and looked at his friend, sadness in his eyes. "What are you going to do?"

"Why should you give a damn?"

Willy handed Eli the manila envelope. "This contains the full report in German, an English translation, and pictures. It is a copy for you to do with as you choose." He patted Eli on the shoulder.

Eli snatched the envelope, unable to offer a thank you. Then he got out of the car and slammed the door behind him. Willy drove off.

Eli leaned his hand against the side of his Volkswagen and wretched on the macadam. After he finished, he slapped the roof hard enough to hurt. He leaned his head against the car and closed his eyes to vivid pictures and deafening noises: glimpses of his mother and father in death, flashes of light and the zing of bullets, scared and angry soldiers shouting, thunderous explosions, and the suffocation of gunpowder blended with blood. Then the cascade of fury hit him - bewilderment, anger, hate, and resentment - all directed at her father. Eli must have stood there in the back corner of the parking lot under the hot sun for an hour until sorrow numbed every other thought and feeling.

He couldn't face Lara right now, so he hid in his office at Company Headquarters. Somewhere around three in the afternoon he pulled the report Willy gave him out of its envelope. It included a picture of the young SS Major Rudolph Kohler before he had the scar through his left eyebrow, or graying temples to mar his perfect brown hair. His arrogance was evident; the malevolence was not. After Eli read the report carefully, he shoved it and the picture back in the envelope, and then drove his jeep down to the tank pads.

He propped his foot on the fender of his jeep, absently watching one of the Charlie Company tank crews change a tread. Further down the concrete runway, other crews greased drive sprockets, tightened bolts, and oiled machine guns. Black plumes, diesel fumes, and the rumble of a revving tank engine cloaked the early September afternoon. I hate Germans, he thought to himself. Then how the hell did I ever let myself get so tangled up with one of them?

He finished his cigarette, field stripped it, and let the breeze blow the few flakes of tobacco away. He wadded the paper into a small ball and shoved it in the left pocket of his fatigues. Then he pulled another cigarette from his breast pocket, packed it on his Zippo lighter, and lit it. He knew if he didn't figure this out right now he was going to lose Lara. But he wasn't sure what to do next. Only two more months and he would be on his way home to Brooklyn - a way out if he wanted to take it.

When he got back to headquarters, it was well past quitting time. Specialist Pierce, the company clerk, had a message for him. "That *Fraulein* Kohler called twice." His dirty smirk bordered on inappropriate. "Wanted to know when you were coming home for dinner. Sounds eager."

What was he going to say to her: Your father was a Nazi? Or should he tell her he loved her, and that's all that mattered? Maybe he should just get the hell out of this country, this whole snake's nest of Nazis. But he could never leave without her. So he grabbed the report, and prepared for the moment of his life, a life which had already seen too many decisive moments. He prayed she loved him enough to handle what was coming.

TWENTY

Eli wanted to torture Rudolph Kohler, punish him for murdering Jews. Taking his daughter from him would be sweet justice. But by the time his tired Volkswagen crossed the new bridge onto Hindenburg Strasse, he was searching for a way out, one that would protect Lara from the stain of her father's sins. What he wanted most was a reason not to have to tell her at all. Yet isn't this what she said she wanted, to know the past? To be absolved of it? To be loved in spite of it? When he pulled up in front of his apartment, he saw her red and white bicycle propped against the side of the building.

The smell of *Frau* Giesler's frying pork chops filled the stairwell. On any other day, it stoked his hunger. Today the odor soured his stomach. He trudged up the steps desperately searching his mind for a way to present this to Lara that would leave her undamaged.

She waited for him, sitting on the edge of the stuffed chair in the living room, hands clasped in her lap. She didn't rush into his arms like she always did. Her brow wrinkled with worry. Her shoulders sagged, and her dress hung on her.

"What is wrong?" she asked.

"What makes you think there's anything wrong?"

"I heard it in your footsteps. Now I see it is on your face." Her fingers fiddled with the silver heart dangling on the chain around her neck.

He fidgeted with the manila envelope in his hand. She looked at it. "I have something to tell you," he said. He walked over to her and dropped to his knees. He took her limp hand in his. "First I must tell you I love you. I want to marry you."

"That is not such an enthusiastic proposal." She forced a gray smile reflecting his sober tone.

"Let me take you to America."

She rose from the chair and inched toward the doorway, her back to him. When he grasped her shoulders and kissed the nape of her neck, she pulled back. "You found out about me, yes? How did you find out?"

"It wasn't hard. Your father didn't cover his tracks very well."

"My father? You are talking about my father?" She looked over her shoulder at him, surprised. "Not something else? I do not understand."

"This is hard to tell you." He took a deep breath, the envelope heavy in his hand. "Your father was a Nazi. More than a Nazi. He was SS."

She turned around to face him, disbelieving. "That is not possible. He was in a prison." She backed away, two-arms-lengths between them. When he came closer, she backed up further.

He held the manila envelope out to her. "Read this. It tells everything."

She moved another step back. Then she raised her left hand and took hold of the envelope. She eased the papers out as if they might ignite if hurried. She started reading. The more she read the more her eyes welled and her hair drooped. She clamped her hand to her mouth and held it there.

Sounds of children playing in the park below and a beeping car horn on Hindenburg Strasse climbed through the open window into the black silence filling the apartment. Lara began to say something. Her mouth opened and closed but nothing came out.

At that moment, Eli would have done anything to take back the envelope and undo what he just did. Too late! He raised his arms and inched a step toward her. She inched a step back without taking her eyes from the page. When she finished, she pushed the papers back in the envelope and looked up at him. He didn't know whether her angry expression was aimed at him or her father.

"*Mein gott*! It's not fair what they say here," she protested. "He loves me. He was the one who stood by me, the only one who did." Her eyes flitted back and forth as though following spiders climbing across the wall. Her pupils contracted to black dots.

Anything Eli said would be the wrong thing, so he said nothing. Her eyes bore in on him. I'm losing her, he said to himself.

"So what would you have me do?" she demanded to know. "Kill him? Is that what you want? Tell me."

"Marry me, Lara. Come to America. Leave all this ugliness behind."

She lowered her head, her palms pressed hard against her hips, one hand still clutching the envelope. The cuckoo clock on the wall chose that moment to announce the hour. When the bird finished and Lara spoke again, her voice was flat and weak, sorrowful.

"*Mein vater*. He is a murderer. He killed babies. How could he do such a thing? He is a monster." Neither of them spoke, each absorbing the unfolding calamity. "His blood is my blood," she finally muttered.

"Don't say that."

Her face twisted in anger at her father, at Eli, and at herself. "This explains. Why I am what I am. Why I did what I did."

"It explains nothing."

Stuff ran down from her nose, pooling on her lip. She sniffled, and then wiped with her finger. She was ready to dissolve. "Every time you look at our babies, every time you look at me, you will see only little Nazis."

"Stop it! It is not in your blood." Desperation seized him. He wanted to grab her in his arms but she looked like a skittish cat about to bolt. "We love each other. I know it. A Jew and a German. Our children will have the blood of both. What better way to end this?"

"It is in my blood."

"It is not in your blood. If it were, then Hitler was right. He wins. Don't you see that?"

"You do not understand." Her voice grew as gravely as sand and cement. Then she screamed, seized by a demon. "I killed my baby, I killed my baby."

"You had a miscarriage. That's not your fault."

"You are so stupid!" she yelled back, smashing her hand down on a stack of books on the end table. "It was no miscarriage."

"What are you talking about?"

She clenched her empty fist and tightened every muscle. He watched, paralyzed, and waited for her to explode. He could smell his own sweat boiling.

"It was an abortion. I killed it. Just like my father killed little babies. Just like the Nazis killed little babies."

Eli leaned his hand on the couch arm to keep from falling over. Decent girls didn't have abortions. He never knew anyone who had one. He stammered, trying to find something to say, but nothing came out.

Her voice quieted; now faint. She looked at him through red-rimmed eyes. "I hoped if I loved you enough, it would all go away." She edged toward the hall.

"Nothing can make me stop loving you."

Lara wasn't listening any more. She grabbed her purse and ran for the door, flying down the steps two at a time, the manila envelope in her hand. It took Eli a moment to recover. He chased after her, but by the time he got to the bottom of the stairs, she was already on her bicycle half way across the park, peddling as fast as her legs would go, her skirt swirling around her knees.

He sat down on the stone steps and buried his head in his arms, forlorn. For an instant, he was relieved that maybe it was over. Nazis, her father, murder, and now abortion. How could there be a good end to this mess? No right answer, and maybe no answer at all. He needed to talk to Grandpa Avi, but that was impossible. And this time Otto Kaltenbach was no substitute.

She needs me, he thought, and I owe her. I'm the one who caused this. So now what? Would she confront her father? Even if she did, how could she come to terms with an abortion?

He decided to leave her alone for the night to sort things out in her own way. Then he would go to her tomorrow and start the healing, together. He had no doubt his love for her would give him whatever strength it took to deal with this. He only hoped her love was strong enough too.

He spent a sleepless night.

TWENTY ONE

The next morning Eli telephoned Lara's house before he left for Holden Barracks. He let the phone ring and ring, but no one answered. He phoned again as soon as he arrived at Company Headquarters, again with no response. He tried again and again until after lunch. He was of no use to anyone, so he cut out early and stopped by Kaltenbach Fotographie. Otto said Lara hadn't come to work today, and hadn't phoned or sent a message. Eli described to him everything that happened the day before, beginning with the report from Willy Speer.

"Lara told me about the abortion some time ago," he said. "Before she met you. I did not know about *Herr* Kohler's history, but it does not surprise me. Many important people in this town, in Germany, have this history." Otto was more resigned than angry, but he shared Eli's worries for Lara.

"Was I wrong to tell her?" Eli asked.

"She will figure it out, as you say, and be back tomorrow. You will see. Be patient with her."

But Eli couldn't be patient. When he left Otto, he drove to the Kohler house at the other end of the old bridge, parked in front, and knocked on the front door. He knocked two more times. When no one came to let him in, he hammered on the door again, so hard it seemed like it would shatter under the assault. Still no answer. He peered in through the ruffled lace curtains covering the front windows. It was dark inside, no movement, no sound, and no lights on.

The following day, and the day after that, he did the same

thing with the same result. He telephoned Otto, and then Margot. Neither had heard from Lara. At the end of each of those days he ran up the stairs to his apartment and through the door hoping to find her there. She wasn't.

By the fourth day, desperation consumed him. He could think of only one avenue he hadn't yet tried. He went to the *gymnasium* - the high school - where Rudolph Kohler served as headmaster. He startled the staff in the school office when he crossed their threshold in the middle of the afternoon, still in his olive army fatigues. A hard-faced elderly woman, the assistant headmistress, hurried out to greet him. He explained he was Lara Kohler's fiancé and the family was concerned about *Herr* Kohler. She told him *Herr* Kohler called two days ago to say he would be gone for a while. He didn't say how long. That was all she knew. Her abrupt tone signaled the conversation was over, and Eli's departure was required.

Eli brooded by himself. Something happened to Lara, of that he was sure. And it was his fault. I never should have told her, he scolded himself. Sure, an abortion was a horrible thing, but she had good reason. She was too young, and under her father's influence. So how could she possibly equate that with what the Nazis did, and what her father did? Well, she couldn't hide from him forever. When he found her he was going to beg for her forgiveness, and then beg her to marry him. Love conquers all, he told himself, and she loved him. He was sure of that.

Eli stopped by the photo shop every day to commiserate with Otto. On the sixth day, Otto had a letter for him that he received in the mail, the address written in Lara's hand. It was postmarked from distant Stuttgart, with no return address. The envelope contained something small and hard.

Eli took the letter outside and sat down by the fountain in the lacey shadow of the nearby tree. He slit the envelope open with his finger. The silver heart necklace fell out into his hand, the one he bought Lara in Nuremberg. How could she possibly return it? She cherished that necklace. He started reading her carefully written note, the chain entangled in his fingers.

My darling Eli,

By the time you read this I will be far away. I will not return to Kronberg until I know for sure you are gone home to America for a long time. Please do not try to find me. No one knows where I am except my mother, and she has sworn on the cross that she will not tell.

I want you to always remember that I love you with all of my heart, like I have never loved anyone. My darling, I will never stop loving you. Having had your love for even a little while is more than I deserve.

You were right about many things, including my father. I never will see him again. But you are wrong that we could put Nazis and abortion and murder behind us. We could never forget and live a regular life like other people, not even in America. You have lost so much, and I am not worthy of the love you give me. You are such a good man and such a loyal one, that you could never have left me, even when you came to your senses and realized how dirty I am.

Do not feel sorry for me. I must do my penance for now to pay off the debts of my father and my own. Someday when that is done I will start my life again. I do not want you to forget me, but I pray with all of my heart you will find a woman to love, one who loves you like I do.

Goodbye my schatzie,

Lara

Eli would not take no for an answer. Never! He shoved the

letter and the necklace in the breast pocket of his fatigue shirt, jumped in his car, and raced over the cobblestones to the far side of the bridge. The lace curtains in the Kohler house were pulled back and the light on the table by the sofa glowed inside.

This time when he hammered on the door, *Frau* Kohler opened it. She looked much softer than the woman he met on his previous visits, more like Lara. "Come in, *Leutnant*. I have been expecting you."

She led him into the tidy living room and motioned him to take the paisley winged back chair. The house was stuffy, silent, and smelled like moth balls. The monotonous tock of the grandmother clock mocked him and his desperate quest. Inge Kohler sat on the couch opposite him, her attractive legs crossed. She pulled her skirt down when she noticed Eli's stare.

For the next fifteen minutes, Eli begged and pleaded with *Frau* Kohler to tell him where Lara was so he could go to her right away. He was even prepared to go AWOL, consequences be damned. She listened patiently and without comment.

Then when she responded, she was as resolute as she was gentle. "*Leutnant*, I failed my daughter once before. I will not fail her again. You see, from the moment I found out Lara was pregnant I disowned her."

Eli leaned toward her, hands on his knees. "You think abortion is always so wrong? Even for a scared, innocent seventeen year old daughter who'd been taken advantage of."

Inge remained composed, as though she didn't hear the accusation in Eli's words. "Some of it was because I thought it was wrong, of course. But there is more to it. We have many secrets in the Kohler family, Rudolph and I. You already know the worst, so I trust you can keep one more secret. You see, Rudy did not come home right away after the war like most of the German men. How could he? He was in an American prison."

Inge went over to the sideboard and filled two small glasses with *schnapps* from the same decanter *Herr* Kohler had used that first afternoon Eli met the family. She handed a glass to Eli, then sat down and resumed her story.

"We were starving, all of us, but particularly the women who had no men. Lara was only six years old then, but so skinny you could see her bones. So I sought out the only men who could give us food - American soldiers. I was pretty then, like Lara. I found a good one, a technical sergeant from your city of Trenton. After a while he came every day, and he always brought food, cigarettes I could trade, and sometimes a toy for Lara. He was a nice man, but he already had a wife in Trenton and did not need another one. Besides, I was still married to Rudy even if I did not know what had happened to him. To make a long story short, as you say, when my soldier went home he left me pregnant. That was only a short time before Rudolph came home."

"Katrin?" Eli said reflexively, embarrassed by her revelation.

"Yes, Katrin. You see, I could have had an abortion. It was easy at that time. So many German women were raped at the end of the war there was much demand for it. But I could not. And I am glad every day I did not. Katrin is such a precious child. So when Lara was in the same situation, I could not understand how she could do it. I underestimated *Herr* Kohler's influence, or that his hate for Americans was so large he would sacrifice his daughter and his unborn grandchild."

She picked up the pack of cigarettes on the coffee table and examined it as if reading the label. Then she went on, looking up at Eli, her eyes glistening.

"You see, Lara's belief in her father is what gave her a sense of well-being. That is who she was. The child whose father was innocent. All the other fathers had to hide what they did in the war. Not *Herr* Kohler, the victim imprisoned by the Nazis.

Well, it was all a lie. She worshipped him. That is why she listened to him when he told her she had to have an abortion. And after the abortion, she could still be proud to have a father who stood up to the Nazis. Only seventeen years old. What was she supposed to do?"

She sniffled, then took a handkerchief from her pocket and wiped her nose. Eli rubbed his own nose with the back of his hand. He waited, holding his breath, not knowing what to say or what new surprise was coming next.

"It was my grandchild too," she continued. "I was angry at Lara as much for siding with her father as I was for the abortion itself. I could not take it out on him so I took it out on her, never letting her forget how foul she was for doing it. I feel so guilty." She blew her nose again, this time more forcefully. "I was wrong, very wrong for many years. I will not fail her ever again."

Eli took a sip of the *schnapps*. This time it tasted more like spoiled grapes than kerosene. He grimaced, but the fire in his throat felt right. "Does *Herr* Kohler know Katrin isn't his?"

Inge took a small swallow of her own *schnapps*. "Yes, but of course he knows. I could not hide it. I was already pregnant by the time he came home. Sometimes I thought I owed him everything for staying with me and raising Katrin as if she was his own. But I knew from the start I made a contract with Satan. He did it for his own pride, and because he needed a wife and home if he was to again be an honorable citizen, hiding his past. It took Willy Speer's report for Lara to disown her father, and for me to throw him out. I warned him not to come back to Kronberg or I would expose his Nazi SS history. He ran like the coward he is. You see, *Leutnant*, we are not all monsters. We did not know what Nazis like Rudolph were doing. The killing of all those Jews. Such a pity." She hung her head, then raised it, asking for his forgiveness.

Eli wanted to argue, to tell her she must have known, as she must have enjoyed the booty Rudolph sent back from the countries Germany plundered. He couldn't say it, so he instead asked her how she was going to support herself.

The house was hers, she said. Her parents left it to her. She would rent out a room and maybe get a job in town or on the base. She was still a good typist.

Eli told her again how much he loved Lara, that he could rescue her if Inge would just tell him where she was. He pleaded until a tear prepared to drop. He wiped it away with the back of his hand.

Inge refused again, irritated this time, and devoid of pity. "If you really love Lara, you must leave her alone. Let her make amends as much as she must. Let her heal. That is what she needs." Then Inge's tone softened again, the voice of a mother. She looked and sounded so much like Lara it unnerved him. She reached out and touched Eli's hand. It felt like Lara's. "You are a good man, but your love makes it worse for her. Go home, Eli. Go home to your family."

He nodded. There was nothing else to say after that. When he left, Inge Kohler put her arms around him and hugged him like a mother hugs a hurt child, kissing him firmly on the cheek. He embraced her. He should have despised Inge Kohler for her steadfast refusal to help him find Lara. But he didn't. She was too much like Lara.

There must be a moment in every great battle when the commanding general knows he has been beaten. That is the way Eli felt. He was out of ammunition, out of options. And still he could not retreat. He had six more weeks until he rotated home.

TWENTY TWO

In the first days after Lara left, Eli continued to plot and plan how he was going to get her back. When he realized that wasn't going to happen, he cursed Harry and Margot for ever introducing him to Lara. And he told Willy to his face what a disaster his report had caused, and how his Nazi obsession had ruined his life. Then he apologized, and blamed himself for ever telling Lara about it. If only he had kept it to himself. Eli felt sorry for himself, but it couldn't compare with the sadness he felt for Lara, trapped in a tribulation not likely to end any time soon.

He could no longer stand to be alone in his apartment. He thought about moving back to the Bachelor Officers Quarters for his last few weeks, but that would take more energy than he had. So he hung out at the Officers Club, still alone. Margot's due date rapidly approached, and Harry stayed close by her. A few of his other friends had already rotated home. The new crop of schoolteachers who arrived from stateside in time for the new school year held no interest. Neither did any of the *frauleins*. So mostly he ate alone, drank alone, and wrote letters home.

One Friday night just thirteen days before he was to leave Germany for good, Eli took a small table by himself in a corner of the Officers Club bar. On Friday nights the unmarried officers, and a few of the married ones, gathered at five o'clock for Happy Hour. A half liter of the best German beer cost only a nickel and shots of *schnapps* only a dime. You could get too drunk to drive on a quarter. The teachers billed in the BOQ around the corner always joined the party.

Just after Eli's beer arrived, Richard Kaine walked into the club and deposited his fatigue hat on the long narrow table by the door in a row with dozens of others. The party in the bar was already underway, the juke box blaring Peter, Paul, and Mary's *If I Had A Hammer*. Captain Ski sat alone at the far end of the bar nurturing a bourbon. Two schoolteachers and an Artillery lieutenant gathered around the slot machine taking turns throwing in nickels. They cheered every time a few coins clattered down with a win.

Uninvited, Kaine joined three newly arrived 16th Armor second lieutenants at the table next to Eli's. He gave a nearly imperceptible nod to Eli. Eli nodded back, and then tried to ignore him. But after one quick drink, Kaine took over the conversation at his table, too loud and obnoxious for Eli not to overhear. He regaled the new arrivals with his oft repeated tales of the glories of the Citadel and the Civil War.

A few schoolteachers and officers took to the dance floor, gyrating their hips and responding to the music's command to *Twist and Shout*. The noise level and the haze of cigarette smoke rose along with the alcohol consumption. When perspiring young bodies answered the call of Chubby Checker's *Limbo Rock*, one particular person caught Richard Kaine's attention.

"Look at that jigaboo," he said, nodding toward Sam Jethroe, a black officer from the 33rd Field Artillery. "He's happier than a pig in barbeque sauce." The black officer bent low, backwards, scooting under the broom stick held low on each end by two other guys from the 33rd.

Everyone at Kaine's table cheered when Polly Sands, a cute little teacher with a blond ponytail, followed Jethroe under the broom stick. "She's gotta' have some nigra' blood in her," Kaine asserted, his face fixed with a false smile. When the song ended, the group around Jethroe and Polly applauded them.

Someone dropped a few more coins in the jukebox, and Ray
Charles crooned *Born to Lose*. The talk at Kaine's table turned
back to favorite subjects: war and women. But Kaine said nothing, and never took his eyes off the dance floor. "Would y'all
look at that," he sneered. "That nigra's dancing with that same
white girl."

Everyone at the table looked over. "You want some of that?"
one of them laughed, addressing Kaine.

"You are kiddin' me!" he spit back. "What white boy's gonna'
wanna' even touch her after a nigra's had her?" Eli bristled. He
stared hard at Kaine, unblinking, trying to blind him with his
glare. Kaine pretended not to notice.

Even before the song ended, Eli got up from the table and
walked over to the light skinned black officer and the blond
schoolteacher. He had seen both of them around the club, but
didn't know either of them very well. "Let me buy you a drink,"
he offered. He ordered another beer for himself. They chatted at
the bar for a few minutes. Then Eli asked Polly to dance, a slow
one by Bobby Darin. He pulled her close to him, cheek to cheek,
and made sure Kaine was watching.

When they finished, Eli marched over to Kaine's table and
stopped, hands on his hips. He hovered over Kaine, glowering.
Conversation stopped, all eyes on Eli.

"Do you want to tell these fine young officers how you wet
your pants during the Cuban Missile Crisis and hid in a supply
truck?" Eli challenged. "And when you're done with that, go
screw yourself." He turned and marched out of the club, not
looking back.

The very next morning, the hammer came down on Captain
John Symanski, relieved of command. Sadness, and a little guilt,
jabbed at Eli. Maybe he could have protected Captain Symanski

awhile longer if he hadn't been so wrapped up in Lara and his own misery.

Colonel Stratton informed Eli himself, as though he had to justify his actions to a short-timer lieutenant. When Eli tried to defend Captain Symanski, Stratton cut him short, reminding him for the past three months Charlie Company led the battalion in disciplinary reports - drunken fights in town, three AWOLs, and one jeep accident by a driver inebriated on duty. Re-enlistments fell to last in the battalion when in better days the company usually set the pace. As a final peg in the coffin, for the past two alerts Charlie Company was last out the gate. Discipline and order had broken down.

The Colonel offered Eli one last chance to extend his tour and take command of a tank company. But by then nothing could entice Eli except Lara's return, and that wasn't going to happen. So the big question was, if not Eli, who would be the new company commander? Any animosity Eli felt toward Stratton for canning Ski dissolved when the Colonel told him Harry Ashby was the new CO.

Eli immediately turned his sights on Richard Kaine, fearful Harry would be saddled with Kaine as his Executive Officer. "Don't worry about Kaine," the colonel replied. "He's already on a plane back to Kansas with a less than satisfactory Efficiency Report. Did you think I didn't know what was going on there?"

A few days later Stratton gave Eli his own final Efficiency Report, a going away present wrapped with a big bow. In it, he wrote *Lieutenant Schneider is an uncommonly devoted officer with leadership skills unmatched among other young officers in this command.* Stratton's high praise buried forever any lingering doubts Eli might have had about his right to call himself an American. He arrived two years earlier eager to succeed, fearful of failing in this world of war-ready tigers. Now he carried the certainty he was man enough for anything, and that included surviving a broken heart.

He shared a last beer with Willy Speer at the Schutzenhaus, down the street from his apartment. Willy didn't get into any arguments with anyone this time. The two good friends sat in a corner of the ancient gasthaus surrounded by the malodorous mingling of German cigarette smoke, German workmen, and knockwurst. Four of the men at the table near the bar laughed and needled each other. Willy kept looking over at them as if ready to start another argument, then thought better of it and concentrated on Eli.

"I am sorry about Lara," Willy offered as they were finishing their last gulps.

"It wasn't your fault. It was no one's fault, except maybe her father's."

"I do not know if I will ever see you again. So I want you to remember something. We are not all Nazis. Some of us are try-ing to do what is right... what is right for Germany. So we can go on living in a civilized world."

"I am proud you are my friend," Eli answered.

Margot had her baby, a chubby little boy, in the army hospi-tal in Wurzburg. They named him Jefferson Harold, after Har-ry's grandfather. The already-evident freckles and red hair marked him as an Ashby. Eli couldn't care less about babies at that point, but he went to meet him at Harry and Margot's apartment as soon as they got home. He brought a silver rattle and a bonnet for the baby and a flower bouquet for Margot. Har-ry pressed Eli to hold little Jefferson. He did so reluctantly, and held the baby as if he were a dead possum. Margot quickly res-cued them both. She went to put the baby and herself to bed, leaving Harry and Eli to share a last beer.

"We're getting Army quarters in three weeks," Harry said.

Eli glanced around the tiny living room and nodded. The place smelled like soiled baby diapers and spoiled cabbage. "That will be good," he replied.

Harry took a swig out of his beer bottle. "Lara sent a present, through her mother," he said. "But there was no note and no indication where she is. Sorry."

Eli fidgeted with his beer bottle. Harry waited. "I still love her," he said softly. "Maybe I always will."

"At least you don't hate every single German anymore."

"How can I and still love Lara. I'd even say a good word about her father if it meant getting her back." He took a long gulp of beer.

"That's a start."

"It's Lara who can't forgive, not me. She can't forgive her father, and she can't forgive herself. She's the one who would have seen little Nazis every time she looked at our children." She also would have seen the child she never had.

His next-to-last night in his apartment at 7 Lindenstrasse, Eli did the only thing he could do. He put a Dave Brubeck album on the stereo, and then sat down to pen a goodbye to Lara.

My darling Lara,

If you are reading this then you have returned to Kronberg, which is a good start. As I write it, I know I love you more than ever, and more than I thought it possible to love someone. You have taught me how to love, how to be loved, and how to forgive. I pray with all my heart you have forgiven yourself. But I also know you were right. We would always remind each other of the hurt that is too deep in both of us. I hope you find someone who will belong to you and give you much love. I hope the same for myself. But even if I

am so lucky, I know there is a place in my heart that will al-
ways belong to only you.
   Goodbye my love, my schatzie.
   Eli

Saying farewell to Otto was almost as hard. Otto promised to give Lara the note when she returned, as both of them knew she would someday.

The Kaltenbach Fotographie shop was as much home to Eli as any place in Germany ever was. He studied the photo of Adriana and Sophie, trying to commit it to his memory. By now they were part of his family. Alongside the picture of his wife and daughter, Otto had hung the picture he took of Lara and Eli at the wedding on the day Eli realized he had fallen in love.

"It is there in your eyes and in her eyes," Otto said. "I have seen much love through the lens of a camera." A kind expression warmed his face, the same one that lighted his face whenever he looked at the picture of his wife and daughter.

Otto reached down and picked up a framed photo that had been on the floor facing against the wall. "Tomorrow I will hang this one, the first of Lara's portraits." It was a close-up of Eli she took one sunny Saturday in June at the Residenz in Wurzburg.

"It shows her talent." Eli was pleased, but a little embarrassed.

"Her heart shows in her work."

Eli didn't want to leave. At the door, Otto embraced him. Eli could smell burned pipe tobacco on the old man's gray cardigan sweater. "I will write you as soon as I can," Eli said.

The old man shook his head. "No. You and Lara each must find yourselves, on your own separate paths. I do not want to be the link that prevents that to happen." He pounded his heart. "But remember me here."

After he left the shop, Eli wandered across the cobblestoned market square, the chilly November afternoon as dark as his own mood. Saying goodbye to Germany and the Army was harder than he could have ever imagined. He looked in the window of the bakery where he and Lara first intrigued each other.

He walked down to the old derelict synagogue. He sat on the bench by the river and thought about his family murdered by the Nazis in Uman. He started to say *Kaddish*, the Jewish prayer of mourning, then couldn't remember the words. But for the first time in his life, he could recite the names of his father, mother, sisters, grandpa and grandma out loud - Joshua, Leya, Rebekah, Anya, Grandpa Lieb, and Grandma Golde. Then he said their names again.

He smiled. In a few days he would be home among his American family: Grandpa Avi, Grandma Sara, his mother Kira and father Jake, cousins Rose and Max, and all those other cousins and aunts and uncles always getting in each other's hair. He loved them all, and they loved him like crazy. He wondered what they would think of their lean, tough hero, two years gone defending America. Glad to see him, that's for sure.

A barge chugged by, the two decrepit rowboats tied up at the dock bouncing in its wake. The last time he sat here Lara was by his side, her torment cresting. He didn't want to let go of the hurt in his heart for her. It cleansed him in some ways.

He walked back toward the *Alte Brucke*, absorbing in his mind every *hausfrau*, schoolchild, and farmer he passed. A grim old man with a cane dressed in an equally old black suit saluted him as they approached each other. Eli returned it with a crisp salute and a smile. The old man smiled back.

Loving Lara had changed him, and he was glad of it. He thought how, on the day he first arrived in this country, his hate for Germans burned in his belly like a bonfire. He condemned them all. Now when he looked around he saw kind grandmothers, dedicated fathers, women grown old working the fields, appealing young men and women trying to be modern, and happy children racing to grow up. Surely there were evil ones among them, like Rudolph Kohler. But there were also good people, like Otto and Inge Kohler. Maybe he couldn't forgive them all. But he could forgive those who atoned and deserved to be forgiven, and those who never deserved his condemnation in the first place. Never again would he judge a whole people with one broad stroke, like some judged Jews.

He stopped halfway across the bridge at the peak of its arch. He leaned his elbows against the stone rail. From here he could see Lara's house. He watched the muddy water of the Main River flow under the bridge, his mind wandering from memory to memory - the excitement of tanks attacking across an open field, and the face of Lara in Nuremberg stretched out on the bed wearing nothing but her glasses. Emotions eddied from satisfaction, to sadness, to love won, and love lost.

He grabbed his fatigue hat when a wind gust tried taking it away. An older *hausfrau* peddled by on her bicycle, its basket filled with groceries. Three teenage girls followed in their school uniforms. A new mint green Volkswagen beeped its horn as it passed around them.

Eli took Lara's heart necklace from the breast pocket of his fatigue jacket. A dramatic gesture felt like the appropriate mark to an ending. I'm not alone any more, he said to himself. The silver chain dangled in his fingers over the edge of the bridge, the river below. Something told him love would come again.

He put the necklace back in his breast pocket, and then walked home.

TWENTY THREE

Eli joined the small stream of soldiers, officers' wives, and army brats pressing through the departure gate of the Rhein-Main Airbase passenger terminal toward the steps of the waiting DC-7 turboprop. He paused at the top of the gangway before entering the plane for a last look at Germany. In less than twelve hours he would land at McGuire Air Force Base in New Jersey, next door to Fort Dix and the Army discharge awaiting him.

The two years had been more adventure than anything he ever imagined. The Army, of course, but mostly it was Lara. It would always be about Lara. Right now, all he wanted was to get home to his family and lick his wounds.

He stowed his travel bag in the overhead rack and took a seat on the aisle. A young woman sat in the seat next to him peering out the curtain. The propellers started turning and the engines revving. "*Auf wiedersehen,*" the young woman said to no one in particular.

He closed his eyes and let thoughts of home stifle the ache. Cousin Max had returned home from the Navy a few months ago; they would raise hell together again. Max probably had a girl lined up for him already, as well as a couple for himself. He believed someday he would find the right girl, but he wondered if he would ever love anyone again like he loved Lara, or if any woman could ever love him again that way. Certainly he could stand a lot less drama next time.

"This is always the most exciting part," the young woman next to him said just before the plane roared down the runway.

When the wheels lifted off, Eli grunted and looked up briefly into her smiling face and sparkling hazel eyes. Then he buried his head back in his magazine, the latest issue of Time with the new German Chancellor, Ludwig Erhard, on the cover. He flipped by that story. He had had enough of Germans.

"My name's Emma Bishop," the cheerful young woman said.

"Eli," he responded without looking up.

"How long were you in Germany?"

"Two years." Leave me alone, he thought.

"Me too. I was a schoolteacher at Ramstein Air Base."

When he didn't reply, Emma opened her paperback, *To Kill a Mockingbird*. Eli glanced at her out of the corner of his eye. Not bad looking, nice reddish chestnut hair, and a tempting bosom. Clean and well groomed in that American schoolteacher way. No more unshaven armpits and hairy legs where I'm going, Eli thought. Girls who bathe every day; he was looking forward to that.

The young woman pulled a Pall Mall from a pack of cigarettes in her purse, and then fumbled around for a match.

What the hell, Eli thought. It's going to be a long flight, and she seems nice enough. He pulled out his Zippo lighter, flicked it open, and leaned over to light her cigarette. She cupped her hands around his, her ringless finger on view. She blew the smoke from the first puff toward the ceiling, and then flashed him a darling smile. Not bad, he thought when she crossed her legs.

"So where are you from?" he asked.

"I'll be stopping in New York for a couple of weeks." A timid twinkle graced her eyes. She giggled. Then she answered his question. "Youngstown, Ohio."

PART TWO

1988

TWENTY FOUR

MONDAY

Everyone gets a second chance, they say. But I wanted a third chance. I messed things up the first time with Lara, and the second time with Emma. I could argue that with Lara it was as much her fault as mine. But Emma was the perfect wife. It never was her fault it didn't work. It was all mine. And Lara's. She messed me up good.

The Lufthansa flight attendant made me hungry just looking at her, her hips just right, her legs muscular, nice behind, and ample breasts. Her braided blond hair wound like a nest on top of her head. *"Sehr geehrte damen und herren, herzlich willkommen an bord."* When I heard those few words of German, I felt my adventure was starting all over again, the same one I ended twenty-five years earlier. I hadn't been back to Germany since. It was a long flight from New York City to Frankfurt. I couldn't help but think about where these last twenty-five years had taken me, and what was now taking me back.

The young woman sitting next to me on that flight home in 1963 was Emma, a schoolteacher returning home from a two-year stint teaching children of the American military personnel. I slept with her two weeks later in New York right after President Kennedy was assassinated. I wonder if we would have hooked up if not for that. Sex soothed our grief. We didn't get out of bed until he was buried.

I didn't write, call or see her again for a year, not until she moved to New York. Youngstown, Ohio was just too small for anyone who had known life abroad. We were married a year after that, and our son came along fourteen months later, an accident but one we welcomed, both then and now. Emma had no objection when we named him Joshua Jacob Schneider after my natural father and the father who raised me.

We had a small wedding, a civil ceremony in New York City Hall. Her parents weren't too crazy about their daughter marrying a Jew, and would have preferred to keep it a secret. Her father was a big deal executive at Algonquin Steel, and her mother a committed member of the Daughters of the American Revolution. My family, on the other hand, embraced Emma like she was their own, *shiksa* or not. At least she wasn't a German. Emma's younger brother Stan and Aunt Beatrice were the only ones from her side who came to the wedding, besides her parents.

Grandpa Avi and Grandma Sara cried when we exchanged vows. It was the last time I saw them happy. Grandma Sara died in her sleep in her own bed only three months later. Theirs was a forever romance made in heaven, one I still longed for. Grandpa went just five months after Grandma. For him, life had no point once she was gone. I still have conversations with him in my mind whenever I'm confused. But at times like this trip back to Germany, I needed him here in person to explain things to me all over again.

I'd like to tell you all about Emma, but let's just say for now that she was as good a wife as any man could ask for, and certainly better than anything I deserved. It's not that I was a bad husband; it's just that sometimes I wasn't there. She, on the other hand, threw everything she had into the box all of the time. When I decided I didn't like the garment industry - the rag business, as Uncle Isaac called it - she embraced my plan to go to graduate school as though it was her idea. She voiced no regrets even though we had to take out loans, along with the G.I. Bill, to get through. She wanted to ask her father for help, but my pride prevented it. So we lived like Dickens' orphans.

She was also a great mother to Josh. Actually, we were both good parents, neither of us ever missing a soccer game, a track meet, a teacher's conference, or a piano concert. We rarely disagreed on anything about raising him, but then we both said Josh pretty much raised himself, a perfect kid right from the start. Maybe that's why we never had any more children. Why tempt fate? We were left to revel in his glory, visible evidence of what exceptional parents we were.

Emma could have complained, or even vetoed it, when my first teaching offer was as a History instructor at Mifflin College, a small traditional school in a small uninteresting town in southern Pennsylvania, far removed from anything. Instead she became a dedicated, charming faculty wife who furthered her husband's career.

I loved teaching and learning about how humankind arrived at this place in its destiny. Each year's flock of new students presented a fresh challenge. They were all bright, most of them spoiled by indulgent parents. My purpose was to help them learn how to think, and maybe understand a little about the human condition. Like all academics, I was expected to carve out a piece of history about which I knew more than my peers. I chose Jewish history in the Ukraine: how Jews got there, how they lived, and how they ended - King Kazimir of Poland who invited them in, the Haidamacks who tried to drive them out, the Hasidics and the Haskalah who competed for their faith, Catherine the Great who confined them in the Pale of Settlement, and the Nazis who endeavored to kill them all.

The Dean of the Faculty, the Chairman of the History Department, and the President of Mifflin College all pressured me to write and publish, write and publish. They tried flattery, bribery, and threats of withholding tenure. I resisted as much as I could, partly because I enjoyed teaching and being with the students, but mostly because I enjoyed being a pain in the ass. I did end up publishing two worthy works that gained me a small bit of international fame. But more about that later. It's important, however, because it is why I was on the plane carrying me back to Germany twenty-five years after I left for good.

In all those years, I never really stopped feeling lonely. But with the help of my shrink, I faced and learned to live with the murder of my family, my own survival, and my convoluted childhood. Dr. Freud, as I called him, helped me see that I had an abundance of people who loved me and would never leave me: Mother Kira, Father Jake, Max, Rose, Aunt Tillie, Uncle Isaac, Harry, and a multitude of other cousins, aunts, uncles, and friends. Above all, there was Emma. Dr. Freud said I just wouldn't let any of them touch me in the tenderest spot in my psyche. As Josh grew up I changed, not entirely, but some. I loved that little boy beyond anything I imagined possible. He touched me in that spot Dr. Freud talked about, the first and only one since Lara.

Back to Emma for a moment, and our marriage. I was a dedicated, attentive husband who tried to give Emma everything she wanted. It wasn't hard for me to see what a gem I had in her. I tried, I really did. But the truth is I never could get Lara out of my system. And every time Emma and I had an argument, and every time I got bored, and every time I felt lonesome, I thought of Lara. I loved Emma in my own way. And Emma loved me, of that I had no doubt. But Emma couldn't love me the way Lara did. And Emma couldn't make me a different person, like Lara did.

Still, I remained loyal and faithful to Emma, except for two very brief flings that meant nothing to me. One was with a post-graduate student from Penn State I met about ten years ago at a conference; the other was the sister-in-law of Bart Wisser in the Math Department. She was just passing through over Christmas vacation six years ago. Both women were slender and reasonably attractive, with dark brown eyes and muddy blonde hair. But both of them were vacuum headed, nothing like Lara, and more boring than Emma. What they lacked in brains, they also lacked in passion.

Speaking of which, Emma and I ceased to interest each other sexually about the sixth year of our marriage. After that, it was all mechanics, duty, and scratching an itch. By our tenth year, we did it about as often as two neutered porcupines. Still, to family, faculty, and alumni, we were as cute a couple as you could be at age forty-three.

Behind the drapes, I went on with my own personal Shake-spearean tragedy, mythicizing Lara, the beauty of our romance, the intensity of her love for me, and the heartrending ending. The more mundane Emma's and my sex life became, the more glorious the memory of what it was like with Lara. The more boring our conversations, the more spectacularly interesting was Lara. And when Emma began to droop a little - not much mind you - the more I fantasized about Lara's taut, lithe body, and adorable ass.

I made a concerted effort to recall and preserve every detail, to convince myself it once was real. It did happen. And she was still out there somewhere. I tried to imagine what her life might be like at that very moment. I genuinely prayed she had forgiven herself and found a good life, maybe with a good husband and three good kids, all of who looked just like her. At the same time, I hoped deep down that she hadn't forgotten me, the love we had, and that she still held a piece of me in her heart.

At first I exhausted myself trying to hold on to my loathing for Lara's father, Nazis, and all things German. It helped keep my ache for Lara from swallowing me. I couldn't be mad at her, so I was mad at the whole German nation. That worked as long as I didn't think too much about Otto, Willy, Margot, *Frau Giesler*, and even Lara's mother, Inge Kohler. Then more and more, West Germany publicly acknowledged national guilt and sought atonement. The government provided reparations to Jews, took steps to build strong relations with Israel, and aggressively hunted down Holocaust murderers for prosecution. With all of that, little by little my antipathy simply faded over the years. When I tried to summon even a smidgen of hate to blunt a sudden longing for Lara, the hate was just no longer there.

I kept in touch with Willy Speer, my old German friend, and even saw him three times when he came to the United States to cover stories in New York and Washington, D.C. I asked him once about Lara, and he told me she had returned to Kronberg, still working in Otto's photographic studio. Then I cut him off. I didn't want to hear any more. I didn't ask again, and he didn't offer.

Harry Ashby was the only one with whom I bared my soul. He worried about me, and saw through me, almost from the time I married Emma. "Lara's gone," he said. "Forget her. Emma's a terrific girl, and you're going to screw it up if you don't watch out." Later he encouraged me to seek marriage counseling, warning we could end up divorced like he and Margot. Of course I didn't have the excuse of Vietnam like he did.

In the early years, Margot still heard from Lara occasionally, but Harry refused to tell me anything about her. I didn't really want to know. It was still early in my marriage, and if I let that whole thing out of the neat compartment to which I assigned it, I would lose any chance at a full life with Emma.

After Germany, the Army sent Harry and Margot to Camp Irwin in California. He was one of the early volunteers to go to Vietnam, as Operations Officer in an Air Cavalry battalion. Seven months after he arrived, Harry landed in a hot zone with his unit, surrounded by an overwhelming force of Viet Cong and North Vietnamese regulars. By noon of the third day, half of the battalion's five hundred men were dead or wounded. Harry himself was hit in the stomach and arm, but he was the highest ranking officer still alive on the battlefield. He stayed on the ground until every last one of his men had been evacuated. For that, the Army awarded him the Silver Star.

Harry was never the same again. He got better after a few years, but he still drinks too much, and the ghosts still wander his corridors. He won't talk about it, at least not to me. For a while after he got back, I worried he might even take his own life. Instead he took it out on Margot. He admitted he hit her a few times, and one time he forgot his four year old son in the back seat of his Oldsmobile in the Sears parking lot. Two years later they were divorced. That's the last I ever saw of Margot. Harry told me she re-married, another Army officer she met while he was gone.

Harry left the Army when, a couple of years after his first stint, they wanted to send him back to Vietnam. If anything good came out of it, it was that he reconciled with his family, on his own terms. With his father's help, he went to work on Wall Street with an investment banking firm and made a success of it. He married again. I was his best man for the second time. Judith is a nice person, more in keeping with his Scarsdale mother's ideal of an Ashby wife. She loves Harry enough to cope with his nightmares, still going on some twenty years later. She is always polite to me, but I don't think she appreciates anyone from Harry's past life with Margot. Harry and I are still best friends. We see each other two or three times a year, usually without wives. We talk on the phone often.

When I told him I was going back to Germany, his first question was, "Are you going to try to see Lara?"

"Not sure," I answered. "Should I?"

"You'll always wonder," he said.

But right then, at thirty-five thousand feet, zooming toward Frankfurt, I still didn't know what I was going to do.

Before I leave the subject of Vietnam, let me say this. I continued to serve in the Reserves for a few years after Germany, and almost got called up in the summer of 1965 when LBJ decided to send U.S. troops into Vietnam *en masse*. I still feel a little guilty about not being part of my generation's war, the one we thought we were going to be fighting in Germany in 1962 and 1963. On the other hand, I get furious when I think of the 58,000 dead Americans, the 200,000 wounded, and the countless numbers too damaged to be full human beings again. A few of the officers I served with, and several enlisted men, were among the numbers - all for nothing, a complete waste. Screw Lyndon Johnson and screw Richard Nixon!

Sergeant Pickett went as Sergeant Major of an infantry division. He was badly wounded and discharged when he got out of the army hospital. I lost track of him after that. Colonel Stratton also went. He never did get that general's star he was always shooting for. When he retired, I started receiving Christmas cards from him, until he passed away three years ago. I never heard another word about Captain Symanski, but I think about him often.

Symanski had been right about Private William Salyer, as he was about so much else. The eight ball I made my jeep driver at the Captain's insistence turned into a model soldier, one of the best in Charlie Company. He was loyal to a fault, and eternally grateful for what I did for him. He named his first child after me, and still sends me pictures now and then.

On my best days, I summon some compassion for my nemesis, Lieutenant Richard Kaine. He went to Vietnam and was promptly fragged by his own men, just like Captain Symanski predicted. What an inglorious way to go. His Confederate ancestors would be ashamed.

Though it's faded some with time, the military left a permanent mark on me - how I walk, how I talk, how I think, and how I act. After Germany, I no longer doubted I had earned the right to call myself an American.

The Lufthansa flight attendant refilled my wine glass. It was nice that they were flying me over Business Class. I loved her accent. It reminded me of Lara's. Enough time had gone by since my divorce that I was beginning to pay attention to women again.

From the first time we met, I did not intend to deceive Emma about Lara, but I did. I told her only enough to lead her to believe it was only an innocuous fling with a *fraulein*. Emma wanted to believe it, and I thought she did until that one big day.

We had just returned home after driving Josh to Carlyle College to start his freshman year. He could have gone to Mifflin College for free as the child of a faculty member, but he always wanted to go to college where his dad went to college, a legacy. We both stifled tears when we drove off, leaving our truly precious little boy behind.

When we finished unpacking our suitcases, we adjourned to our family room. Emma poured two glasses of red wine and handed one to me. "You'd better sit down," she said. That's what she always said when she had something serious to discuss. My first thought, given the timing, was that she had a health issue. I took my usual spot on my leather recliner. She sat down next to me on the couch, never taking her eyes off of me.

"What's going on?" I asked.

"Eli, I want a divorce."

There was a kind, firm quality to her voice but the words landed like an unexpected punch in the gut. I nearly dropped my glass. "What are you talking about?"

"Our marriage was over years ago. You know that. We've both been holding on for Josh's sake. He's on his way now, and there is still time for both of us to start new lives."

"You can't do that," I responded, a little too strongly.

She touched my hand. For a woman who had just asked for a divorce, she seemed more concerned about me than herself. "You're a good man, Eli, and a good father. I'm sure you love me in your own way, just like I love you in my own way. But we both know there's always been a third person in our marriage. I thought by being a good wife I could make you forget her. I couldn't. She won." Emma took back her hand.

"But I love you," I protested. "Tell me what I have to do." Panic clawed my insides, driven by a resurrected fear of being alone again. Emma had been there for me for the past twenty-three years.

"We'll make it as easy on Josh and each other as we can."

"Why now? After all these years?" I pleaded.

"A couple of years ago I came across a picture in your desk of the two of you. I wasn't prying. I was just looking for a postage stamp or something, and there it was. She really is very pretty. I saw the way she looked at you, and the way you looked at her." She cupped her wine glass with both hands, looking down at it, then back up. "I'm not blaming you. You can't help it, but you never looked at me that way. Then there was the note she sent you. I guess it was when you split up. You kept the picture and the note all these years. I couldn't pretend anymore."

The old cuckoo clock I brought home from Germany twenty-three years earlier chose that moment to announce that it was five o'clock. When it stopped, I gathered my thoughts and continued my plea. "Emma, I'm so sorry. I haven't seen her or been in touch with her ever. You have to believe me."

"I do believe you. But I know any girl who looked like her caught your attention. Like that cheerleader, and like Bart Wisser's sister-in-law."

"You knew about that?"

"Don't look so surprised. Wives know these things. But husbands don't." A hint of triumph touched her lips. "I slept with Figg Newton about five years ago."

"No, not Figg Newton." I was shocked Emma would sleep with anyone, but not him of all people. She had too much class. His real name was Newton Figg, Chairman of the Political Science Department, a real jerk, not even remotely handsome.

"It was only once, and only to get even with you."

"Why are you telling me now?" For the first time since we sat down, a bit of anger, jealousy really, darted through my mind.

"When this is over, I don't want you to carry around a lot of guilt over your flings with those two bimbos. I know they meant nothing more to you than Figg meant to me. We're even."

It took almost two years to settle all the details and the legal mechanics. We ended it amiably, thanks mostly to Emma. She asked for little. Josh took it as well as one can hope, in a thoughtful, caring, and intelligent way, as sorry for us as he was for himself.

The end of a failed marriage, no matter how civil and justified, leaves a residue of defeat and loss. I felt all alone again. Emma moved back to Youngstown where her parents still lived. I moved into a small apartment not far from campus.

My new book, *The End of Uman*, hit the book stores at almost the same time our final divorce decree came through. It was my second popular history, non-fiction written from the heart for the general public. It centered on a young German lieutenant who in his testimony at the Nuremberg War Trials recounted the murder of all of the Jews in Uman - all except me.

The new book followed on the success of my first popular history, *Two Brothers from Uman*, published three years earlier. Before he died, Grandpa Avi gave me all of the letters my Grandpa Lieb wrote him from Uman over a thirty-five year period. That book came right from deep inside me. It gave me a chance to know my two grandfathers in a different way, and to use my accumulated academic research. Together, the two books released me from the grip of my past.

It's not entirely accurate to say no one read my earlier academic research papers. About ten years ago I decided I needed to return to Uman and place a marker at the place where my family was murdered. But when I applied for a visa from the Soviet Union, it was rejected - barred for life. Apparently my discussion in one of my first scholarly papers of Ukraine complicity in the Nazi massacre of Jews didn't sit well with the Soviets. But things are changing in the Soviet Union under their new leader, Mikhail Gorbachev. Hopefully I will be allowed to take a trip to the Ukraine soon.

Before that first book, I wrote many academic papers which no one read, except maybe a handful of academics, and those Soviet censors. Now several hundred thousand people read *Two Brothers*, to the genuine admiration of most of my fellow faculty, and the resentment of a few like Figg Newton. My publisher told me early demand for *The End of Uman* indicated it would far exceed *Two Brothers*, particularly because of strong international sales. My agent told me Germans and Israelis were big fans. It seems the world still can't get enough of stories about Nazi atrocities. Perhaps we all continue trying to understand it, even after all these years.

Willy Speer had a lot to do with my strong sales in Germany, and he was the reason I was invited to speak in Frankfurt the next afternoon in front of a huge conference of historians from across Germany. I had been told to expect wide press coverage.

Willy gained fame as a young man from a series of articles he did in the mid-sixties about the Frankfurt Auschwitz trials, one of the first in which Germans tried other Germans for war crimes. He was scrupulous with his details and brutal in his condemnations. That earned him a position with *Munich Rundschau* - Munich Panorama - one of Germany's largest and most important news magazines. Over twenty years, he rose to editor and publisher. He made sure my books were well-covered both in his magazine and other media where he had influence.

"*Herr* Schneider, please bring your seat to an upright position." I startled out of my reverie, sure I had heard Lara's voice and felt her touch. But it was just the attractive flight attendant with the nice legs. I snuffed out my cigarette and then did what I was told.

Willy would be there to meet me as soon as I cleared customs. One of his first questions was sure to be whether I planned to visit Kronberg. I still hadn't decided that. There wouldn't be any point to it if I didn't try to see Lara while I was there. I didn't know if I was brave enough to do that, not after twenty-five years. What would I say?

TWENTY FIVE

TUESDAY

Nearly six hundred accomplished German historians and three hundred hand-picked graduate students crammed the Kultur Hall of Goethe Universitat to hear me speak. The standing ovation at the end sent goose bumps up my spine. Right after that, a respected commentator interviewed me for a television documentary on the Holocaust. He was most flattering. At such moments, I couldn't believe this was happening to me, a little known history professor from a little known small Pennsylvania college.

Willy clapped me on the back as we pushed our way through the last of the crowd, out the main door of the old brick building, and into the pleasant May afternoon sun. "How is it you Americans say? You punched it out of the stadium."

"Hit it out of the ball park."

"Yah. That is it. Hit it out of the stadium." He laughed, as pleased with himself for arranging the event as he was with my performance. "You had them eating from your hand when you praised Germany. You, a Jew and an American army officer."

"It's true. Germany's the only one that's stood up, recognized its past, and atoned for it. Look at the Austrians, electing a damned Nazi like Kurt Waldheim president."

"We have done a good job killing our Nazi ghosts here in West Germany. But someday soon the Wall in Berlin will come down and we will have to do it all over again in East Germany."

"Gorbachev started withdrawing Soviet troops from Afghanistan," I said.

He continued on with his thought. "But any time there is even a small suggestion of Nazi renewal, we have to reassure the world again that we are now a democracy. It is okay. It is the stain we must wear for deeds done in our name by our fathers."

"Maybe someday."

Halfway across the Campus Commons, just when serious conversation threatened to darken a beautiful day, two studious young women intercepted us, begging me to sign their copies of my book. The plain one made me feel like a rock star. The other one looked good enough to eat. She made me feel like an old lecher.

Willy noticed my awkwardness with the two girls. After they ran off with smiles on their faces, he said, "You are not fifty yet, still a young man with time." He wanted to ask me if I was going to go to Kronberg to see Lara, but he waited. At the moment, I still couldn't answer the question myself.

That evening we met before dinner in the plush, near-empty bar of the Park Hotel where I was staying, just down the street from the Opera House. The last time I visited Frankfurt in 1963, the elegant old building was still a bombed out skeleton, left standing as a reminder of war's cost. Since then, they rebuilt it exactly as it was before the war, down to the last nail.

"So if I stay in Germany a few days, what big changes am I going to see?" I asked as soon as we sat down at a small round table in the corner. A piped-in Elton John song played softly in the background.

Willy's eyebrows rose. "Stay? Why would you stay?"

I ignored his question. "I didn't notice as many American soldiers walking around town."

"They are all still here, but they are more hidden, less obvious." He took out a pack of HB cigarettes from his shirt pocket and offered me one. I declined and took out my own pack of Tareytons. When he lit up, I remembered how fowl German cigarettes smelled, a combination of donkey dung and wet rope.

"The food is still the same," I offered. "And the wine. That's good." I ordered a Spaten beer when the stern-faced waiter came for our order. Willy did the same.

"Konrad Adenauer is not Chancellor anymore," he laughed, knowing I knew that. "Now it is Helmut Kohl. We may never get rid of him. But you'll see more Mercedes, fewer Volkswagens. Same ugly men's suits and ladies' dresses, but made from better material. Houses painted in brighter colors, no more gray. No more smells of human manure in the farm villages. No more oxen in the fields, only big powerful tractors. And everyone is fatter." He patted his own slender stomach. Willy still looked the part of the handsome, blonde Aryan, but he couldn't help that.

"So should I go to Kronberg?" I asked.

Willy had been waiting for that question. Now he stammered a moment, searching for the right response. "That depends. Why do you want to go? What do you expect to find?"

"Lara. Why else?"

Willy nodded and took a sip of his beer. "She never married, you know. When she came back to Kronberg, she went to work for *Herr* Kaltenbach again in his photography shop. He died a few years after and left the shop to her."

I breathed, relieved for the time being. "What else?"

"No man that I know of, but then I do not go back to Kronberg often since my father died. She turned the shop into a photo gallery showing and selling her own work. She is quite accomplished, mostly portraits and photographs of children. She is somewhat famous in Germany. I have used her a few times to take pictures for the magazine. We used one on the cover last year."

A portly, well-dressed man at the next table must have said something funny because the attractive young woman with him let out a forced cackle. Willy frowned in their direction.

"What is she like now?" I asked Willy.

"I really do not know. I have one of my editors work with her, never me directly. I hear she is still quite beautiful."

"So, do I go?"

TWENTY SIX

WEDNESDAY

Who was I kidding? After twenty-five years of self-inflicted hurts, there was no way I was going to be this close and not attempt to see her, particularly now that I knew she had never married. That gave me something to think about. I wondered if I had anything to do with it. She promised she would never stop loving me. Maybe she hadn't.

The next morning I boarded the train from Frankfurt to Kronberg, just an hour run. A young second lieutenant in his army greens sat in the seat across the aisle from me looking as keyed up as I must have looked the day I reported in to the 16th Armor. A jeep would probably be there to meet him. For me it would be a taxi to the Kronberger Hotel, a small place on Hindenburg Strasse close to town, just down the street from my old apartment. I didn't know if I would be staying just for the night or until my plane flight home in three days.

The train pulled into the old Kronberg train station. Nothing had changed in twenty-five years, not even the sign on the side of the building or the worn green tile inside. It didn't feel real, but real enough to make my knees knock and my stomach coil. What would I do when I saw her? What would I say? What would she do? What if she wasn't even there? Then what? I almost hoped she wouldn't be. At least I could tell myself I tried.

The young lieutenant drove off in a 16th Armor jeep driven by a boy, a soldier who looked young enough to be a Cub Scout. A dozen newly-arrived enlisted men in fatigues piled in back of a two-and-a-half ton truck. The smell of diesel exhaust up my nose turned on my subconscious. I searched inside myself for the courage this place always brought out in me.

Before I left home, I packed my image outfit just in case: tan chinos, classic blue button-down shirt, navy blazer, and cordovan loafers - my college professor dress uniform. I went to the bathroom for the tenth time since I checked into the hotel, and then inspected myself in the mirror for the twentieth time.

"This is crazy. What am I doing here?" I asked myself. The walk from the Kronberger Hotel to Kaltenbach Fotographie was only a few blocks, past the old tower wall and the *Rathaus*. Some children played in the park across from my old apartment building under the watchful eyes of their mothers. The trees and bushes had grown dense in twenty-five years.

I hurried as though this was a trip to the dentist I wanted to get over with, and then be on my way back home. But I had to at least try to see Lara, maybe close a chapter, and then get on with my life.

Willy was right. Kronberg remained a quaint German farm town, but one with fresh, bright colors that made it shine as though it were a set for a Disney version of Hansel and Gretel. The Lutheran church at the end of Kaiserstrasse looked well-dressed, like an aging grand dame with fresh makeup. The facade had been painted a mustard-gold against pure white stucco, its slate onion steeples washed clean.

I stopped by the familiar old fountain in front of the shop and took a deep gulp of the early afternoon baby blue sky. A cigarette would taste good right now. A few cars rumbled over the cobblestones behind me toward the *Alte Brucke*, more Mercedes now than Volkswagens. Two *hausfraus* on their bicycles headed in the opposite direction. I snuffed out my cigarette and field stripped it, stuffing the filter in my chinos pant pocket.

The stenciled *Kaltenbach Fotographie* still marked the traditional show window. The old door, painted new, looked like it had been there since the Hundred Years War. I peaked in the window, everything unfamiliar. The old camera shop's show cases, back office, supply room, and dark room had been removed, the interior transformed into a much larger, open-spaced ultra modern photographic gallery. Pewter-gray tiles covered the floor, and framed photos of children covered the white walls. Toward the back, a stainless steel, glass topped coffee table and three ugly German-modern stainless chairs sat in front of a three-quarters high false wall.

A well-dressed middle aged man and stout, dark-haired woman stood in front of one photo, he with his hands in the pockets of his suit pants, she pointing and talking. He nodded. There was no sign of Lara. I breathed a sigh of relief and turned to leave, then looked back when the overhead spotlight caught the photo image of old friends. There by the door, Otto's photograph of Adriana and Sophie hung in its usual place. Next to it, Otto himself stared back at me, a close up of the weathered old man as I knew him. "Eli, please come in and say hello," his kind smile seemed to say. "Let me fix you a cup of tea."

Just as I was about to turn the doorknob, a professional-looking woman scurried out from behind the false wall with a couple of pamphlets in her hand. She handed one to the man and a larger one to the woman. They nodded, exchanged a few words, and then brushed by me on their way out the door. A little bell tinkled.

There she was, Lara, not a fantasy but a real person. My heart beat so hard I thought I would have a seizure right then and there. One look and I was in love all over again. Or maybe more accurately, still in love. A car honked its angry horn on the street behind me. Another answered back, angrier.

She had filled out a little, more like her sister Katrin, but she still looked and moved like a ballerina. A small smile caressed the corners of her lips. Her now-short muddy blond hair swept behind her ears, accented with small diamond stud earrings. Her tapered charcoal pants, calf-high black leather boots, and loose-fit off-white silk blouse would have looked stylish even walking down Fifth Avenue in New York. Her black framed glasses gave her the same devilish look she wore in Nuremberg when she wore nothing else.

Just as I was about to turn the doorknob and go in, she looked up. Her eyes widened, startled. She raised her fist to her mouth and silenced a scream. I pushed the door open and stepped in.

I waited twenty-five years to see him just one more time. Then I look up and there he is, peering in the window of my studio like he did in the beginning. But why did he have to come now, just when my life is at last comfortable. When I see him, I raise my fist to my mouth and bite down so hard I leave deep teeth marks. I can hardly breathe when he turns the doorknob and walks in. "Eli. Is it really you?"

"Yes, it's me." I must have been grinning like a Cheshire cat.

Her smile was more guarded. "It is nice to see you." She raised her arms and we hugged a chaste hug as distant as one you give when you run into your old First Grade schoolteacher in the supermarket. But even in that brief hug, I smelled eucalyptus.

The gallery was empty except for the two of us. We both shuffled, uncomfortable, not knowing what to say next. "You have a beautiful gallery," I finally offered.

"Let me show you," she said.

It didn't take an expert's eye to see that these photographs were taken by someone of extraordinary talent. There was a sensitivity to her works that could only come from the deep wounds of a scarred soul. Most of the photos were of children of all ages, shapes, and circumstances. One looked like a little Hasidic boy with his sidelocks. We stopped to admire one of the few adult images, a stern middle aged woman with graying hair and kind eyes. Then we paid homage to Otto, Adriana, and Sophie.

"I was so surprised he left the shop to me," she said. "But he had no one else."

We were running out of superficial things to say. A moment passed, then another. Maybe it was time to just leave, but I couldn't, not after coming all this distance and all these years. "Let's go have a cup of coffee. Is the old bakery still there?"

She thought for a moment, and I waited as though the next decision she made could change my life. "It is different now," she said. "But we can go." She called out to her assistant, a stylish young woman who had been working at a desk behind the three-quarters high wall. She said something in German which probably meant she was going out for a while.

She walked across the cobblestones with the same purpose I remembered. I hustled to keep up. "The Combat Zone is gone," she said, gesturing toward the two streets running off the square by the *Rathaus*. "The soldiers are better mannered now that there are more women in the American army. They do not need German girls so much."

About ten minutes into our coffee and pastry, I was feeling this was about as exciting as dating your dowager aunt. Her guard was up, presenting me with a solid facade. But there was still something interesting about her. I was determined, but every time I tried to turn toward the personal, she shut it down. The only things she wanted to talk about was her work and mine.

*I cannot believe I am sitting here with him. I want him,
but that is what got me in trouble before. I cannot let that
happen again. Keep him at a distance. Do not let him talk
about what used to be. It is no more and can never come
again. I wonder if he is married. He is not wearing a wedding ring.*

"I read both of your books," she finally said. "They are beautiful. I think I got to know you like I did not know you before."

"They gave me my freedom. Understanding my real parents
and grandparents. Getting rid of all that hate."

That opened the conversation a little. I told her about my
failed marriage with Emma, trying to be kind, but also trying to
minimize my love for my ex-wife. I probably talked too much
about Josh. All-in-all, not a good way to ignite an old flame. I
switched to my academic career as quickly as I could. She listened attentively.

Finally I stopped talking and let her start. She had little to
say. Her mother was still alive, living in Wurzburg with her sister Katrin. Katrin had been married for sixteen years and had
three children, a boy and two girls. "I am their Auntie Lara," she
said. Her nose wrinkled. "I love them much."

"And your father?"

She clasped her china cup in both hands and looked down into the pool of coffee. "I never saw him again. Maybe I could
have forgiven him, but he did not want forgiveness. He was
proud of what he did. He said his only regret was that Hitler had
not killed more Jews. It's strange, but he liked you." She raised
her chin, her eyes empty. "He died two years after you left." She
sounded as indifferent as if she were talking about an former

acquaintance of little consequence.

"I'm sorry," I said.

"*Macht nichts*. It does not matter." She looked into my eyes and held her gaze there. The smile still curled on the edge of her lips. I couldn't look away.

We had a history together, and that is what I wanted to talk about. I tried introducing it with mirth. We laughed together about our first date, stepping on each other's toes as we danced. But she quickly cut me off as I tried to continue down that track.

"I know you would like to talk about old times," she said. "But I do not remember so much."

How could she forget when I have been carrying every detail with me for twenty-five years? It wasn't fair. I was getting nowhere.

"I must return to the gallery. "It is almost time to close, and I have to make some phone calls."

"Can I see you for dinner tonight?"

I must end this right here! Right now!

"I am so sorry, but I am busy tonight. Maybe some other time."

Some other time? As though I hadn't come four thousand miles just to see her. We walked back hardly speaking. When I accidentally brushed against her, she moved away as though I were contagious.

"It was nice to see you," she said. We did not even exchange the obligatory hug. Instead she stuck out her hand for the single-pump German handshake.

"Goodbye." I slammed the door a little too hard when I exited the gallery. I walked back to the hotel fuming. What a disaster. I wished I had never come.

When I entered my room, I threw the big medal-balled key on the end table and my blue blazer on the bed. That bitch. She knew exactly what she was doing. She did it to me twenty-five years ago, and she just did it again.

I stretched out on the bed with my clothes on and closed my eyes. I was bleeding. I saw her. She was real. And she had a hold on me as firmly as she ever had. How was I ever going to lead a life, fall in love again, with Lara owning me like this? I had to find a way.

Tonight I would eat alone, and tomorrow morning be on the train back to Frankfurt, and then home.

The jangling telephone jolted me out of my stupor. "I will meet you in front of your hotel in fifteen minutes," she said. "We will go to dinner." Then she hung up.

I ran some cold water over my face, gave my teeth a quick brush, checked myself in the mirror, and ran down the steps. Right on schedule, she pulled up in a newish silver Mercedes, one of those small diesels they don't export to America. She had changed into a bright blue spring dress patterned with tiny yellow and white flowers.

"We will go to the Golden Kreuz in Iphofen. Yah?" she said.

One of our old haunts - a good sign. "Sounds good to me," I answered.

She drove with the aggression of a race car driver, upshifting and downshifting, jabbering away, glancing over at me and smiling as she hit a hundred kilometers an hour on a narrow two lane road. I would have died of fright if not for her beautiful legs, her dress gathered well up her thighs. Did she have any idea? I found myself aroused with little provocation.

I suppose I expected to find the same unblemished youthful ballerina I last saw twenty-five years ago. Instead I found a handsome, mature woman with character, embellished by a few crow's feet around the eyes, imperfect hands, and wrinkles on her neck. What was the same was the human warmth and inner beauty projected in her dark brown eyes, and that smile I had not forgotten. I was as enchanted as ever.

Iphofen was no longer the manure-saturated farm town I remembered. The old houses, cobblestone streets and town walls were the same, but everything was painted and immaculately clean, with numerous Opels, BMW's, and Mercedes parked at odd angles in places meant for hay wagons. The Golden Kreuz wasn't the Golden Kreuz I remembered. Graceless modern wooden tables and rust colored curtains replaced the old ones that had probably been there since Bismarck. But the food and drink were what I remembered. We both had the sauerbraten with spatzle and red cabbage, which we devoured with the same ferocity we had the first time we came here together. When we finished, we raised our forks in tribute to each other.

We also polished off a bottle of good Franken wine. By then, we were both giddy, and I was in love. We talked about books, movies, and music. The tables around us had filled up, even in mid-week, mostly with younger well-heeled men and women, a few with children.

"Do you still like jazz?" I asked.

"Oh yes, very much. Chubby Checker, Beach Boys, Elvis Presley." She looked serious, but with a mischievous twinkle. "A joke, Yes?"

"Just like before."

"Yah, just like before."

We settled into a comfortable, encouraging familiarity. "Are you free tomorrow?" I asked.

"No, not tomorrow," she answered too quickly.

"Dinner?"

"I do not think so."

I probably would have eventually crept up on the subject, but just then an unexpected thought burned me like a spark from a coal furnace. "Do you have someone else?"

She stared out the leaded glass window for a moment. "It is complicated."

"Complicated." My jealous heart sank.

"You have been away a long time."

"Well I'm here now," I snapped.

Her eyes held mine. Neither of us said anything. Conversations from tables around us ebbed and flowed in a tongue I still could not understand. The smoke from her cigarette curled from her fingers to my nose. She looked like she was hunting for an answer in my face.

Those flecks of silver in his hair make him even more handsome than I remember. He is so interesting and funny and kind. But look at those lines in his face. He has known sorrow. I hope I am not the reason his marriage failed. I could not live with that. I want to grab him in my arms and comfort him. But I cannot let one evening with him after twenty-five years upset everything I worked so hard to construct, every hurt I have worked to repair, and the fragile balance. No, when dinner is over this must be the end of it. I must find the strength to say goodbye. It is not his fault, but I will not let my heart be broken again. It would not be fair to give him hope when there is no hope. But look at the way he looks at me. I hope I am not looking at him the same way. This wine is making me tipsy. I must stop before I do something I will regret. I cannot let him kiss me. I do not know what I would do.

She knocked the ash off the end of her cigarette and took a slow puff. She opened her mouth to say something, closed it, and then spoke. "Tomorrow night I will make you an omelet. Nothing more. Just an omelet." She didn't look at me when she said it.

When she dropped me off in front of the Kronberger Hotel, she let me give her a kiss good night, but only one. It tasted like well-fermented honey, moist and delicious. When I tried for a second helping she pulled back behind the steering wheel. "Until tomorrow," she said, starting the engine. "Thank you for a pleasant evening."

Pleasant? That's the best she could do? I wondered how serious she was about this other guy, and what I could do to throw a monkey wrench into it. It couldn't be too serious or she wouldn't be seeing me again. Yet she seemed troubled by the need to break a date with him.

Why did I do that? Why did I ever offer to make him an omelet, in my apartment? I feel the same old urge as though I were a young girl again, not a dried up old raisin. I am frightened, and cannot let this get out of hand. Still, I must see him again before he goes for good. Gertie will not be very happy with me when I telephone and cancel dinner with her again. I am not being fair to her. Why did I let him kiss me? If I had had another glass of wine I would have gone up to his room and then who knows where we would go? Do I still love him? Yes, I think I do. But I loved him twenty-five years ago, and I still found the strength to walk away. It was better for both of us. Or did I make a mistake? An omelet. That is all it will be, and then I will send him on his way. This time he will not come back. What would Mother say if I told her? She would say I am crazy to let him go again. But

Gertrude, she will always be here for me, safe. She loves me too. He is going to expect more than an omelet. I cannot let that happen. Every time I am involved with an American I am nearly destroyed.

She was a successful businesswoman, an accomplished artist, and prominent in her community. Then why did she seem to be the same scared, insecure girl she was twenty-five years ago? For a moment I flattered myself, considering the possibility that the mere sight of me had unnerved her. But that wasn't it. She was still troubled in her soul in spite of her achievements. In fact, it was probably her pain that drove her creativity. Maybe I was an uncomfortable reminder.

I got one thing answered that day: I still loved her. I never belonged to anyone before Lara, and no one ever belonged to me. That's the way it was once, and that's the way it should be again. I thought about what Captain Symanski always told me: "When in doubt, attack!" That's what I was going to do. And I only had two full days more before my flight home.

TWENTY SEVEN

THURSDAY MORNING

My plan was simple: convince her to spend the day with me, charm her with my wit and wisdom, mix in a few memories, and then launch a full assault in the wake of an omelet in her apartment. I took the time over a breakfast hard roll, cheese, and bitter black coffee to think up clever remarks and brilliant insights sure to impress her. My uniform of the day was navy pleated twill pants, a blue and white checkered shirt, black suede slip-ons, and a light tan jacket for the chill of the early May morning.

When I walked in the gallery door, the clock in the *Rathaus* tower struck ten. Lara looked pleased to see me, not at all surprised by my earlier-than-agreed appearance. I presented my plan for us to spend the whole day together. She readily agreed, and told her stylish assistant she would be gone for the rest of the day. The young woman gave me a professional nod of the head by way of a greeting, and then a critical appraisal as we left the shop.

"I must show you some things in town," she said as soon as we left the shop. "Then we drive out to the base so you can look around." She was excited like a child who wanted to show her parents her new art project, her previous day's reserve diminished.

We turned up the street next to the *Rathaus,* the Combat Zone where drunken G.I.'s used to chase those German girls who were willing. Now it was just restaurants and shops for the townspeople. We stopped about halfway up the street. "Look here. Do you see these stars in the sidewalks?" She pointed down.

Brass stars were embedded every few yards, up one side of the street and down the other. "Yes. Very nice. What are they for?"

"Each one marks a spot where a Jew lived when they were attacked on *Kristallnacht* in 1938. You know about *Kristallnacht*, yes?"

I nodded. "The night of the broken glass. Organized Nazi thugs attacked Jews everywhere in Germany. They destroyed Jewish homes and shops. Killed some, beat up many. Burned down synagogues."

Her voice caught, her face stern. "We put these stars here to honor those Jews."

"Who is 'we?'"

"The Kronberg Jewish Memorial Society. I was chairman when we did this." She said it with a touch of pride. Then she looked toward the market square. "Come. Now I must show you the best part." She set off with her purposeful gate, impervious to the restrictions of her tight black skirt and jacket.

I hurried to keep up. Re-living a Nazi past wasn't going to get me to where I wanted to get with Lara. But she was tackling this with enthusiasm, not remorse.

When we turned right at the *Alte Brucke*, I knew where we were headed - the old synagogue. At the big blue front door, she pulled out a key from her purse and opened it.

"We made this into a museum of Jewish people in Kronberg. There are of course only a few old Jews left now, but they come here some days and pray."

We stood together admiring the stained glass window behind the bema, the raised platform for reading the Torah. "It is beautiful," I said. And so it was. But it was filled with dark memories for me. When we came here twenty-five years ago, Lara was on the verge of a breakdown, and our ending near.

As we were leaving, Lara pointed out the memorial plaque to Otto, Adriana, and Sophie Kaltenbach. She tried to rush by another plaque commemorating the restoration, chaired by one Lara Kohler. I stopped and acknowledged it. When I praised her for leading this significant undertaking, she dismissed it as though it were nothing of importance. But we both knew it was part of her atonement.

She followed me to the bench behind the synagogue, along the river. We sat down, the morning sun warming us. She didn't resist when I took her hand in mine. "You did a marvelous thing here," I said.

"We all have the burden to recognize and remember. I can never make up for my father's sins, only my own. I try. I still work at the orphanage, but there are not so many orphans now. That is good. And people do not care so much about brown babies."

My indiscriminate hate for Germans and Nazis was long gone, and I told her so. What she did to honor Jews and atone for Germany's past made me love her even more, but I couldn't say that. What I really needed to understand was whether she had forgiven herself for the abortion. I didn't know quite how to ask. "Lara, are you at peace?" I finally asked.

Why did he have to bring that up? I can live with our Nazi past. But the abortion will be with me forever. I no longer think about it every day. But I do think about it, and wonder if it would have been a little boy or a little girl. I understand now it was something I could not help. I was so young. I trusted my father completely, and he said this is what must happen. I did not know then that he himself was a Nazi butcher who thought nothing of killing babies.

She let go of my hand and laced the fingers of both her hands together in her lap. When she spoke, she spoke softly. "You want to know if I have forgiven myself for the abortion. Yes, I have. But that does not mean I am not still punished. That will never end."

She stared out at the river, watching a barge loaded with coal churn by. The diesel smoke polluted the perfume from the flower bed next to the bench. She continued. "The mistake I made with the American G.I. is not the problem, you see. Even the abortion I can forgive. I was a scared little girl, bewildered by what was happening to me."

"You've paid enough." I meant it, but it sounded so feeble. It wasn't hard to see that pain was still there, pain I would have given anything to suck out and take on myself. "Have you been to a counselor? A psychiatrist? I went to one before Emma and I split up. It helped." I didn't want to mention he also helped me deal with losing Lara.

I looked at her, but she would not look back, even when she answered my question. "I do not intentionally punish myself. I know what is in the past cannot be undone. But what can never go away is the feeling someone important is missing. They say people who have lost a foot still can feel the foot long after it is gone. That is how it is for me. I still feel my child. Maybe a little girl or a nice boy like your Josh. I do not know which it was."

She stared at the ground, searching for a thought. She looked up when she found it. "Try to imagine that you know of Josh's spirit, but he is not here, and never has been. That is what it is like. I feel my child's spirit."

My mind was blank, and she had nothing more to add, so we

listened to the cars passing on the street behind us. After a couple of minutes, I took her hand in mine and kissed it. "I am sorry," I said.

She nodded her head and then withdrew her hand. She glanced at her watch and stood up. "Come. Let us visit the base," she pronounced with a delicate smile, as though we had never had this dark discussion. When I tried to hold her hand again, she pulled it away to search prematurely in her jacket pocket for her car keys.

My visit to Holden Barracks was like chasing clouds. Lara waited in her car while I stood in front of the old Battalion Headquarters looking across the parade ground toward Charlie Company. On the day I left twenty-five years ago, I did the same thing, wondering what was in store for me.

If I needed anything to remind me I was a worn out old combat boot, a puzzling column of very short soldiers marched toward me in full backpacks, helmets, and slung rifles. When they were on top of me, I realized they were women in full combat gear. Women hadn't been part of my army.

Tanks still lined the runway as they did in my day, but the M-60s were gone, replaced by the new M1 Abrams tanks. I still could have climbed in the turret of one of our old tanks and gone right into battle, but I had no idea what was going on with these new ones.

Our drive around the rest of the base was empty of nostalgia. Some of it looked almost like it did, though without the polished sheen. A number of nondescript army-issue buildings had replaced noble ones that used to mark Holden Barracks as a formidable former German army post.

The majestic old Officers Club would surely capture my nostalgia, I thought as we walked up the wide stone steps. The heavy, carved oak door could still withstand a battering ram. But inside, cheap knotty pine panels had replaced the fine plaster walls and oak wainscoting. This was someone's idea of redecorating. The old polished parquet floor was covered over with cheap floor tile.

Memories can sting and tickle almost at the same time. I could once again hear the roaring tank engines, smell the gunpowder, and recognize the excited voices crackling over the radio. I could see my own young face and that of all the others. Some of them were dead now, and I was old.

I hadn't said much for the past half hour, and Lara left me alone with my bittersweet reflections. She drove slowly back towards town. "I miss Harry," I said. "Not like he is now, but how he was then. I miss Margot too."

She reached over and patted my leg. I covered her hand with my own. She let it rest there until she needed to downshift. "I miss Margot too," she said. "She is not the same any more either. She still loves him you know. But when he came back from Vietnam, she was afraid of him."

"Do you ever talk to her?"

"Not so much. The last time she came here was five or six years ago. I do not like the new man she married. He is in the Quartermasters." She said it as though supply officers were some kind of lesser life not to be admired like an Armor officer.

Visiting ghosts was one of the reasons I came to Kronberg, but not the important reason. A sour mood wasn't going to get me anywhere, so I forced it back in its hole like I did over the years with other bad memories.

"Do you remember after our first date you told Margot I looked like Paul Newman."

Lara giggled like a schoolgirl. "Yes, I remember. I am so embarrassed. Margot was not supposed to tell you."

If not for that, I might never have asked her out again, I thought. Then I said out loud, "I'm ready for an omelet."

"First I have to buy some eggs. We'll see if the chickens have laid any today."

After a quick stop for eggs, bread, and cheese, Lara turned on to Lindenstrasse. She stopped at number 7, my old apartment. I thought she was making another stop on my nostalgia tour. Instead, she turned off the engine, grabbed the sack of groceries, and said, "We're here." With that, she opened her car door and got out. I opened mine and followed her, dumbfounded. "I live here," she said in response to my startled look. "In your old apartment."

The outside of the stone building looked the same, and so did the staircase, though both had been scrubbed and buffed. Most of the best times with Lara - and the worst ones - happened in this apartment. Of all the apartments in Kronberg, why did she pick this one?

She seemed to be reading my mind. "It is close to the gallery. I can walk, even in winter." We climbed the familiar stairs. All that was missing was the smell of *Frau* Giesler's frying pork chops.

"Is *Frau* Giesler still here?"

"She died. And so did *Herr* Giesler. So now I rent from their daughter. They all remembered you and Harry. *Frau* Giesler said you were cute."

"And what did you say?"

She looked at me and smiled, shy. "I agreed with her." She climbed a few more stairs, and then added, "A lot has changed." Her poker face sent the message she intended.

TWENTY EIGHT

THURSDAY EVENING

When she unlocked the door, I expected to walk into my apartment just as I left it twenty-five years earlier, preserved as a museum for my memories. Instead I found a place which bore little resemblance to my old bachelor's pad. Interior walls had been removed so it now opened into one large space covered with shiny hardwood floors. Clean, bright white baseboards and crown molding accented warm beige walls. New cream counter tile topped cherry kitchen cabinets. Even the bathroom had been moved from its privileged spot near the front door to the back end next to the bedroom. Lara decorated her home with comfortable, stylish contemporary furniture in hues of soft blue.

She took off her suit jacket. "I have to get out of this outfit. Nothing fits me anymore," she said, heading for the bedroom. "Pour us some wine. There is a bottle in the refrigerator. Have a look around."

I opened the door of the small refrigerator. Inside, everything was carefully arranged in orderly rows: Olives, pickles, mustard, and associated condiments on the left, two wursts and two cheeses in the middle. Beer and wine on the right. Vegetables, oranges, and lettuce lay neatly stashed in the bin below. I didn't look in the freezer compartment, but the meats were probably arranged in alphabetical order. I poured two glasses of chilled white wine and set Lara's on the counter top. I filled hers a little fuller than my own, remembering how alcohol used to stoke her appetite.

Outside the window in the courtyard below, a squirrel ran through the sprouting vegetable garden first planted by *Frau Giesler* after the war. Light afternoon sprinkles began to mist the air. I took a tour, getting to know Lara through the home she created. I was also searching for evidence of a man friend - the undefined competition.

Lara placed everything precisely, arranged as if prepared for a photo shoot, even down to the manicured philodendron in regimented planters. The wall clock from her mother's house was the only thing that looked familiar to me. I went right for the three nicely framed pictures on the sideboard. The first was her sister Katrin with her husband and their children. Next to it stood a picture of her mother Inge, much older now, with a granddaughter. At the end, set apart, there was one of Lara with a hard gray-haired woman. They had their arms around each other's waists, smiling, probably taken on vacation in the Mediterranean. There was no picture of anyone who might have been her special man. That was a good sign. Maybe he wasn't so special.

There is no doubt I love her, I told myself. But in thirty-six hours I would be on my way back to Frankfurt's airport and then home to a busy schedule of book appearances and presentations. There was no leeway. Time was running short; I was going to have to make my move now.

She came out of the bedroom humming what might have been *Edelweiss, Lili Marlene*, or a combination of the two. She had changed into an outfit of sandals, a blue denim skirt, and an untucked flannel shirt unbuttoned to her chest. Without her glasses, she looked like a young girl again. I wanted to have her right then and there.

Why did I put this on? Look at the way he looks at me.

Maybe I should button one more button. Macht nichts. *He will be gone soon. Still, it is nice to have a man look at me like that. Particularly this man. Why do I let him affect me so? I feel like a schoolgirl. How foolish. But would it hurt if I kissed him just once? Maybe later, after we eat our omelets.*

She looked so cute in her apron, and so appealing when she brushed her hair back behind her ear and licked her lips. Was she flirting? It was much easier in the old days when all I wanted to do was get her into bed. I still wanted to do that, but now I desperately wanted all of her. I tried not to show how nervous I was. If I asked her to marry me, could she possibly say yes? At this point it seemed like a long shot, but one I had to take, mindful that last time I asked, she ran away.

We ate our omelets slowly, relishing each bite. The table was so small our knees touched, sending needles up my legs.

"Do you like the omelet?" she asked.

"Delicious."

"It is better than the liver, no?" She laughed, recalling that long-ago day.

I grinned back. "I always enjoyed shoe leather."

She gave me a playful punch on the arm.

Between bites, we talked about photography and teaching, but in a more private, personal way - how our hearts entered our work, and how our work affected who we had become. I didn't understand a word of the technical jargon she threw off so casually, but her charged expressions and the sound of her voice hypnotized me. She in turn listened with rapt attention to my commonplace theories of history's relevance, as though they were the most original insights yet offered in the Twentieth Century.

I couldn't be sure, but at times it felt like she was inviting me to go further. Other times she seemed to distance herself, preparing to say goodbye.

I could listen to him talk forever. He is so interesting, so appealing. I hope it does not seem like I am flirting with him. After tonight, he must go away and I will never see him again. I must not think about that or I will cry.

I had to find out about the man she's was seeing, but she wouldn't talk about him. So I figured if I offered some intimate, unflattering details about my two meaningless dalliances while married to Emma, she might reciprocate.

"No more American soldiers after you," was all she offered. "They are all too young now. And German men are too interested in only making money."

"So?"

"So I gave up about eight years ago." I was relieved to hear that, but confused. When I tried again to bend the conversation back to her boyfriend, she rebuffed me with talk about her good friend Gertrude Steiner.

"I met Gertie about six years ago," she said. "When *Mutti* - my mother - went in the Wurzburg hospital for her appendix to be removed. Gertie was a nurse there. She still is, only now she is the head of the department. She was very kind to *Mutti*, and Katrin and me. We became good friends. You would like her. We get along well. We go shopping, we go to dinner, and sometimes we take a trip. Last week we went to a piano recital at the Residenz in Wurzburg. Chopin."

"I thought you didn't like classical music."

"I don't, but Gertie loves it. She does not like jazz. Or Elvis." She laughed. "Or books."

After we swallowed the last of our omelets, I helped her do the dishes. She washed and I dried. When the plates and the frying pan were put away, I refilled our wine glasses, and followed her into the living room. Daylight petered out. Fresh spring rain began to pelt the windows. It felt cozy.

Lara sat down in the comfortable chair and I was forced to take a seat on the adjacent couch. I leaned toward her, wine glass in both hands. Now or never. "Of all the apartments in Kronberg, why did you choose this?"

She brushed away an invisible speck of dust on the coffee table and then took a sip of wine. "I always felt safe here," she said. "It is where I was happiest one time."

"With me?"

She squirmed in her chair and took another sip of wine. "I prayed for years someone, maybe you, would come and save me. *Mutti* kept telling me if anyone was going to save me I would have to do it myself."

"I liked your mother, particularly at the end. She loves you."

"I know."

"And so do I."

She wouldn't look at me. The wrinkles around her eyes made her look so sad. "Eli, please. No. You talk as though love is all that matters."

"It is." A gust of wind splattered raindrops against the windows like handfuls of pebbles.

"I have my life here. My work. My gallery I have struggled to build. My sister. My nieces and nephew. I love them. I am their Auntie Lara. They need me too. And *Mutti*. She is not so young anymore."

"You can't let ghosts haunt you the rest of your life."

"You sound like *Mutti*." She glanced over at me, a fleeting look.

I'm not going to give up so easily, I thought. She doesn't love this other guy. I can tell. I waited for her to continue.

"I know you are lonely," she said. "I can see it."

"And so are you. Even if you have a friend, he's not me."

She turned red in the face. She took a long sip of wine. So did I. The last song of the Dave Brubeck record finished, the room now silent except for the rain running down the gutters outside. She rose and walked over to the Grundig record player. She slowly leafed through her albums until she came to the one she was looking for.

Frank Sinatra. *In the Wee Small Hours.* It hit me in the gut. We made love to that song many years ago. Was she giving me a message? I got up from the couch and intercepted her before she reached her chair. "Dance with me," I invited, holding out my arms.

Her pensive mood dissolved. She laughed and kicked off her sandals. "So if I step on your toes I do not hurt you so much."

"Me too." I kicked off my loafers.

She smoothed her skirt, and then smoothed it again. She swallowed.

I put my right hand around her waist, and raised my left for her to hold. Her hand trembled. Then she snuggled into my arms and relaxed. My heart thumped. She melted into me, her head against mine, her warm breath on my ear. She felt like she always felt and smelled like she always smelled. I wanted to lick her. *This love of mine goes on and on,* Sinatra reminded us. *You're always on my mind....*

She purred when I nuzzled her neck. Then she let go of my left hand and draped hers around me. We abandoned pretense and wrapped both arms around each other. We swayed back and forth to the music, more an embrace than a dance. I could feel her hardened nipples against my chest; she was not wearing a bra. I slowly maneuvered her toward the couch. She pushed her-self against me, feeling me. She lifted her head and invited me with her eyes and wet lips. I kissed her, and she kissed me back. She tasted like brown sugar. She couldn't possibly tell me she didn't love me anymore.

We dropped onto the couch still clutched together, unlocking our lips long enough to keep from falling. I eased her onto her side, me pressed against her. Her breathing came deeper and faster. "You cannot want me," she groaned. "I am a dried up old raisin."

"I like raisins," I responded.

I kissed her open mouth. Our tongues touched. She gripped my rear with both hands and pulled me against her.

I moved my hand from her hip down to the entrance to her skirt. My fingers petted the inside of her soft warm thighs and slowly slid up. She trembled. My god, this was really happen-ing. I tried vainly to control myself. So familiar, and yet brand new. Was she with me in this moment, or somewhere else, tied up in her fears?

She was as dry as she had warned. When I stroked her, she jerked. My gently probing finger provoked a painful squeal. "We'll go slow," I whispered. She gulped and kissed me so hard I thought she would break my teeth. Slowly, ever so slowly, she moistened to my touch. She tensed involuntarily, and when she snorted loudly I unzipped my fly. I started to push her skirt up to her hips.

Just at that moment, she shoved me away so hard my one knee crashed onto the hardwood floor. I muffled my own cry of hurt.

"I cannot, I cannot." With that, she heaved herself up from the couch and stood, turning her back to me. She struggled for air, or she was sobbing, I wasn't sure which. How could she stop like that, right in the middle? No man I knew could do such a thing.

Sweat washed my brow. I cupped both hands over my nose and mouth. My chest heaved with each deep breath.

"I have disappointed you," she said. "I am sorry."

"We will go slowly."

"I cannot."

I was confused beyond words, and a little angry. "What the hell is going on?" I stood up, challenging her.

She swayed back and forth, eyes closed, as though she were praying. "It is complicated."

"Everything is always complicated with you!"

She turned toward me, glaring. "I did not order you to come here," she shot back.

"Be honest," I demanded. "Is there someone else?"

"You have no right to ask."

"For the love of God, don't you realize I love you? I want to marry you."

"Stop it." Angry, in a voice I hadn't heard before. She covered her mouth as though she were trying to smother herself. She couldn't even talk. The color drained from her face. "I cannot marry you," she finally said, steely, emotionless.

"Don't run from me," I begged. I couldn't face being alone again, without her. Yet I felt as helpless to stop her from running as I was twenty-five years before. I reached for her, but she backed away.

Her tone tempered, maybe regretting the cut of her sharp words. "You have made me feel like a woman again. Thank you for that." She shook her head slowly. "But I cannot."

"So this is the end? How our story ends? It can't be."

My life was full and I was content until he appeared. It

must end now. There is too much pain. And when I tell him everything, it will be over anyway. I want to be with him, but it is not so easy. It is selfish. It is not fair to Gertie. It is not fair to him. How do I let go of him? He will hate me.

Her lips trembled, tears formed, her shoulders slumped. She wouldn't look me in the eye. Silence. There was something important she wasn't telling me. "I don't get it," I said. "I know you love me."

She hesitated. "This is not so easy to say."

I kept my mouth shut, scared of where she might be going next.

She took a few steps away from me, toward the corner of the room. She turned her back again. The Sinatra record stopped. The grandmother clock tocked into the emptiness. "I have a friend, a very good friend. Her name is Gertrude Steiner." Lara's voice was flat and deathly weak.

She proceeded to tell me she and Gertie were companions, or something like that. Of course with Lara nothing was as simple as it sounded. It had started out as a friendship, a closer friendship than Lara had felt with any girlfriend since Margot. But then it became more than just a friendship. They saw each other almost every day except when Lara was traveling for her business, or Gertrude had night duty. Gertie took charge of Lara. She made her feel safe, taken care of, protected.

They started taking trips together, renting only one twin-bedded hotel room to save money. One night Lara cried out in her sleep, and woke from a nightmare. Gertie crawled in bed with her and comforted her. She held her and kissed her, and Lara fell back asleep.

Lara insisted she never touched Gertie in that way, and only watched Gertie touch herself because it made Gertie feel good.

Lara liked how it aroused Gertie but, as Lara reminded Eli, she was a dried up raisin who didn't need that.

She loved Gertie in her own way, but not in the way Gertie loved her. She could never love a woman that way, she said. Gertie wanted them to move in together, but Lara kept putting her off. She couldn't keep saying no much longer. Gertie was a very strong woman, used to being in charge. Usually Lara liked that. She was tired of making decisions, and didn't make very good ones, as she reminded me.

She stopped talking and turned around, toward me. She looked intently at the ceiling as though following a bug on a journey. Lost in my own maze, I wasn't sure I understood her words. What was she telling me? Was she trying to get rid of me, finally and for good? "What do you mean?" I asked when I could think of nothing else to say. My face must have revealed my confusion, but she might have seen it as condemnation.

"Do not judge me." She glowered, cold as ice. "You have no right."

Then a thought broke through. "Are you a dike?" A question, not a statement. As soon as I said it, I wanted to yank it back. Too late.

"Do not dare use such an ugly word. It is not like that." She shot more darts at me.

I was jealous beyond words, totally unprepared to compete against a woman. But Lara wasn't a lesbian. She couldn't be. And I loved her anyway, whatever she was. "I don't care," I answered back. "Come with me."

She stared at the wall as though she didn't hear me.

"You have a responsibility to yourself. And to me."

"Do not talk to me about responsibility." Her eyes narrowed to slits, her lips firm.

I reached out to her. "Just take my hand. It's not too late."

She kept her distance. She had the same look on her face she had twenty-five years ago, right before she bolted for the door, down the steps, and out of my life.

"Why did you come back? What did you expect from me after all of these years?" A tear dripped out of her eye and ran down the side of her face. Another followed. She kept staring through a glaze.

"You know why I came back. For one more chance."

"You were always a romantic," she scoffed, an unfamiliar sarcasm. "You want so much for love to be real. You probably still believe in Heaven and Hell."

"You have to make a choice."

"For God's sake! Do you know what you are asking? Oh, God! Just go."

"Maybe this was not a good idea, to come here," I said with all of the resolve I could muster. "I'll love you forever, but if I leave this time, I'm not coming back."

"Then go. Now!"

"You can't mean it. Tell me you never loved me."

An unlit cigarette dangled there between her fingers, pointing at me. She flicked her lighter and tried to light it, but her lighter wouldn't ignite. She threw the cigarette on the spotless floor.

"Love you? Of course I loved you. Like a Greek god. A myth. Not a real person. Now here you are a lifetime later, pretending to be Eli Schneider. Well you are not him. You are someone else. Someone I do not know. Someone I have never known."

She paced to one end of the room, then back again, eyes fixed ahead of her.

"You're making no sense," I responded, the last of my will weakening.

She stopped her pacing. Her eyes constricted, fuming. "What

do you mean, I make no sense?" She paused, then she attacked again. "To hell with you."

"You ran away."

"Do not talk to me about running away. I had to save myself. But why did you not come back? Because you married that whore. If you loved me so much you would have come back. Every day I prayed you would come back for me. You did not come. Do not tell me now you love me. I do not believe you."

I did not recognize the ugly, belligerent woman shouting at me. What started as such a pleasant day had turned into a disaster, a war I was losing. I tried to get hold of my shaky voice and shaking hand. "If you want me to go I will go. But I want you to have this so you will always know." I reached into my pants pocket and pulled out the silver chain with the heart pendant, the one I bought her in Nuremberg, and that she gave back when she ran away. I handed it to her.

Fog covered her eyes. Her face contorted, wounded and defiant. She stared at the necklace. Then she threw it on the floor. "Stop it!" she shrieked. "You mean nothing to me."

"You destroy every chance we have," I hollered. "You're pathetic."

She stared and I stared back, both of us frozen. She leaned forward, snarling, every muscle in her face strung tight. I didn't know whether to run or keep fighting, so I stood there like a tree stump, bewildered, waiting for the hurricane to blow me down.

Perspiration wetted her forehead and across her upper lip. Her face turned red as a pepper. "You want to fuck me," she screamed. "So come. Do it. That's all you ever wanted. To fuck me." Her eyes flamed, her teeth bared, and rage smeared her face. She grabbed me by the arm and yanked me toward the bedroom, moving with rapid, determined strides.

What the hell is going on, I asked myself? She tore off her

skirt and stripped off her shirt before I could even unbutton my own shirt. She jerked at my belt and unzipped my pants.

Now I was the one who tried to slow things down. "Lara, you don't have to do this."

She rammed her lips against mine, biting down with her teeth. "Do it!" she grunted. She pushed me to the bed, and steered my hand to her. Then her guiding hand took charge of both of us.

Reckless urgency swallowed us, frantic, out of control, like two crazed monkeys in the jungle. Nothing else mattered, mindless. Her legs wrapped around me, slippery strokes. Growls, groans, whimpers in my ear, her breath hot against my neck, then violent thrusts. She bit deep into my shoulder, branding me. Hold on, hold on. Whatever this was, I didn't want it to end. Then her whole body shuddered, she cried out my name, and I could no longer hold on. We crested like a tsunami, frenzied, the bed destroyed, our bodies shining with sweat.

I was dazed, confused by the sexual violence of this gentle woman, like nothing I ever experienced before. Every part of my body palpitated. Her scent enveloped me. What had just happened? We laid there holding hands, sheets soaked, staring at the ceiling, panting. I had no idea what she was thinking until she raised my hand to her lips and kissed it, then pressed it against her breasts. "I love you," she said, at first quiet and tentative, like a new thought. Then she shouted it. "I love you!"

How long I waited to hear her say those words. I could have lain there forever, heads touching, drained, and feeling more complete than anything I thought I would ever know. We held hands for a long time, listening to the cars splashing by on rain-soaked Hindenburg Strasse.

The second time was unhurried and gentle. She mounted me, looking in my eyes the whole time, moving slowly, sighing, and bending to kiss me tenderly. I gripped her hips, and then cupped her breasts in my hands. I squeezed her smooth white cheeks between my fingers. She smelled and tasted like a ripe grape - warm, sugary, and moist all over, familiar. When she began tremoring, she whispered "love me," and pressed her puffed lips hard against mine.

Before we fell asleep, Lara got up and made us toast and or- ange juice. She moved languidly, wearing only a seductive smile and her black-framed glasses, letting me drink in her un- clothed body. She looked like the statue of a Greek goddess come to life, still young with only a hint of a pooch and ripening breasts.

She brought the toast and juice into the disheveled bed. We fed each other and licked the jam from each other's fingers. We talked of love, she no longer reluctant to bare her heart about me, and I no longer guarded. We were two young lovers again. But when I touched between her legs, she flinched. "I am sore," she giggled. "It has been a long time. Maybe again in the morn- ing." That was okay with me. I wasn't so young anymore my- self.

I pressed for commitment from her, almost certain I had won the war. She hesitated. "We will talk about it in the morning," she said before sliding into the crook of my arm, her hand on my chest. I nestled my nose in her eucalyptus hair. We cuddled under the featherbed, the sound of rain on the rooftop above us.

We held each other until we were nearly asleep, neither say- ing anything. But I had one more sentiment to deliver. "No mat- ter what happens next, I will love you until the day I die. That must count for something."

She didn't answer. I thought she had fallen asleep. Then she turned her head and kissed me on the cheek. "It does."

I feel good, warm deep inside me, different. What happened? It is like I exploded and now I am a new person. For all these years I have been tied up like a chicken, a victim, always trying to please everyone except myself. No more! Now I please myself. But I want to have my cake and to eat it too. I want Eli, yet Gertie must be considered. I want my life as it is; I want it to change. I must choose, but I always choose the wrong thing. I run when I should stay, and stay when I should run. It doesn't matter, I always make a mistake. This time I must be right. I cannot expect more chances. I must be strong. Am I being selfish?

TWENTY NINE

FRIDAY MORNING

I awoke to sun beaming in the bedroom window, the musky smell of sex in my mouth, and the sound of Lara shouting, arguing loudly on the telephone with someone. I picked up my boxer shorts from the floor and opened the bedroom door to hear better. Lara was speaking German, only a few words familiar: *Nein, macht nichts, lieben, mein schatzie.* I couldn't get the sense of who she was talking to or what the argument was about. Maybe it was about me. Was that good or bad? I shook the spider webs out of my brain.

Her tone was more than loud, and more than angry. It was defiant, intimidating like a Gestapo interrogator. Then she softened, almost cooing. She talked so quietly I could barely hear her. Trying to make up? Then another angry outburst. She slammed down the phone, and stomped into the bedroom.

She wore the same outfit she did two days earlier when I first saw her: charcoal pants tucked into black boots. Only today she wore a modest black scoop-necked top. "Stay here," she commanded, lightning in her eyes. "I will be back in one hour. Then we talk." No gentleness from last night's lovemaking lingered on her tongue. I was too bewildered to object.

She stomped out again, slamming the apartment door behind her. I heard her boots thunder down the steps like Harry's and mine used to do. What caused that? I could only guess.

I rubbed the sand from my eyes. A note rested on the pillow next to mine telling me the coffee was on, bread and wurst waited, and I could take a shower. In the bathroom, fresh towels were piled on the counter next to a woman's Gillette disposable razor, her shaving cream, a new toothbrush, and a fresh bar of soap. I used them all, including her shampoo and deodorant.

I imagine now Lara striding with purpose through the park and then marching rapidly across the cobblestones toward a rendezvous with Gertrude.

> *Gertie cannot talk to me that way. I will not allow it. I must make her understand I love her just the way I love my Mutti, and my sister Katrin, and my nieces. But I cannot love her the way she wants me to love her. I cannot. I love only one person like that, Eli. Only him. Forever. This time I will not make the same mistake. If she loves me, she will understand that. How can I explain it to her when she is so angry with me? She will refuse to be my friend anymore? Did she threaten me? She should know that is no way to persuade me. I cannot push him away again. That was the biggest mistake of my life. When I am with him I am not afraid. But she is so strong and I am so pathetic. Can I do what I need to do? Fight for myself? She said she hated me. She could not have meant that. She frightens me when she says such things. Be strong, like Eli. Be strong. How dare she call me a bitch, a whore? Eli has seen the worst of me, the ugly parts, then and now. How he can still love me I do not know. I hate to do this to Gertie, but I can never be what she wants. Never. I love him. To hell with it, I'm going to be with him no matter what.*

What the devil is going on? Where did she go? I couldn't figure it out. Lara was so different this morning than I had ever seen her before. Am I still in this ballgame? I wondered. Did I want to be? Yes, of course I did. I meant what I said before we fell asleep. But what if she says yes? I can't live here and she can't live there, in America.

Strange that in a moment like this, Emma was the one person I wanted to talk to right now. She understood me like no one else ever understood me, but more like a sister than a wife. She would probably tell me what Lara told me: I am a hopeless romantic who expects everything to turn out like in a fairy tale, and then I'm forlorn when it doesn't. I can't let go. If I could, I wouldn't be here in Lara's apartment - my old apartment - waiting for who knows what.

I tried eating some wurst and bread, but all I could choke down were coffee and cigarettes. Every few minutes I checked my watch again, nervous. This was the moment of my life, and I knew it.

A rumble from outside sounded like a passing army convoy, probably trucks, tanks, and armored personnel carriers. A trace of diesel fumes climbed in the open window, or was it just my memory? Maybe some young second lieutenant was being forced to say goodbye to his *schatzie* for a while as the battalion headed to the field. I hoped his path proved easier than mine.

The clock struck ten. Lara had been gone for more than an hour. I paced, and examined every spec of the apartment, anxious. I hallucinated at the window overlooking the shaded garden in the courtyard below. The apartment again felt like home, but oddly different. The clock bonged ten thirty. Had Gertie convinced her? Resignation replaced desperation. In all these years, Lara had been with me. If I left this time without her, she would be gone for good.

When I could stand it no longer, I at last heard her unmistakable tread on the stairway, then the turning of the apartment door lock. I ran, stopping three feet from her, afraid to hope. She stopped and smiled that adorable smile that always took my breath away. The silver heart I bought her in Nuremberg hung around her neck, nestled between the humps under her black top. There stood a pretty young woman with startling dark eyes and muddy blonde hair, twenty-five years washed away.

I brushed her bangs out of her eyes and smoothed her hair behind her ear. She leaned her forehead against mine, and then raised her eyes. Her hand touched my cheek.

A beauty glowed in Lara like I had never seen before, and an unfamiliar sureness carried in her voice. "I did it," she said. "I told Gertie I loved you and only you. She was not happy. She said some filthy things."

"Are you sure about this?"

"I told her you fucked me." Lara said it as though she enjoyed saying that word, a bad girl for a change. I doubt she ever said it before last night. I smiled and waited for her to continue. She giggled. "I did not say it quite like that. I said we made love together. And that it was wonderful. That you were gentle and sweet, even when I was not."

"I think you told her too much."

"I had to tell her everything. No secrets. Not anymore. And do you want to know the funny thing?"

"There's a funny thing?"

"I do not feel guilty, and I do not feel ashamed."

I meant to be calm and composed, but I couldn't manage it. My voice was throaty, full of pebbles. "So now what do we do?"

She glanced down the hallway at the unkempt bed. Then she took me gently by the hand, and led the way.

When we finished, we clung to each other for a long time. She purred. So many unanswered questions still bounced through my discombobulated mind. I wanted her warm body next to mine every night. "Marry me," I said, then held my breath.

She was ready for my question. "Let us wait for now, but maybe later," she answered, not at all dismissing the idea.

Her response disappointed me, but I liked this newly assertive woman. She had it all figured out. "So what are we going to do?" I asked.

"I will come to America at the end of June to live with you for four months. Then you will live with me here in Germany for four months, and four months we will be apart."

I love this good man with all of my heart. We will try this. If it does not work, I will spend all of my days with him, in America if necessary, married if that is what he wants so much. Anything to make him happy. But I will never lose him again.

"Do not make any new friends while I'm gone." I tried to make light of it, an offhand remark, but inside some doubts lingered, some jealousy.

She touched my cheek and kissed me lightly. "Do not worry. I have made my choice. Maybe it is the first one in my life I am sure of."

"What if I can't stand being away from you for four months?"

"Then we will figure out something else."

"What are you going to do in America, and what am I going to do in Germany?"

She laughed and nuzzled her cheek against my cheek. "I will take nice pictures of American children. And you, you will write another book, your best one yet."

"Another book? What about?"

"The daughter of a Nazi major who falls madly in love with a handsome American soldier. And they live happily ever after."

The End

ACKNOWLEDGMENTS

Thank you:

Ann, my wife, for making this a better book.
Andy Weir, Carla Skladany, Denny Lemaster, Jan Skladany,
Lynda Steele, Steve Kofman, and Tom Brunner
for molding the early drafts.
Bob Berkowitz, David Bryant, George Marcellino,
Marlene Kofman, and Neli Ilies for polishing the late drafts.
Beth von Emster, my daughter, for telling me
when I was finished.

AFTERWORD

Two Dickinson College classmates of mine instigated this story, Carla Seybrecht Skladany and Allan Sidle. When Carla finished *A Fine September Morning*, her immediate reaction was, "Now I need to know what happens to Elias," the little boy introduced at the end of the book. Allan's reaction was, "Your next one has to be about a young Jewish army officer serving in Germany in the Sixties." He said it knowing he was describing me many years ago.

It took about a year for me to turn my attention to writing a new novel. When I did, I melded Carla's and Allan's thoughts into a plot. Many thanks to both of them.

Despite Allan's suggestion, this story is *not* autobiographical. Yes, I did meet and marry Ann, my wife of fifty plus years, in Germany, but she was an American, there teaching the American dependent children. I never knew anyone like Lara Kohler or Eli Schneider. They are entirely creations of my mind. In writing this story, however, I did draw on my own experiences as a lieutenant in a tank battalion stationed in the small Bavarian town of Kitzingen. And I did borrow some of the traits of people I knew, locations in and around Kitzingen, and a few on-duty and off-duty incidents.

I made one conscious compromise with authenticity. Namely, I cleaned up the crude, uncensored language used by young men in an all-male combat unit far from home. Though my army buddies might complain about this, I did it in consideration for the more genteel audience who might read *Lara's Shadow*.

Hopefully none of the flavor of the time and circumstance has been lost.

Just like Eli's mother, my mother was with me on the hot, humid August afternoon in 1961 when I went to the Berwick Post Office to pick up a registered letter sent to me by the U.S. Army. It was from my new battalion commander, Colonel E.R. Brigham, welcoming me to the 1st Battalion, 68th Armor of the 3rd Infantry Division. This is how I learned I would soon be on my way to Germany. The Berlin Wall had gone up just days earlier provoking a military crisis, the massed armies of the United States and the Soviet Union facing off on the other side of the Atlantic.

My mother's reaction when she learned I was ordered to Germany was much like that of Kira Schneider, Eli's mother - horror. I was full of bravado, insensitive to her fear for me, a Jew among Germans. It was only sixteen years since the Holocaust. When you are twenty-two years old, sixteen years seems like a long time ago. Today, it seems like the blink of an eye. It must have felt even shorter for my mother. She had lost a Greek cousin in Athens to the Nazis.

To me and most of the young officers I served with, President John F. Kennedy was King Arthur and we were the knights of his roundtable. We saw ourselves as brave and gallant, engaged in the noble struggle of good versus evil, Freedom versus Communism. We were equipped with the best, most modern arms and trained to a fine edge. Many itched for the balloon to go up so we could prove our worth.

We came close during the Cuban Missile Crisis in October of 1962. Our battalion was deployed north of Wurzburg, close to the East German border, waiting for the larger Soviet force to attack. We were ready, and maybe eager. It never dawned on me that, if war erupted, I might be one of the causalities. That's the perceived invincibility of the young, and why the young fight the wars.

I am proud of my service. Together with an army of dedicated, capable young men, we helped deter a war with the Soviet Union. But what we did cannot compare with the sacrifice of those who fought in Vietnam. Many of those I served with in Germany were among them. A few died there, one after he came home. Some others were wounded, and all were scarred. I was in the Reserves at the time of the big buildup, and narrowly missed a call-up.

For Americans, foreign travel was rare in the early sixties, expensive and inaccessible. The only people I knew who had been to Europe were those sent there by the Army, Navy, and Air Force. I myself was eager for adventure and requested assignment outside the United States.

The Germany I experienced was still recovering from the war, still largely agrarian, but industrializing and growing at breakneck speed. A large part of the citizenry was of modest means. Quaint villages dotted the Bavarian landscape, with mostly small family plots in the surrounding farmlands. Women routinely worked the fields, most often with their men, but sometimes without. The latter were the war widows struggling to keep it together. Reminders of the war remained in bombed out buildings in nearly every city, and in memorials like the concentration camp at Dachau outside of Munich.

My mother and father were tolerant people. I learned about the Holocaust while growing up, but hateful speech about Germans would have been out of place in our home. So I arrived determined to like Germans, and over the next two years they gave me many reasons to do so. I didn't particularly think about the likelihood that many people I came in contact with on a daily basis had probably been Nazis, that some had fought in their army, and that a few may have been participants in atrocities committed against Jews.

What was it like being a Jew in Germany so soon after the war? It was nothing especially noteworthy. The subject of my being a Jew rarely came up. Occasionally a German would make reference to my German-sounding Fleishman name. Sometimes I would just smile. Sometimes I would quietly say my name was Jewish. In rare instances, like after I visited the Dachau concentration camp, I defiantly threw it in their faces, proclaiming I was *ein Jude,* without a trace of a smile. Regardless, their response was usually one of polite indifference, perhaps practiced.

They seemed more interested in the fact I was a U.S. Army officer than the fact I was a Jew. More than one German bought me a beer because we were now allied in opposition to the Russians. Many of the men of the right age proudly proclaimed they had fought the Russians on the Eastern Front, as though we were allies in that war too. None of them admitted to having fought against the Americans. "Then who the hell were we fighting?" we used to joke. I did not know then that vastly more Germans and Russians fought and died on the Eastern Front than did Americans and allies in the West.

In general, being part of the U.S. Army in Germany in the early sixties felt somewhere between being an occupier and an invited friend. All Germans tolerated us because we were their only bulwark against the Soviet Union and Communism. Some resented us, but most appreciated us, particularly those who benefited economically from our presence. Still, the U.S. Army was an overwhelming presence in their lives.

Americans were everywhere. American military and civilian vehicles clogged their streets and roadways. American tanks and troops conducted maneuvers across their farmlands, often with destructive results. Americans crowded their towns, the horny young enlisted men obnoxiously rowdy on Friday and Saturday nights. It took us a while to realize that young German men saw us officers as especially unfair competition for the affections of German girls. We had cars and prized American dollars in our pockets they could not match.

When I graduated from college, I was proud to have friends of different religions, races, and ethnic origins. I was an idealistic, open-minded liberal, hopeful that people of good faith could all get along regardless of their dissimilarities. When I looked at the Army, I saw blacks, whites, and Hispanics working and living together, mindless of race; many of them were seemingly friends.

Today I am embarrassed to admit how naive I was, blind at that time to the deep racial divide present in those soldiers' off-duty lives, the paucity of black or Hispanic officers, and the attitudes of many Germans toward African-Americans. These German attitudes were often encouraged, maybe even instigated, by the attitudes and behavior of white Americans.

The summer of 1963, my last summer in Germany, was also the last summer of American certitude. Some would call it a time of innocence, others a time of idealism, and still others a time of blind arrogance. Whatever it was, we still believed in our righteousness and our God-given purpose as the bastion against all things evil. We believed in the unique goodness of Americans. We did not yet acknowledge that racism in our country was systemic. We did not foresee the horror of Vietnam and the deaths of so many of our young men yet to come. We were a confident, unified country, bound by our magnificent triumph in World War II, the saviors of democracy. But as Bob Dylan sang, *The Times They Are Changing.* Little did we know.

By the end of 1963, President Kennedy was dead, a loss felt as acutely as if he had been a member of the family, but felt in a different, ominous way. Escalation of the Vietnam War came next, then Ghetto riots, along with progress in civil rights.

The 1964 Civil Rights Act was a landmark for African-Americans, but it also drove a spike in the institutional anti-Semitism lingering in America. Jews could now no longer be barred from jobs, housing, and public accommodations simply because they were Jews. Private colleges could no longer set fixed quotas specifying an upper limit on the number of us who could be admitted.

In 1963, many older Germans still denied their part in the scourge of Hitler, Nazism, and the Holocaust. "We didn't know," was their steadfast assertion, evidence and logic to the contrary. But the next generation, their children, had begun to challenge them. The parents didn't like the questions their children were asking, and the children didn't like the answers their parents were giving them.

Among the Americans, there was still talk about the collective guilt of the German people, and whether there was a flaw in their basic character - in their blood - a flaw that drove them to make war so often, and to murder six million Jews. That is nonsense! The German nation has done vastly more to confront the heinous crimes they committed, or were committed in their name, than any of the many Europeans who colluded in murdering Jews. They have acknowledged and atoned to an extraordinary extent.

My intention in writing *LARA'S SHADOW* was to make it about acknowledging our trespasses, atonement, forgiving others, and forgiving ourselves. The book says that, no matter the act, there can be redemption. The capacity to forgive is as important to our own well-being as is being forgiven.   But forgiveness doesn't come for free. It must be earned. In the end, it is not about collective guilt and collective forgiveness. It is about personal guilt and personal forgiveness.

Alan Fleishman

AUTHOR'S PROFILE

ALAN FLEISHMAN is the author of two earlier successful novels, *Goliath's Head* and *A Fine September Morning*. Before becoming an author, Fleishman was a marketing consultant, senior corporate executive, university adjunct faculty, corporate board member, community volunteer, and served as a U.S. Army officer in Germany. He hails from Pennsylvania where he graduated from Berwick High School and Dickinson College. The father of a daughter and twin sons, the grandfather of seven, today he and his wife Ann live with their Siberian cat, Pasha, high on a hill overlooking San Francisco Bay.

www.alanfleishman.com

71372707R00148

Made in the USA
Columbia, SC
25 May 2017